WORKING CLASS VEGAS VAMP

The Vegas Underground Book 1

AM Scott

Lightwave Publishing LLC

DEDICATION

To my sister and brothers. I'm glad we're there for each other—love all of you!

CONTENTS

CHAPTER 1

A ROCK-HARD FIST DOUBLE-TAPS the shiny black bar under my polishing rag. Before I can react, citrus, incense, and ginger with a strong undernote of rusting iron assaults my nostrils. My spirits sink, but I keep the rag moving and reinforce my pleasant, welcoming expression. Then I look up and meet the ancient vampire's gaze.

Klaus Theoden slides onto the stool in front of me. My least favorite customer first thing tonight—for the third time this week; five unending nights last week. The hot billionaire has a hard time understanding the word no. I suspect my primary attraction is "playing hard to get"—even though I'm not playing at all—so I try to be bland and slightly servile. But the Night King of Vegas rankles me too easily. "What's your poison tonight, Mr. Theoden?"

"Call me Klaus, and you, of course, Charlene Flammen." One corner of his lush lips rises, but I know he isn't smiling. He never does.

I slide the list of top shelf liquor across the bar in front of him, adjusting my tone to bored. "Not for sale. What would you like off the menu?" Wealthy, gorgeous Theo is sadly predictable, demanding the most expensive and exclusive items. But high prices don't equal good taste.

I turn and reach high for the Pappy Van Winkle Reserve, our most expensive bourbon whiskey, kept just for him. Occasionally some other rich dude trying to impress orders it, but even at the hottest drag show in Vegas, few will pay $500 a shot, double the usual bar price. But Fantastique is on the pricey Vegas Strip, where nothing is cheap.

A few months ago, a tech bro bought a bottle and tipped me a glass. After a single sip, I passed the rest to Troy; he raved about it all night long. It didn't taste all that different to me, but I'm not much of a drinker. Of alcohol, that is.

I turn back to Theoden and raise the bottle along with a single eyebrow. When he doesn't say anything, I shrug and pull a fresh cloth to polish the bottle. He likes to play games. I don't. I finish polishing and put the bottle back, then grab the next, an equally expensive tequila, ignoring Theoden's attempts to burn a hole in my back. Laser eyes aren't one of his many advantages. But his mere presence, night after night, worries me more than enough.

After waiting on the table behind Theoden, Janice grimaces at me, and continues her rounds. Troy remains at the other end of the bar, casting wary glances at us. They both know Theoden is here for me, the working class vamp who escaped his control.

Turning me was a rare mistake on Theoden's part. Caught in the crossfire of a mob shootout in the Starlight Casino in 1966, I dragged my dying body out the back door to see the lights of Vegas for the last time. Of course I told the blond hottie with the ice-blue eyes that I wanted to live—everyone does. But even as a regular, he didn't know the real me.

He saw a middle-aged woman fighting the effects of age with makeup and moisturizer, making perfect drinks, and entertaining her customers. He, like so many of the businessmen leaning on my bar, probably believed I made my real living on my back. But they were all wrong.

Flattery gets you a long way if you do it right. I keep the banter light, with just enough bite to intrigue and get the big tips. Theoden isn't the first man who has followed me out a door after a shift, thinking I was actually been interested. Most of them take the "no thank you" with grace. The few that didn't got my spiked high heel through their foot and a punch between their legs—if security didn't get them first. These days, I use a taser—much less effort, more effective, and less likely to end in a lawsuit. And an official escort out the unmarked employee exit after each shift generally prevents issues.

Too bad for Theoden that his first genuine conversation with me were the last gasps of a dying woman. And too bad he didn't take the time to demand the usual assurances of undying eternal loyalty, because I would have turned him down flat. I've been chained to a man before—I'd literally rather die. Theoden's sloppiness cost him, and he keeps trying to rectify the mistake without admitting he has messed up. In reality, his ego keeps me alive.

Fool.

But in return, I have to fight his sporadic attempts to bring me back under his control with brains, not brawn. Or money. He has billions, a legion of beholden and besotted followers, and he isn't stupid, just arrogant.

Pity, that. Stupid men are easily led.

Roger, the latest in a long string of show managers, stomps to the bar, stopping near Troy, and crooks his finger at me. Since I work for the man, I go, dragging my feet. But I already know the answers, and so does he.

Roger leans close, speaking in my ear. "Char, you've got to do something about that guy. He's not buying, and he's taking up valuable real estate."

Sun-blasted Theoden. Still, I'm not a pushover or stupid. "You want him out? Get security to throw him out. Or ban him from the bar." I lean back and meet his gaze. "Not. My. Job."

Roger scowls. "You know I can't do that."

"I'm not doing it. Or anything else with him. And if you order me to do what he wants, I'll take it to the cops. Want to go down for forced solicitation?" Roger is human; he doesn't know I'll never go to the authorities. I have better options.

Except I don't. Not with the night ruler of Vegas determined to own me, for some reason known only to him.

"No, that's not what I meant!" He holds up his hands like he's surrendering, then drops them. "But if he keeps coming in and throwing out those 'mess with me and die' vibes, I'll have no choice but to let you go." He shakes his head. "I don't want to. You're a great floor manager and an excellent bartender. You make my job easy. But we can't have that kind of buzz kill at the show, and you know it."

I keep my expression placid, but my heart sinks. I've noticed Theoden's dampening effect; it isn't surprising Roger's picked up on it too. Finding a new job is a hassle I don't need. I've been in this one for years, outlasting manager after manager, because I am good—no, I'm great. I keep the customers happy and solve staff and performer issues before they become problems.

But tonight, no one came near me. They'd assisted each other or asked security to step in.

No one wants Theoden's attention. "I don't know what you want me to do, Roger. I'm not giving that man an inch." I'd planned on staying here a couple more years and building my emergency funds higher. But maybe it's time to leave. I'd go someplace with a gloomier climate, far from Theoden's influence.

"I don't know either. But the big bosses will notice eventually, then you'll be gone." He taps the bar. "Figure it out."

Roger isn't a bad guy, but he isn't the brightest, either. When I return to my end of the bar, Theoden sneers, drops a few hundreds, and leaves. The night drags on, but we finally close the bar and ready it for the next night. Matias, the security chief, escorts us out. I grab my taser and walk away. The locals don't bother me, and most of the drug addicts are passed out or on the Strip, harassing the tourists.

After two long Vegas blocks of crumbling concrete, flashing neon, and wary homeless, I tap in the gate code for my lousy Paradise Road apartment complex. Climbing three flights of stairs, I avoid the wobbly railing and the soft spots in the concrete walkways, unlock my door and step inside. Nothing moves.

After locking the door, I slide the heavy security bar into place and cross the cheap, stiff carpeting to the sliding glass door. Through the closed door, the disgusting stench of unfiltered cigarettes and marijuana singes my nose and clenches my fists. My downstairs neighbor is smoking again.

My need to decompress outweighs my disgust. I drag the sliding glass door through the oxidized track with a whoosh. The inevitable desert grit rumbles and the door bangs against the frame. The grumpy woman downstairs is likely to leave another note on our door, but I don't care. My ass hits the canvas chair on the tiny balcony, and I unzip my thigh-high platform boots, kicking them off to land with a one-two thump on the living room floor. Then I loosen my corset. I can breathe deeply again—too bad that vampire myth, along with the perfect face and superhero strength, is wrong.

Being a drag show bartender pays well, but the required costume isn't comfortable. My feet throb, my wrists ache from tossing bottles, my ears ring from the loud music, and my body is stiff from walking the length of the bar over and over. If only I'd been turned in my twenties, rather than mid-forties. But I'd be dead, because like many escaping their small towns for the city's bright lights, I was a fool. Older and wiser Char has learned from her early mistakes, and that helps me survive my new life, or facsimile thereof.

Flicking the fan in the corner on blows the smoke away, replacing it with cool desert air laden with vehicle exhaust. Pulling a blood box from my oversized tote, I stab the straw through the foil, and suck down the thick, lukewarm, life-sustaining brew, ignoring my craving for the good stuff straight from the source. I sympathize with my neighbor's addiction because I have my own.

But mine is a necessity. Still, I minimize the harm my survival creates, no matter how my inner darkness fights the chains of will I've forged.

With the flick of a fingernail, I shred the box's seam and lick the last traces of blood from the foil. I crave that taste—and hate my desire. Even the boxes—a mix of herd animals with a little human, the equivalent of a protein bar—are delicious.

Sated for the moment, I retreat to my sanctuary, where I sleep the day away.

Or die the day away, depending on who you believe. Since I left Theoden's lair early, I don't know which is true. Nor do I care. Over the decades, I've learned the difference between many of the myths and truths on my own, and I'm better off for it. So many vamps believe everything they're told, forging their own chains.

Inside my room, I bolt the steel door, secure it with steel bars across welded brackets, and press the rubber seals tight over the tiny seam. A clever invader would attempt to go through the walls instead, but one of the most attractive parts of this barely working class apartment complex is the abundance of concrete block walls. The only flimsy wall in my suite is between the bedroom and bathroom. I've placed metal bars across the only window, then laid bricks and another set of bars, making my lair secure.

In a fire, I'll die, but I'm not really living anyway.

A jet thunders through the sky above the apartment, the first of many taking off today. Vegas never sleeps, it's true. But every thinking being has to at some point, for mental health if not bodily. I throw the sheet back, flop on my ridiculously expensive but supportive mattress, and rather than worry about Theoden, I meditate until the sun rises at five twenty-seven.

Then I drop into a darkness that Vegas visitors never see.

CHAPTER 2

WHEN THE SUN FALLS below the horizon, I wake. The sheet still drapes my body, and my security measures are in place. My phone, and my body, tell me it's nine minutes before eight, and the sun is down. I breathe into my daily meditation. When the singing bell chimes on my phone, I rise, pull on a workout bra and shorts, and begin my yoga routine. The double dose of mind-body work might seem like overkill, but control is key to surviving a hostile environment surrounded by temptation.

When I'm done, I stare at the ceiling and wish I could fall back asleep like a human. But wishes aren't horses or gold bars, so I get ready for my day—or night, in reality. Vegas is almost perfect for a working-class vamp—plenty of decent paying night shift jobs, ever-changing management that doesn't ask questions, and special service providers are readily available. For example, I have alternate identities, including disguises, ID, transportation, and cash secured in different locations around the city. A hidden safe under my bed holds my first and best escape costume.

Sadly, I don't have alternate, permanent light-safe lairs. I might get shelter for a day or three from a few of my friends who hate Theoden as much as I do, although none of them have his power or money. They have something better—the loyalty of found family.

But anyone will break under enough pressure, so I'd be hesitant to ask for their help, even though Theo rarely goes to those extremes. Money and influence work better for what he wants. Plus, he pretends to be civilized, when in fact, he is anything but. Lots of humans and paranormals have found that out the hard way.

But thinking about the admittedly hot billionaire vampire doesn't pay my considerable bills. I shower, moisturize, paint my face, and curl my silver-streaked hair into beachy waves.

Then I put on my black leather cropped halter top and cover it with a bolero jacket. Tuxedo pants and thigh-high platform boots round out my look. I make more tips wearing a short skirt with spike heels, but it isn't worth the hassle of dealing with drunk idiots who don't understand the word no.

Nor is it worth the temptation to teach them the error of their ways.

Gathering my bag and keys, I unlock my lair, with plenty of time to suck down a blood box before a brisk walk to the bar. Ride shares are expensive and every penny I save strengthens my safety net.

At the back door of Casino Royale, I hold my card to the lock and enter my code. After trudging up the mostly empty, plain concrete hallway to the back door of the Fantastique, I enter the staff room, put my platform boots on, and throw my things in my locker. Swiping my card across the closest terminal, I clock in and bring the house lights up. Under the bright LEDs, the shiny black and silver plastic looks cheap and cheesy, but with stage lighting, it turns glamorous and glittery. Hopefully, Theoden won't ruin tonight's ambiance, too.

Over the next hour, staff and performers trickle in while I prep the bar, slicing fruit and filling trays. Troy pours ice into the bins. "Going to be a slammer tonight." His combination of tuxedo pants with suspenders, bow tie, and no shirt makes him extra popular with bridal parties. "Hotel is full of tech-bros."

"Ugh. Those guys are terrible tippers." Janice tosses her long, straight, honey-blonde hair over her shoulder. "And they don't take 'no' for an answer. Hope Security's on top of it tonight." Janice wears her usual shiny black satin corset with ribbon lacing over a short, tight skirt. Even on towering stilettos, she glides through her tables holding heavy trays overhead without spilling a drop. Being a werewolf helps.

"No worries. We got you." The gargoyle security team lead, Matias, nods from his post at the end of the bar. His dark suit, gray-tinged skin, combined with a little natural glamor, makes him hard to see against the dark walls. I know he's there, but only because I can hear him breathing. Once the show starts, he'll fade into the background until a threat brings him out. Then, his six-six height and massive shoulders do most of his job—except for the idiots too drunk for common sense.

"Thanks, babe!" Janice throws him an air-kiss.

Troy growls. "I'll protect you." Her pack mate isn't a fan of interspecies dating and has delusions of pack leadership.

Janice wags her finger in front of Troy's face. "No, you'll stay behind the bar, or Char will have your blood for dinner."

He sneers but glances at me. I stare back, licking my upper lip. I'll never take blood from him, but he doesn't know that. He turns away, stacking cocktail shakers at his station. Janice laughs and twirls her tray.

I don't let my amusement show. Pack leadership is unlikely if he can't stare down one working-class vamp.

After I solve the inevitable last minute performer crisis, Matias opens the doors. I peer around his massive body and breathe a sigh of relief. Theoden isn't waiting at the VIP rope. Maybe I caught a break tonight. I trot backstage, nodding at Security guarding the stage door on my way, and Tanya gives me the final set list.

But when I return to the bar, Theoden's sitting in his usual seat. And the owner of the Casino Royale, Don T. Ald, slouches next to him, with a fleet of men in somber suits surrounding them.

Tonight is a very bad, no good, awful night.

I'd seen the owner here exactly once, watching the police arrest the *Fantastique's* manager for embezzlement. His appearance now can't be good for me. My feet slow, but despite the dread weighing me down like an anchor, I continue. Better to know what is going on—avoidance does no good.

When Theoden spots me, his lips compress and his brows rise, then he reclaims his usual stoic expression. "Charlene, a bottle of Pappy's with enough glasses for all of us. Doubles." He waves at the suits. Roger hovers on the outskirts, obviously uncertain of his role in this show. As he should be—he's outclassed big time.

I turn and reach for an unopened bottle, keeping my expression blank, despite the sinking sensation in my stomach. After placing it on the bar, I gather glasses, and pour two triples for Theoden and Don immediately, then check with the minions. "On the rocks or straight, gentlemen? Raise your hands for rocks." Hands go up—split half and half. I grab tongs and the special "kinky boot" ice cubes, each landing in the glass with a tink. Then I pour generously; no reason not to when Theoden is buying the bottle.

"Pour for yourself and your two colleagues as well." Theoden lifted his glass—straight, no kinky boots for him—and nods.

I hold back a grimace and deliver glasses to Janice and Troy, exchanging raised-brow looks with both. Then I fill a glass with water for myself. I already know I don't want to toast this moment.

One of the suited minions points at a paper inside a leather folder in front of the current casino owner. "Sign here, here, and here, sir." Don scrawls on the paper, then slides the folder in front of Theoden. He signs and hands the folder to the man standing next to him; a stamp thumps on the paper, and the man notarizes both signatures.

Theoden's attorney takes the documents. "Sirs, we'll send official copies to your offices." He holds up his glass. "Congratulations, Mr. Theoden."

Bloody daylight—I'd been right.

Don slaps Theoden on the back and holds out his hand. "I hope the Royale is as good to you as it was to me." He shakes Theoden's hand and tosses back his drink like it's cheap swill, thumping the heavy glass on the black plastic. "I'll enjoy the Malibu bikini babes while you fight the desert heat, the tourists, and the headaches. Best of luck." Sliding off the stool, Ald totters out the door, waving without turning. Half the legal staff follows.

Theoden's lawyer snorts. "He'll be back in less than six months. Guy doesn't know when to quit."

"That's true. But it won't be this casino." Theoden clinks glasses with his lawyer, then turns to me. "You're not going to congratulate your new boss, Charlene?" He purrs my name in his deep, rumbling voice and raises his brows.

I stare at him while I review my assets. Another year would have been better, but I can do it now. Holding his gaze, I pour my water in the sink and undo my apron, taking my casino ID out of the pocket and placing it on the bar in front of Theoden. "I quit." Then I walk away without glancing back. Troy gasps. Janice's snicker cuts off abruptly.

Matias joins me before I reach the locker room. I glance at him while I unzip my thigh-high boots and pack everything in my tote. "Making sure I don't rob the place blind on my way out?"

He snorts. "Standard procedure, you know that."

I grin at him and rise. "I do. Thanks. For everything."

He opens the back bar door for me and we weave through busy minions pushing carts filled with booze and food, hurrying to fulfill their master's orders. I revel in my freedom, pushing thoughts of my next steps away to enjoy this moment.

At the door, Matias steps out first, looks both ways, then beckons me out. "I've enjoyed working with you, Char. I wish I could offer you something other than luck, but I can't. I need this job." He holds out his hand.

I shake his cool, rough hand and smile. "Oh, I know. I've burned my bridges. Take care, Matias, and tell the crew and cast goodbye for me. I'll miss most of them."

"Will do. Watch your back. Guy buys a casino for you and loses? He'll be out for blood." His big head swings back and forth, his brows drawn together in worry.

I snort. "I can't believe he thought it would work. Hope he loses his shirt on this lousy place and you all get better jobs."

"Don't worry about us." He jerks his head to the side, away from the door. "Get going. Fast."

I trot away, eager to leave Theoden's territory. At the edge of the Royale's property, I step across the invisible border and slow slightly, my anxiety dropping.

A long, black limo pulls up beside me, the passenger side window rolling down. "Ms. Flammen, I've been directed to give you a ride."

The worry returns, but I keep walking. "No thanks. Not interested in anything from your boss. Bye now." If I get in, he'll drive straight to Theo's tower.

The window rolls up, but the limo shadows me until I let myself in the gate at the Paradise Road apartment. Then I break into a run, thudding up the stairs and down the hall to my front door. Unlocking the door, I slam it open—no need to care about the neighbors anymore.

I yank all the blood boxes from the top shelf, put them in a bag, and head for my room. Inside, I secure the door behind me. On my phone, I log into my bank account, send an extra month's rent and transfer everything but the minimum to my Bitcoin wallet and off-shore accounts. Then I do the same with my other bank accounts.

Grabbing my big suitcase, I pack practical clothing, leaving my pricey uniforms behind. My toiletries and makeup go into my smaller suitcase, along with the blood boxes. I shove two changes of clothes in my tote bag, on top of my emergency escape supplies.

Lifting the bed, I unlock the safe underneath, and toss the gold, silver, and cash into the tote bag. I fasten a thin pouch with more cash, cards, and ID around my waist, then jam my feet into white tennis shoes with one sole higher than the other. As a last safety measure, I drop a pre-paid credit card in my bra. Next, I grab a short gray wig, a loose, flowered dress, and a pair of gold-framed glasses. In the bathroom, I wipe the makeup from my face and lighten my brows to silver. After putting on the dress, I slide the glasses and wig into place and add short white gloves.

The charmed wig instantly transforms me into a harmless old woman. I round my shoulders, and the uneven shoes make me limp, enhancing my appearance.

Cameras in the hallway could catch me, but I'm not leaving through my front door or my living room balcony. I roll my suitcases to the closet, pull the hidden lever, and yank the folding stair off the ceiling; it lands on the floor with a bang.

At the top, I enter the code, undo the padlock, and withdraw the security bars, then heave the hidden door up. Springs keep it from banging on the roof. Warm desert air blows through the opening. I grab my suitcases and place them quietly on the roof, then join them. Crouching, I close the hatch and secure it, then lower the fake air conditioning tower into place, covering my escape route from casual eyes. Or a drone. I scan the skies but don't see any, and I'd moved the rooftop security cameras away a long time ago. Removing my phone from the pocket of the ridiculous mumu, I take the sim card out, break it in two, and throw the pieces across the roof.

When the next airplane roars above me, I lift my suitcases and tread carefully across the roof path padded with rubber mats to cover any noise. At the far side of the big complex, in a nook between a staircase and the building, I uncoil a rope from the front pocket of my smaller suitcase and lower my luggage to the ground. Then I follow, rappelling down the rough stucco wall, and roll my cases to a slightly dented silver 2003 Nissan Sentra. Pretending it takes all I've got, I struggle to load the cases into the trunk and drive to the front of the complex. A series of elderly women have used this vehicle to run errands for years now, but they all knew it could disappear at any time. Alice, the current "owner," rarely drove anymore; she wouldn't miss it.

Leaving the car running, I slide my keys, gate fob and a pre-written notice of intent to vacate into the mail hatch on the manager's office door, along with a note about how to get through my additional security measures. Then I remove the battery from my phone, dropping that and the phone out the window as I leave the lousy apartment complex for the last time.

I won't miss the place, not one little bit.

CHAPTER 3

Leaving the lights of Las Vegas behind, I drive along the highway outside Red Rocks Canyon Park, right at the speed limit, and find a slot in a small parking area on the side of the road. Technically, the park is closed, but stargazers sneak in all the time. Taking my tote plus a low camp chair from the back seat, I follow the pre-scouted trail into the rock formations. After half a mile, I check my surroundings and leave the path. Fifty feet later, I sprinkle cayenne pepper on my footsteps, put on a crime scene technician's suit, and make my way to a cave I'd discovered. I'd spent many nights finding bolt holes in and out of the city, and that preparation would pay off now.

I'd left a small pile of pebbles marking the unique rock formation. Rolling a two-foot diameter stone away from the entrance buries the pebbles. I wriggle through the opening, pushing the chair and tote in front of me. Last time I'd been here, nothing resided inside, but that could have changed. A rattlesnake, scorpion or spider bite won't kill me, but it won't feel good, either. I haven't seen any animal tracks outside, so hopefully, my lair will still be safe for the day. I click the flashlight on, hoping the light causes any critters to scatter.

After crawling fifteen feet under the stacked rocks, I emerge into an opening. It isn't a true cave but a place where eroding hoodoos and boulders have crashed into each other over the years, leaving a five-foot diameter hollow. Inside, I block the entrance with another boulder, set up my chair, sit, and turn off the flashlight, looking for any hint of sky. Despite not seeing any stars, I unfold a wildland fire shelter. After draping it over my body, I fasten it to the chair's high back above my head with Velcro, then slide my feet into the far end, and shove the sides underneath my arms. If any sunlight penetrates my lair, the combination of reflective aluminum foil, woven silica cloth, and fiberglass should keep me safe. I'd heard of vampires surviving full sunlight for a day in a fire shelter. Not something I want to try, but my now-precarious future means I might not have a choice.

As the earth rotates, bringing the sunrise closer, I suck down a blood box and review my actions. Despite my care, I'm traceable; if Theoden had discovered my car, he could have put a tracker on it. He also could have put trackers on my suitcases or clothing—if he'd penetrated the security on my room, which was difficult, but possible. Or someone could have stuck a tiny tracker on me in the crowded back hallway of the casino on my way out, but I'd take care of that tomorrow. Anything small enough to hide on my skin wouldn't have the power to penetrate all this rock.

He also could have used traditional methods; a drone could have followed every car leaving the apartment complex last night, backed up by people in vehicles. I hadn't noticed anyone following me or anything in the air, but I'd be moving fast when the sun went down tomorrow. I drank a second box and waited for unconsciousness, praying I'd escaped.

God might not care about vamps, but it didn't hurt to ask.

I wake and listen, then open my eyes to pitch blackness. Clicking my flashlight on, I pull the fire shelter off, ignoring the crinkling noise. If they followed me to the park, Theoden could get a were to find me, even at the new moon. If they survived the cayenne pepper, they might hear the shelter or my suit. But the sound is unavoidable, so I ball the shelter up and slide it into my tote bag, then stand and stretch, loosening my body.

No time for my usual meditation and yoga–speed is literally life tonight. Rolling away the stone blocking my temporary lair, I crawl out and listen again. Hearing nothing but the wind and a few insects, I climb the stack of boulders I'd slept under. My Tyvek suit rustles, but the ever-blowing Vegas wind rattles the dry vegetation, covering my noise.

Looking back at my car parked along the road, I see only one other vehicle and a yellow tag on my windshield. The other vehicle, a small SUV, appears empty and doesn't match the cars from last night. The tag could be an official warning to move the car or a note from Theoden's people—no way to tell from here.

Decision time. Do I risk checking and possibly keep the car and my supplies? Or leave it all behind just in case? If they'd tracked my vehicle here, they'd probably find me quickly, no matter how fast I hike. I had to move or Theoden would have weres or drones on my tail soon.

Speed is more important. Removing the isolation suit, I climb down and stuff the thing into my tote bag, then take a different route back to the trail. Exaggerating my shoe-caused limp, I shuffle along the official trail to my car, then yank the tag. My shoulders sag in relief—it's an official warning that the vehicle will be towed after 24 hours. I toss my chair into the back seat.

Inside the car, I start it and drive just over the speed limit along the highway, despite the fear urging me to move faster. I'll head north and leave Vegas—forever. I have an online acquaintance in Salt Lake City; I can beg shelter for the day if I can reach him. And he still lives there. And he's willing to cross Theoden—as Theo grows richer, fewer and fewer people risk his displeasure.

If I can reach Oregon, I can hide out in a lava tunnel for a night or two. But that means making good time tonight, driving two-lane highways in the middle of nowhere. If I hit a deer or some other furry critter, I'm true dead. Or I'll find out if the shake-and-bake—the wildland firefighter's grim nickname for the fire shelters—really works.

But I have to go north first. My head itches; the wig charm is running out. At the end of the loop road, I turn northwest on Highway 95. I'll head for Reno, and if I can't get farther, at least I won't fall into Theoden's clutches.

I'm physically attracted to him—he's hot—but I know better than to get involved with wealthy, entitled men. I've learned the hard way. Once they get you, they use you and throw you away, taking what little money and self-esteem you have left, leaving you with nothing. They want women to beg them for help, and I refuse to do that.

I'd survived and recovered last time, but I'll never make the same mistake twice. Affluent, connected men are nothing but trouble. Leaving Vegas is the smart thing to do, so I drive onward.

My headlights spear the darkness, but if I had human eyes, they'd be completely inadequate. Fortunately, I see better than most. I've avoided all furry critters determined to commit suicide by old lady car for an hour now.

Suddenly, headlights in both lanes make me squint, joined by flashing blue and red. I brake. Turning around before a roadblock will only get me chased. If I'm lucky, the State Police are looking for a fugitive from the nearby prison.

But I'm fairly certain my luck has run out.

CHAPTER 4

I STOP NEXT TO a uniformed State Patrol officer and roll down the window. Forcing my voice to a high, quavering tone, I ask, "What's the problem, officer?"

He shines a flashlight in my face, moves it through the entire vehicle, and returns the beam to me. "License and registration, please, ma'am." He holds out his hand, palm up.

"Of course." I open the glove box and remove the registration, then pull my fake driver's license from the pocket in my tote bag. Handing both through the window, I keep up my act, squinting and shading my eyes from the bright lights with a trembling hand.

The officer steps away, using the microphone attached to his shoulder to announce my fake name and the associated ID numbers. My identity should hold up; I'd obtained it years ago and never used it.

The officer returns, handing my documents back. "Please open the trunk, ma'am. We're searching for a fugitive."

I frown. "The only thing back there are suitcases. My granddaughter is about to have a baby." Although, I hadn't checked my trunk after I returned from my hideout; that may have been a mistake.

"Open the trunk, ma'am." He places a hand on his weapon.

I consider objecting again, but that will blow my cover. "All right." I punch the trunk button, sending the lid upward.

The officer draws his weapon and moves to the back of the vehicle. "Clear!" He slams the lid down and returns. "Thank you for your cooperation, ma'am. Please move ahead to the next station."

"Next station?" I'm not faking my puzzlement, but the officer steps away, looking for the next vehicle. The police car in front of me rolls out of the way, so I ease the accelerator down, stopping next to another man with a raised hand. This man isn't wearing a uniform, but with another row of vehicles blocking the road in front of me, I can't do anything but comply.

A dog's paws land on my window frame and a big, black, wet nose pushes into my face. I rear back, but it's too late. A rough tongue rasps along my neck, followed by a bark in my ear, making me wince again.

That isn't a dog. I put a hand on the snout and shove, rolling up the window, while paws scrabble against the glass. "Get that thing away from me! That's disgusting!" A fully shifted werewolf during a new moon—Theoden is playing at the high roller tables tonight.

Before the window closes, a nightstick shoves into the gap. "Ms. Flammen. Step out of the vehicle."

Nothing left to do but bluff. "I don't know who you're talking about, young man. Remove your stick, now." I keep my tone high and quavery, then snap the last phrase. I don't use command voice often, but I'd found it fairly effective, and it took less time than mesmerizing.

The stick slides away, until the werewolf clamps his massive jaws around the baton, halting it. With the moon far from full, it's probably the alpha werewolf, and my command means nothing to him. I'd never met the Vegas Pack alpha; Janice said he despised the Strip. She'd also implied the alpha hated Theoden as much as I did, and yet, here he is, running me down like a rabbit.

The Nissan can't ram through the roadblock, and fast as I am, a were in wolf form will easily catch me on foot. The last line of official vehicles blocks a bridge, so driving off either side means a drop the car can't handle. The riverbed is dry, so I can't lose the wolf in the water. Assuming I can get out of sight, which is unlikely.

I've got no options.

The wolf drops the nightstick, but both bodies block the door. I yank the useless wig off my head and sigh with relief when the itching stops. Taking the glasses off, too, I glare. "Well, if you want me to get out, move! Men." I shove the door, expressing my loathing in the only way I have left, and stand, bringing my tote bag with me.

The werewolf crowds me, while the man extends his arm, pointing beyond the roadblock. "There's a car to return you to the city, ma'am. I'll get your luggage and someone will drive your vehicle back." The wolf herds me through the line of police cruisers to a waiting limo. Theoden loves his fleet of shiny black cars, and the convenient drivers even more. Transport and dinner, all in one.

The wolf's huge jaws clamp the back door handle and pull the door open before the driver's door opens. A woman steps out—another werewolf. Long, dark hair cascades over her shoulders, framing a face men will fight over. "You better not scratch that!"

The wolf snarls, and the driver jumps, then bows her head. Then he shoves the top of his massive head against my bottom, urging me into the vehicle.

"Rude!" I glare, but get in. With the wolf at my back, I can't run. I slide onto a plush leather seat. Typical limo, with bar service, except this bar includes bottles of blood wine. I don't want to be here, but since I am, I'll take advantage of the amenities.

I reach for a bottle, but the werewolf jumps inside, knocking my arm away. "Watch it, dog." Leaning forward, I grab the bottle. The wolf ignores me, curling up on the bench in front of me and putting his snout on his paws. He is huge, taking up the entire seat, and nothing but lean muscle over solid bones.

Yeah, no way I'd outrun a wolf built to take down elk or buffalo. Or maybe a mastodon. I open the bottle and take a long drink. Delicious; a willing donor combined with a decent red wine. But nothing less than the best would do for Theoden.

A snarl draws my attention to the alpha—he glares at the bottle in my hand. I snort. "You've got a lot of nerve. I need blood to survive. You're running free women down like a fox hound for the so-called Night King of Vegas. I know which is worse." His dark brown eyes meet mine, and his lip curls, but his protest subsides. After holding my gaze for at least thirty seconds, he looks up and away, then turns his back on me. I tip the bottle back. No reason to show up sober. Theoden has me in his evil clutches, and my days of freedom are gone. Drinking might be the only way to survive the nights ahead.

The car speeds away from the scene of my defeat. Hopefully, Theo will get bored quickly. I can't imagine what he wants from me, a middle-aged, working class vamp. Not when beautiful, young, human women and men throw themselves at his feet, vamps bow, and werewolves serve him. Meanwhile, everyone else does their best to avoid his attention. I'd tried, but he'd chased me down.

Probably because I'd escaped his command from the start. I drank again. I still didn't know why he'd turned me without promises of fealty and loyalty. Perhaps he'd already figured out I'd never accept his terms? He certainly hadn't expected me to walk away from his luxurious high-rise home only a month after my turning.

The lights of Vegas grow brighter, and I drink faster. I'd rather not remember the coming conversation. And I need some courage, even if it's fake. Finishing my bottle, I reach for another, but a massive, rough paw pushes my hand away. Lip curling, the werewolf growls.

"Really? I've been avoiding Theoden for years. My freedom is gone. If I want to drink my way into captivity, why shouldn't I?"

"Because we're here, Ms. Flammen," the driver says. "Take the elevator—you'll be sent to the correct floor."

Great. Off to my doom.

CHAPTER 5

"Thanks for the smooth ride. Hope you find a better employer and a better alpha soon." I hitch my tote bag to my shoulder and get out, walking to the only door available—a shiny chrome elevator. The alpha werewolf stays right behind me—I know he'll herd me into that glossy box trap if I run. Or maybe drag me by my ankle.

If there was another exit, I'd try even with Beowulf on my heels. I slow, and he nudges the middle of my back. I spin. "Hey, don't rush me to Mordor, okay?"

He snorts but backs off an inch. "Gee, thanks." As I get closer, the door opens. I drag my feet, but eventually enter, and the door shuts. After a stomach lightening trip up, the door slides aside, revealing a semi-circular foyer that fairly screams "vampire lair!" I step onto slick black marble shot with red veins. The walls are dark, red-tinted wood, and security cameras festoon the blood red ceiling. Two big men in dark suits hold small machine guns, the straps resting across broad shoulders.

The bearded man on the right pulls a phone from his pocket and taps. A section of the wood wall slides away, revealing a gorgeous reception area that announces a spoiled billionaire with dark tastes lives there. More black and red marble flooring, leather and chrome furniture, beautiful hand-knotted Persian rugs, then the room ends with a sheet of glass overlooking the Vegas Strip with a long balcony that starts to my right. I'm sure that light-proof shutters close automatically before sunrise.

The clean-shaven man points into the room without taking his eyes off me. "Please make yourself comfortable, Ms. Flammen. Someone will be with you shortly."

I try to smile, but I'm pretty sure it's a grimace. I trudge forward, and the wall slides shut, trapping me inside. Alone—the werewolf didn't follow. I'd miss him, except he's Theoden's lackey. The impression of modern luxury with a grim edge continues. Black and white abstract paintings decorate the deep red walls, a bar of dark wood and black leather stretches fifteen feet long, and priceless antiques rest on the occasional tables scattered throughout the seating areas. Everything is clean, almost sterile, without any hint of habitation or presence, except a whiff of Theoden's expensive cologne, and the fainter scent of iron. A shiny showplace, not a home.

I could test the doors, but there's no need to bother. I can't see them, but I'm certain cameras and more security watch my every move. Since Theoden will undoubtedly make me wait, I'll get wasted. Behind the bar, I open the refrigerator—as I suspected, it's packed with blood wine. Taking the first bottle, I pop the cork and drink deeply, while strolling to the window. The red in the limo was good, but this white—tinged rose with blood—is excellent.

Outside, neon glares from extravagant edifices, competing for the title of most outrageous, while at the bottom of the glittering monuments to money, tourists gawk and rush to empty their pockets. On the gritty concrete behind the flashy Strip, workers scurry to fulfill visitors' dreams and fill banks with fleeced cash.

Every casino owner wants more and more, and none more than Klaus Theoden. Not happy with simple money, he is out for blood. And mastering every being in his domain.

"Charlene," Theoden whispers in my ear.

I spin and throw the bottle at him. I was alone a second ago!

He jumps to the side, and the glass shatters on the floor, spraying shards and blood red liquid across the shiny black marble. The wine almost blends in; black marble is a wise choice on Theoden's part.

His brows rise. "I knew you'd be unhappy, but I didn't think you'd physically attack me."

I roll my eyes and try to control my jack-hammering heart. "That's what you get for startling me. And abducting me." I glare. "You deserve far worse."

His shoulders rise a tiny bit, and his right eyebrow quirks higher. "Perhaps." Unbuttoning his designer suit jacket—black as his heart—he sits on a couch, sprawling across two seats. "Come, join me." The very picture of a king secure on his throne, all he needs is a crown on his brow and slave girls at his feet.

I lean against the window. "I'm good here." I'm not sitting at his feet, next to him, or within arm's reach. Fighting him is impossible, but I will not put myself in harm's way, either. Not that it matters. I'm trapped here, and he is fast enough and powerful enough to kill me at any time. So I have nothing to lose.

"Suit yourself." He stares at me for a good thirty seconds. I don't look away, living with the discomfort of staring a predator down. I control my reactions, and he'd better remember I'm a predator, too.

"Do you know why I brought you here?" One corner of his lips lifts ever so slightly.

I hold back a snort. "Because, like a three-year-old, you can't understand the word 'no'?"

He crosses his ankle over his knee, displaying a red sole. "I understand, but I choose not to obey the commands of a baby vamp who ought to know her place."

I don't bother holding back this time and blow an obnoxious raspberry. "I didn't give you any commands except the one to leave me alone. I'm never going to be your lackey, slave, or plaything." I lean forward. "My body might be stuck here, but you don't own me. And you won't." I'd rather die for good. He ought to know that by now.

"We'll see." He waves his hand as if he is shooing a fly. Not that an insect would dare appear inside the monument to cash he inhabits. "I didn't bring you here to prove a point. I don't need to prove I rule Vegas."

I don't bother to hold back my eye roll, either. "I think there's a few men out there who'd disagree with that assessment." They are all the same kind of man, though. Ruthless, ambitious, and rich.

"If I wanted to rule all of Vegas, I would." He brushes non-existent lint from his jacket sleeve. "But that would be more trouble than it's worth. Besides, I believe that competition is good for everyone, including me." His lip curls slightly. "But when I play, I win. Always."

I yawn, not hiding my disdain for his villainous monologue. Eventually, he might get to the point. Or I'll pass out with the sunrise. I hope for the first but accept the second is more likely. Theo has enough years as a vampire to hold off the effects of the sun to some extent.

"There's a threat coming." He leans forward, trying to demonstrate his sincerity. Which is as fake as the rest of his pretty package.

"A threat to you, to me, or an existential threat?" I quirk a brow. "Because if it's existential, I believe the answer is forty-two."

"What?" His brows almost meet.

I want to laugh but keep my expression serious. "Forty-two." I say it very slowly, like he is a child. When he continues to gaze at me, clearly confused, I repeat my words. "Forty-two. That's always the answer to life, the universe, and everything. Why don't you know that?" Too bad none of his guards are here. I'm sure someone would be snickering by now. But that might be fatal, so it's just as well.

"You are misinformed. Forty-two is definitely not the answer to this particular existential threat to all supernaturals." His jacket vibrates. Whipping out a phone, he swipes and holds it to his ear almost faster than I can see. "What?"

With that kind of speed, he can separate my head from my body before I even realize he's moved. I push my fear aside. He'll get as little pleasure from my captivity as possible.

"Put it on the screen in here." Theoden moves to the end of the room, leaving a breeze in his wake.

I stay where I am but turn to look. A view of the exclusive shops on the first floor of the building appears, the name of a trendy jewelry designer flashing on one side. Clearly shot from the ceiling, the edges have the warping of a fish-eye security camera. Well-dressed patrons mix with tourists in shorts and t-shirts in the wide mall, a few of each filtering past the security guard at the door.

A man in a suit and a girl in a short, tight, shiny red dress enter the store. In passing, the girl does something to the guard—probably shocks him with a taser—and he falls to the floor. Lights flash, and a metal grate falls from the top of the doorway, but the man holds up one arm and stops it. He must be a gargoyle; no other supernatural can hold against that kind of pressure.

Before the security gate hits the man's hand, a mob of people wearing black hoodies, sweatpants, gloves, and masks sprint through the door, smashing glass cases and scooping jewelry into bags. In less than thirty seconds, they leave. The girl in the red dress rolls the guard out of the way with one high-heeled foot, and the gargoyle lets the security gate fall. Then they run after the mob.

The cameras switch, following. At the front of the shopping mall, bars drop, securing the doors, but the mob leaves through a shattered window, the gargoyle and the girl somehow disappearing into the group. Outside the mall, the mob scatters, some climbing into vehicles immediately, while others keep running. They probably get picked up farther down the block. A flash of red on the back of a motorcycle might be the girl, but the gargoyle has disappeared.

The video plays again, but I watch Theoden's jaw flex and the hand not holding his phone clench into a fist. "Figure out who they are and find them. Now." He listens, his anger clearly increasing. "That's what I pay managers for. Fine. I'll be down shortly. Increase security in the casino, but don't shut anything down. Not yet." He slides his phone into his jacket and rolls his shoulders. Then he turns to face me. "Our discussion will have to wait." He strides out, heels banging against the marble, and the wolf alpha enters.

I ignore the wolf and cross to where Theo had been, watching the smash and grab. The wolf joins me, but I ignore him. I've seen video of this kind of attack before, but it's gutsy to steal from the king vamp. Were they all supernaturals or just the two out front? From the speed of the attack, I think the mob are all some sort of supernatural, but probably not all gargoyles because they aren't known for speed.

The attack was expertly executed, but surely Theoden's people will find enough evidence to identify at least one or two of the perpetrators. If they're caught, I truly doubt they'll be wandering Theo's penthouse lounge with me. Theo clearly thinks this might be a distraction for a larger heist in the casino, but perhaps I can take advantage of the chaos.

I stroll towards the bar, looking for a lighter and a propellant of some sort. Wolves aren't fans of burned snouts. Hair spray is ideal, but unlikely. If all else fails, high-proof alcohol and a rag make an excellent Molotov cocktail. Before I reach the bar, a high-pitched noise makes my shoulders rise, and the wolf, ducks his head between his paws, trying to cover his ears.

Glass tinkles, a warm wind blows the delicate drapes across the windows, and a man wearing skintight black steps inside. The security shutters I'd suspected slam down, but the man holds up one hand, stopping one shutter over his head, like the gargoyle downstairs. Muscles bunch in his arm and chest, but he doesn't waver. His other arm comes up, firing a weapon into the werewolf. The muffled thwap indicates it is an air-powered weapon, but whether it is a drug dart or a lethal impact round doesn't matter; I have to get out now, even though it means leaving my bag behind.

I squeeze by the man holding the shutter, noticing that his face is striped black and white. I don't know if the colors are paint or natural, nor do I care. Stopping at the glass railing of the balcony, I turn, searching for ropes or ladders, but there's nothing. The man got to the balcony somehow; he has a way out. A high-pitched whistle, and the dark edges of the balcony shift.

Dark gray, low-to-the-ground shapes jostle, white striped faces glancing at me, then focusing on the doorway. They stream into the luxury lounge, huge claws skittering against the dark marble tiles. Badgers—a lot of them.

I don't know much about werebadgers, other than to avoid them at all costs. Vicious and stubborn, they never stop.

"Hey, you know where the switch for the shutters is?" The man in the doorway turns to face me.

"No. This is my first time in this room. Hopefully my last." If I knew where security was, I might be able to get out on my own.

"Not a fan of the Vamp Chief?" His eyes narrow.

I meet his gaze straight on. "No. I'm not one of Theo's and never will be." I leave out that he'd turned me; that matters only to vamps.

"Find me something to hold this, and I'll help you." He puts his other arm up, both of them trembling.

I don't want to get trapped on the balcony or inside, but all I see is flimsy furniture. Then I spot the answer—metal torch holders. I run to the stand at the corner and yank, the iron rods heavy in my hands. I pull them close and half-drag the awkward load to the door, standing them next to the man in a row.

"Thanks, darling." The man lowers his arms.

I hold my breath, but the rods don't collapse. "How are you getting out of here?"

A white grin flashes. "With you. Let's go." He takes my hand, dragging me to the railing. "Hope you're ready for this." He picks me up, bride-style, then holds me out over open air and drops me.

CHAPTER 6

I scream, clutching his neck.

He jerks his head away from me. "Stop screeching. You could break glass. Hang on tight for a second." He lets go, and I clamp my wrists tight, scrabbling for a grip with my toes on the glass. Miraculously, there is a tiny ledge. The man reaches around my waist, and a click sounds. "Now, I need to turn you around."

"Turn? Are you kidding me?" I'll never let go of my death grip around his neck.

"I got you. There's a belt around your waist." He clamps his hands on my hips and twists me. "Let go."

I blow out a breath and release my grip on my wrists. I'll have bruises tomorrow. "Okay."

"Got to toss you a little. Don't flail your hands around. When I've got you, find that ledge with your heels."

"Toss me?" I rise and spin in the air and can't hold back a squeal. Then his massive hands grip my hips again. The lights of Vegas highlight the scene of my death, far below. I scrabble against the smooth glass with my feet, then improbably, find that tiny perch. "Okay, my heels are on the ledge, but..." I reach back and grab the railing on either side of the man. If he lets me go, I won't be able to hang on long, but at least I have a chance.

Straps flop over my shoulders. "Gonna get a little familiar now, sorry." He bends slightly and reaches between my legs.

I almost jump but don't want to lose my tenuous perch. Latches snick, and the straps tighten. I assume I am harnessed to the man. "Yikes." That is a lot of pressure in a sensitive spot.

"Good thing you're short," the man says in my ear. "I'm bringing you back to this side. Then I'm going to unlatch you for a minute. Stay here."

He grips my hips again, pulling me up and sliding me over the railing. A quiet snick-snick, and I am on my feet again. He strides to the doorway, where the iron torches are still holding the shutter open, ducks inside, and whistles.

He could have put my harness on while I stood on the balcony. Dropping me over the side was cruel. I'll take his offer of a way out because I have no alternatives, but I'm not sticking around. Only dangerous people enjoy terrorizing others.

Rustling and the clicking of talons on marble signals the badgers' return. The torches clang against the balcony and the shutter slams down. The badgers rush to the railing, grasping the top rail with their long, deadly front claws.

I knew they were strong, but can they really boost their massive bodies over the railing? And if they do, what then? Badgers can't fly.

The man joins them, pulling a tether from the first badger's back. The badger's teeth clamp on it, then it hurtles its body up and over the railing, falling like a rock. I spin and peer over. A parachute deploys, and the badger sails away.

"Hey, come help. Pull the red tether and hold it out so the badger can bite down."

I turn and reach for the harness on the badger next to me. It turns and bares its teeth at me. I recoil, then realize it's waiting, not threatening. I grab the only red cord I see, sticking out from a bulging backpack, and hold the end out to the badger. Long, thick, sharp teeth clamp down, then the badger launches over the railing and is gone. I move to the next, and the next, then only the man and I are left.

"Turn your back, darling, and let's blow this popsicle stand." He makes a spinning motion with one finger.

I snort and spin. His firm hands clamp on my waist, and I hold back an instinctive jump. A latch clicks, and I rise into the air, the straps between my legs pressing hard. I am trying not to think about how we're getting down. No matter what, it won't be a comfortable ride.

"This could get a little dicey." His hands fasten on my hips again. "Legs up and over."

I lift my legs, thankful for my strong stomach muscles, and let them slide over the railing. The lights of Vegas sparkle and dazzle my eyes, and my heart pounds at a rate it hasn't since I was alive. I've been afraid since I was turned, but never completely terrified. Still, the man got here somehow and probably has a parachute like the badgers.

"Don't scream." Soft lips brush my ear, then his hands release me.

I fall. The ground rushes up to meet me, and I clamp my lips together, but I'm sure whimpers break loose. After what seemed like forever, I jolt upward.

"Oof. You're different than carrying a badger." I twist, trying to see above me. "Stay still. I know it's scary, but it's hard enough to steer a double load. Don't make it harder." He laughs. "Just lay back and enjoy the ride."

Typical guy—making innuendo-filled jokes. "Right. Because that line has always worked."

"Hey, just trying to reassure you. We'll be fine, gliding gracefully all the way to the scene of the crash." His voice is velvet; low, soft, and strong, and his body is cool behind mine in the hot desert air. With all his muscles and the way he held that security shutter up, I'm fairly certain he's a gargoyle. But he could be some other kind of supernatural. I'd never researched the whole range of possibilities; I have enough to deal with those who came my way through my job. Or threaten me.

"I thought we'd coast farther, but I underestimated the load. And no, I'm not calling you fat." He chuckles. "A badger would have been just as bad. Or maybe worse." He sucks in a breath through his teeth. "We're at a steeper slope than I'd like, so I'm going to jettison you early."

"What?" He'd better not drop me. We're still at least a hundred feet in the air!

"Don't worry. You'll have a safe landing. Just gonna get a little wet."

I look ahead. Plumes of water blast into the air—the Bellagio Fountains. They are playing "Fly Me to the Moon." I bark a laugh at the irony.

"Sorry I can't actually fly you anywhere. The best I can do is glide. But despite the fact that I'll be getting a beautiful woman soaking wet, I'm happy it's you. If I dropped one of the badgers in the water, they'd come up swinging with those nasty claws. Can't do much damage, but it still doesn't feel good." His low voice is rich with laughter. "You're not gonna claw me, are you?"

I ignore the beautiful woman comment. No one is beautiful wearing an old-lady mumu, no makeup, and hair squished under a wig for more than twenty-four hours. He's a flirt; the habit is undoubtedly helpful, if unnecessary for a guy with muscles like his. I already couldn't remember his face, but gargoyles have glamor; he must have precise control I haven't seen before. "No. Not much point." I hold up my right hand. "My nails are short and round. Besides, you got me out of there. You could dump me in the nastiest golf course pond around and I'd be thrilled."

"Fair warning. I'll release you first, then I'll keep gliding. I'm hoping my glamor holds so no one spots me. But they'll see you. Get out of there and get moving. Do you have somewhere to hide?"

I hadn't planned on returning to Vegas, so I hadn't made any arrangements. I have plenty of emergency bolt-holes around the city but no way of knowing which are still safe. And half of them rely on my access to the Stardust. But that isn't the gargoyle's problem; it's mine. "Sure. I'll be fine. Thanks for the save. I owe you one." I hate saying it, but it's true.

"You helped me, and I'm pretty sure losing you will annoy Theoden. And it might please the wolf alpha. So we're even. Especially after the lousy landing coming up."

Please the wolf? He's part of the problem, not the solution. We spiral down over the water. The song and show ends, and the crowd disperses. I scan the mass of people, searching for large groups I can blend into. Although blending in when dripping wet isn't easy. A crowd of young women wearing tiaras and sashes while drinking huge frozen drinks remains near the south side of the fountain railing, dancing to the music. I point. "There. Near the bridal shower."

"Good choice. One more drunk girl. Although, you won't exactly blend in. That dress is hideous." We glide lower, the spiral tighter.

"I know." But wet, it would cling. And I have an hourglass body, so all I have to do is tie a knot at my waist, and the dress will look better, if not exactly like a sparkly bridesmaid outfit.

"Well, Char Flammen, it was a pleasure flying with you. I hope you get away clean." He laughs. "Keep your eyes on the horizon, don't anticipate the landing, and raise your legs, because I'm not sure how deep this thing is. Better to break your tailbone than your ankles."

He knows my name, but I don't know his. We drop suddenly, my stomach rising, then I rise for a split second.

Gravity takes hold, and I fall like a rock.

CHAPTER 7

BEFORE I RECALL WHAT he said, I hit the water, my arms and legs flailing. "Ah!" I clamp my lips shut and try rolling to the side, but my bottom hits the concrete. I get my feet under me, standing with my head just above the water, chlorine making my eyes water.

Flashes of light are probably cell phone cameras. I swim to the nearest dark point, grip and roll over the bulky concrete railing, then crouch. The flashing never stops, so rather than trying to blend in, I run. Sprinting full speed, I careen through the crowds, grateful my orthopedic shoes stay on despite their squishy state. The difference in sole height isn't important when I'm on my toes.

I run north, dodging people and flinging water everywhere. I can lose any pursuit in the shops outside the Horseshoe. Hiding in the crowds on the escalator to the pedestrian bridge crossing Las Vegas Boulevard, I turn sideways, watching for followers. While I watch the sidewalk below, I run my fingers through my hair, slicking it back, then gather the material of my dress to one side, tying a knot at my waist. Water cascades down, getting my feet even wetter. But that tightens and shortens the dress, letting me blend in better. I didn't notice anyone chasing me, so I continue, merging with the tourists. On the other side of the boulevard, I enter the nearest drugstore. I buy flip flops, a sun hat, and pink heart-shaped glasses, using the prepaid credit card tucked into my bra. I have cash in my waist belt but don't want to draw attention getting it out.

At a shop outside the Horseshoe, I buy a tight, short, sparkly black dress and a tote bag purse, almost wiping out that card. Then I enter the Horseshoe like I belong there and walk towards the back of the casino to the bathrooms. Using paper towels to dry off a little, I change into my new dress in a stall. Throwing the old lady dress and shoes away, I stuff the hat and sunglasses into my bag. I also pull some cash and a key out of my waist pouch.

Leaving the bathroom, I sit at a nearby $1 slot machine and feed it the rest of my credit card. The best way to stay anonymous in a casino is to play the slots.

A server finds me before the stench of cigarettes drives me away. "What can I get you?"

I don't recognize her, but since she's middle-aged, we probably have mutual acquaintances. I glance at her name tag. "Can I get sparkling water with lime, please? And is Tricia working tonight, Sunny?" Her name is as fake as her smile.

"Sure, although you look like you could use something stronger. Tricia's off tonight, sorry." She saunters away before I can ask for anyone else.

But I quickly figure out my next move. I pull the card from the machine and get up, dropping it on Sunny's tray on her return trip, grabbing the plastic glass of water. "Thanks. Have a good night." Strolling into the shops connecting the Horseshoe and Paris, I sip and watch for anyone tailing me in the dark shop windows, but my footsteps are loud in the empty hallway. I take an abrupt left, turning for the parking lot. Throwing away the glass, I enter the brightly lit area.

Despite the lights, there are plenty of shadows if you know where to look, and I do. The Horseshoe, formerly Bally's, was one of my first jobs in Vegas, ironically, as a cocktail waitress. I enter a stairwell, putting my hat back on. At the bottom, a freight elevator door is secured behind me, and large metal doors block the way in front of me. I hold my breath and insert my old key. It turns, and no alarm sounds. Since silent alarms are normal—guest experience is everything in Vegas—lack of noise isn't a guarantee. But I know the renovation money went to the front of the house, not the dregs of the support equipment.

While bright lights and security are important for guests, no one cares about the employees cleaning the parking lot. Inside the concrete room, rolling garbage cans are pushed against the walls, while brooms and other hand tools hang above them. Most of the space is taken up by an industrial sweeper. The sharp scent of industrial cleaner mostly overwhelms rotting garbage and stale cigarettes.

There is no way to lock the doors from the inside, but with a little ingenuity, I can secure the space. I wrap an electrical cord in a figure eight around the old-style crash bars so they can't be pressed down, which also ties them together. Then I roll the sweeper close to the doors and tie the ends of the electrical cord to the machine.

It isn't perfect, but it ought to work for a day. I know they don't clean the lots every night, and it's the best I can do, so worrying is useless. I will, of course, but that will end when I pass out. I put the seat on the sweeper back, grab a garbage bag for a blanket, and find the most comfortable position I can.

While I wait for the sunrise, I think about the night and all the mistakes I'd made. My biggest mistake was moving too soon. I should have stayed another day in my cave. I could have moved my vehicle after the first night, then driven away safely the next. Even Theoden might have trouble running official roadblocks two nights in a row.

Then, before the terrifying ride out of Theo's lair, I should have grabbed my tote bag. I had more money, cards, identification, and lair options in there. Those are all compromised, as is everything in my suitcases and car. Of course, I have more disguises and ID stashed, but I have to get through the coming day. If I am discovered here, I'll end up naked in the morgue and give some poor worker a heart attack when I wake. Or more likely, Theo has someone there, and I'll find myself in a cell in the tower.

I'd rather be naked and free—that's easier to fix. But for now, I have no choice but to relax and hope I wake up here tomorrow.

CHAPTER 8

I WAKE, BLINKING IN the faint glow of a few electrical indicator lights, hunger driving me to move. When I stretch, the lights pop on. I'd survived another day—yay me. Now to hope no one waits outside, then get out of the casino without getting spotted on a security camera. That will be the real trick; speed is the only answer, despite the attention that might bring.

One of my many storage units is nearby. Assuming no one has broken in, I'll have another identity, with clothes and cash. And an electric bike, which can get me to a vehicle. If Theo hasn't covered every casino with his people. With any luck, the raid on his fancy store in the tower has slowed his attempts to find me. That distraction won't last, but soon, I'll be gone. I should have left long ago, but the thought of starting over was overwhelming. And more than a little terrifying.

But first, I have to get off the Vegas Strip. Theo could have had weres out all day sniffing for me, figuring I'd only get so far, but searching Vegas by scent is almost impossible. Thousands of people from across the world bring unusual food, perfume, and cologne with them. Plus, I'd taken a dip in the chlorine-laden waters of the Bellagio. Add in the prevailing scent of marijuana and alcohol everywhere, along with the new moon, and it becomes an almost impossible task. If he's done his research and finds my friends, they'll have a better idea of where to search, but getting it out of them will take more than a few hours. Plus, I know people at every major casino—and most of the minor ones, too. I don't want to put any of them in danger, though.

I doubt Theo will think of a parking garage cleaning closet, but his people might. Time to go. I undo the cord and replace everything, then open the door. No one is waiting for me, so that's one bit of luck. Hopefully, it will hold long enough to put my skills to use.

I can use two vampire traits semi-effectively: speed and mesmerizing people. I'd be better if I practiced more, but expending that effort increases my need for blood. Tonight, I'll employ both traits despite the downsides.

I walk up the stairs into self-parking, slowing within sight of the casino entrance. Families and couples often drop off their luggage, then a single driver parks. I can follow a car through the garage and steal the fob before the driver realizes what I've done. Nightfall brings more gamblers and tourists, which means more opportunities. And if one doesn't appear in the next ten minutes, I can move to another garage.

I saunter, watching carefully for my chance. A family van, then a luxury SUV pull up and unload. Waiting, I lean against the wall where I can see the long drive to the drop point and mime smoking a cigarette. No one will look closely enough to see I don't have one. But I can't stay long, or a security camera will focus on me, and I'll be identified.

Then the perfect target careens into sight, and I smile.

From the erratic steering and loud music, the driver is drunk or distracted. Loud male voices whoop and holler. Perfect—I'll be doing the area a favor by stealing the car and getting these idiots off the street. Screeching to a halt, the car stops, and five young men pile out, going to the back of the SUV and stacking luggage on the concrete. I move closer, blending into the crowd. The driver is at the back too, arguing with one of his friends about his bags.

Grinning, I sprint through the crowd, hop into the driver's seat, and throw the shifter into drive, stomping on the gas. The key fob rests on the console—lesson one of driving in town: keep the fob deep in a pocket. The car beeps, complaining that the tailgate is open, so I glance at the controls, press a few buttons, and eventually, it closes. I speed along the behind-the-casino road, jolting over the unending speed bumps, and turn onto Paradise Road. I slalom through the traffic like a ski racer at the X Games. Then I turn onto Flamingo Road and slow to match traffic, which is still ten miles an hour over the limit.

When I spot the popular local chain restaurant Blueberry Hill, I park, leaving the fob in the car. I wipe the steering wheel and door handles with a sticky, alcohol-soaked napkin, then sprint down a side street. Keeping my speed up and taking my hat off, I keep going, running through the shadowed parking lots of the numerous low-cost nursing homes in the area. They all have cameras, but not casino-quality. Once out of that area, I slow to a walk, starving.

Maybe I should have waited at the restaurant and found a victim. But no. I control my hunger. Speed and distance are my only chance. I'll get money and transport, then sate my need for sustenance. Reaching the storage facility, I enter the code into the gate and another into the door, climb three floors, and unlock my five by five unit. Inside, I change into dark leggings, a tight-fitting concert t-shirt, cross-trainers, and a bike helmet. I open the false bottom on the cheap overstuffed chair, purchased for this exact reason, and pull out a hip pack with cash, pre-paid credit cards, a pack of cigarettes, and a new identity as Lena Sparks.

Maybe the name is a little too on the nose, but it's better than Charmaine Flame, the first one the forger suggested. Picking something close to my current name is easier to remember, but also easier to find. However, Lena Sparks is a real person; a bike messenger doing a booming business. I can't use her identity for long, but that's okay—I have a plan. I get the bike outside and ride to my next storage facility, using a convoluted route not easily followed by a car.

Inside that facility, I pull the cover off my rusty 2001 Subaru Forester and check the tires—they still look full. If not, I have a tire pump. Opening the back, I slide the e-bike inside, close the door, get inside and drive away. I won't try to leave Las Vegas—after last night, that seems foolish. Plus, I need to feed before I find shelter.

Driving towards Henderson, I find another popular chain restaurant and park. I hate taking advantage of people, but at this point, I am literally starving. Unfortunately, buying blood boxes will get me picked up in a heartbeat. In the country, I could find a large animal, like a horse or a goat. But in Vegas, I need an adult human. And not a drunk or someone higher than a kite, which at this time of night, becomes challenging.

But out here in the suburbs, it's possible. I pull out a cigarette and wait for my victim to appear. Vehicles pull in, carrying groups and families, but finally, a single man parks near me. I walk towards him. "Hey, got a light?" I keep my voice low and sexy and think "look at me" at the man.

The man turns, scans my body, and then looks into my eyes. "Sure." He digs a lighter from his pocket and hands it to me without looking down.

He doesn't look away because I don't let him, pushing my will into him. I control my revulsion at my action and walk backward. He follows. "Thanks. But that's not what I really want." I smile slightly and move into the shadows behind a big blue SUV, keeping my focus on his eyes and sending my thoughts to him, telling him I'm safe and he wants to make me happy. I don't know why this mental ability works, but it did, most of the time. Putting the lighter back into his pocket, I take his hand, rubbing his wrists over the raised, throbbing veins. I move my hands up to his elbows, rubbing the insides, while keeping his gaze. Shoving my thoughts at him, I ask him to surrender, to make me happy.

He pushes into my body, and I allow it but rest my head against the vehicle to keep his eyes on mine. His hands grip my hips.

I whisper, "If you want me, say you're mine."

"I'm yours," he slurs.

Completely under my spell. "Such a strong man. A good man. A generous man. You want to give me everything, don't you?"

"Yes. Everything." He shoves his pelvis against my stomach.

He is under my command. "Close your eyes and you'll have your wildest dreams." He closes his eyes, and I turn us around, leaning him against the SUV. Then I raise his arm, lower my fangs, and lick his inner elbow several times. Each time, he shudders. Knowing his skin is numbed, I bite down and drink, counting to mark the minutes and pulling away after taking a pint. I lick the holes until they close, then release his arm.

I don't want to stop—it takes every bit of resolve I had to let go—but I won't injure or kill. Bad enough that I have to steal someone's will and body to live.

The man flops against the SUV. "You had the best time with your perfect woman. You'll have a wonderful, happy life." I tuck a hundred in his pocket and leave, getting in my car and driving away. The man will wake soon and never know how he ended up with an extra hundred dollars. He'll remember a sexy encounter with an amazing woman, but then the dream will fade. Hopefully, my affirmation will stick with him longer.

I know, from listening to gossip at the drag bar, that I can enthrall a person easier and faster than most vampires. Perhaps it's because an old vamp turned me, or maybe it's an innate talent, or a combination of both. I've always been persuasive. I'm certainly not asking Theo. He'll never tell me the truth, anyway.

Even though I need the ability to stay alive, using it makes me sick. The mesmerizing is the primary reason I'd left Theo's den as soon as I could. He and his friends take anyone they want, for as long as they want, without any thought for the consequences. A lost day in Vegas isn't unusual, and most people recover, laughing it off. But a week away from your significant other, then stumbling back claiming no memory and the police dismissing the experience with a "you're lucky to be alive" platitude ruins marriages and lives.

Decades after I'd left Theo's lair, I'd served a group of Theo's lackeys laughing about a social media group they'd found called "Lost in Vegas." The group contained hundreds of people who'd come for vacation or work and couldn't remember anything.

After I got off work, I looked up the group. Some people had obviously overdosed on alcohol and/or drugs, but a majority described the symptoms of mesmerization. A few individuals claimed to be law enforcement, many offering official phone numbers. Some requested direct messages; obvious creeps and scammers. But there were also indications that a serious group was forming to investigate and punish those responsible.

I'd warned Theo that he was playing with fire, but he laughed it off as the fears of a baby vamp. The older vamps didn't understand the power of social media or the strength of large numbers. Which is stupid because humans have banded together to take out vamps before and been successful. Theo knows that but chooses to ignore it.

Just one more reason to stay far away.

Maybe that was the existential threat he was worried about. If so, he'd created the problem—he can deal with it.

And if I get caught in the fallout, I'll be angry, but I deserve punishment, too. I am part of the problem, even if I only take the minimum I need to live.

I have a more immediate problem, though. I have to find shelter for the coming day, and then I'll leave Vegas. Maybe I should drive out now while Theo is dealing with the attack. But he is experienced, has lots of people, and he's intelligent. He can keep searching for me and expand that search to find his attackers. I'll be better off lying low for a while, then getting out.

I don't want to risk any of my acquaintances or friends, so it's back to natural lairs. I drive south to Sloan Canyon National Conservation Area. Like Red Rocks, I've found plenty of places where stacked rocks have left hollows to hide in. Every vehicle I've stashed around the city—and I have three more, all "owned" by people in care centers—has an emergency pack with a fire shelter and something to sit on. Sadly, blood boxes have quick expiration dates, and no one has managed to successfully dehydrate blood so that it retains the qualities that keep vamps alive.

At the south end of the city, I find a quiet neighborhood to park in, pull my emergency pack and my bike, and ride. Sneaking into the park on a bike is easy, and I reach my chosen hideout fast. Stashing the bike out of sight, I crawl through the narrow passage and come out in a small hollow. I unfold my little chair and pull out the fire shelter. There's a few hours before the sun rises, but after last night's close call, I'm happy to relax for a while.

Besides, I need the time to plan my next move. I have to avoid Theo and all his people, while also avoiding all my friends, and then get out of town. While I want to go north, maybe I need to go south instead, at least temporarily. Out of the Vegas area, I can swing back north. But I haven't scouted light-safe lairs to the south, while I have to the north. No matter which way I go, it will probably be more difficult than I anticipate.

I've never figured out why Theo is so determined to control me after he's allowed me decades of freedom. First, he'd turned me without any of the usual blood vows of fealty and obedience, after a few nights of casual conversation. I've learned that's almost unheard of; most vamps who can turn others will only consider those who've served them for many years, people they know well and often, intimately.

After I'd gained control of my urge for blood—something I'd also accomplished much faster than most—I'd left Theo's without fanfare, never guessing that was odd. Or that Theo would be angry about it. Or that he could probably find me whenever he wanted to but had left me alone. I'd been blissfully unaware, staying with a female vamp who'd visited Theo one evening and offered to help me. I hadn't known Cerise saw me as a rival until she told me. After I laughed at the idea of me as Theo's consort, she helped me find a job and a safe place to live.

I hadn't stayed in either for long, and I'd remained far away from Cerise. Especially after I'd heard Theo had rejected her bid for consort. Which was too bad; she'd be a much better choice for the job. I doubted Theo wanted me in that role; he had legions of beautiful, intelligent women vying for his attention. Sure, I'm clever, but I've never gotten past high school. And I appear too old next to Theo, who looks like he's in his twenties.

That's not a mystery I can solve. My problem is getting out of Vegas. I should have bought a burner phone before I got here to research routes. But I hadn't. Instead, I can decide how many days I'll remain in this spot. Two is a good starting point, if I move my car every night. I can change it out with my others as well, but that means returning to Vegas proper. I've stashed nothing to the south, a failure in proper planning.

I really can't make any more decisions until I get more information. After I survive another day, I'll check with some of my south end acquaintances and see if anyone is watching them. I'm pretty good at spotting tails and surveillance. I might miss an older vampire with the gift of shadows, but most of them are too proud to do footwork.

The night is almost gone. I shake out the fire shelter, pull it over my body, and release the chair sides to flatten it. Then I wait for the blackout of day, hoping I wake up alone.

CHAPTER 9

I WAKE AND CRAWL from my den, leaving my chair and shelter there. Risky, but if I get caught by Theo, he'll shelter me from the daylight—in a cell. If I get caught by the sun, it's my own fault. Outside, the air is heavy with heat and dust, and the bright lights of the Vegas Strip shimmer in the distance, smaller casinos flashing nearby.

I retrieve my bike and take a different route back to the popular area of the park, then roll to my car. When I am less than two blocks away, I notice dogs barking and howling. Dogs love me, so something else is upsetting them. Many dogs don't like weres. I turn away from my car at the next intersection. I'll get a burner phone, call a ride share, and retrieve a different vehicle.

I thought the Vegas Pack was independent. But from the way the Alpha herded me into Theo's car—his nose on my backside left an impression—that isn't true. No sense in taking chances that they've tracked me down.

A man turns the corner in front of me. A woman appears across the street, then another on the block ahead of me. I stop, but they continue towards me, so I continue forward, then turn to my right and churn my legs, riding along a rough alley. Feet pound behind me, and two figures appear in front of me. I ditch the bike and run for the stucco-covered wall to my right, but a woman crouches on top of it before I get more than a single step.

They have me cornered. I stand with my back to the fence at my left, knowing any were can easily jump it and get behind me. Men and women stalk towards me, stopping in a semicircle about fifteen feet away. None of them will look in my eyes; they keep their gaze on my feet or forehead. I am caught, at least for now, but I make myself relax. Showing fear might be deadly.

They remain in place while I inspect each of them. Although their height, coloring, and ethnicity vary, each person is in outstanding physical condition. Each is alert, some ready to spring, others seemingly relaxed, but none of them are friendly. They are almost certainly weres, probably wolves, coyotes, and other canines. Generally, you don't see cats in these numbers unless it's a lion pride, and supposedly we don't have any near Vegas. Other were species are rare, and I don't know much about them. They definitely aren't gargoyles. They have a certain sheen to their skin, and when they stand still, they blend into the background.

After about five minutes, two people shift to the side, and a man walks through the gap. He isn't the tallest man there, or the biggest, but he is definitely in shape. He has an air of command, his own mesmerizing quality. While mine cajoles, his demands, rather like Theo's, but with a lot more intensity and menace. He must be the pack Alpha.

I cross my arms and tap a toe. He might intimidate his pack, but I'm not one of his. He stalks across the empty space surrounding me, stopping within arm's length, and meets my gaze. I stare back, but don't try to push my will on his. Even if it works, there are too many others here. They'll keep him from doing anything like letting me go.

I'm not sure how long we stare, but I have to concentrate to keep my anger and fear active. He doesn't push for submission exactly, but rather a feeling that I'd be safer with him.

Neither that, nor any other technique is likely to work on me. I've been around too long to put my happiness, security, or welfare into the hands of another. I want to roll my eyes, but I won't be the first to drop our stare-off. Maybe I should try mesmerizing him; that will make him blink. It will also make him hostile, and I'm not ready to go there—yet.

"Alpha, we're drawing attention. Cops inbound." The volume is low, but the man's words are clipped and business-like.

"Copy that. Team One, get my vehicle. Team Two and Three, return to your usual activities. I've got it from here."

I huff. "Do you?"

He raises a heavy brow above his deep brown eyes. "Unless you'd like to keep our stare-off going until sunrise?"

"If going with you means returning to Theo's control, yes. I'd rather burn." I mean every word.

His head rears back, but he doesn't drop my gaze. "I have no intention of bringing you to Theoden."

"Intentions don't mean much. Especially when you've shoved your nose into my butt doing just that."

Someone snickers, but it cuts off abruptly. "Sure that was me?" A thick brow rises and his lips press together.

"Absolutely? No. Fairly certain, yes. Simple deduction, Watson. I'm surrounded by canines who call you alpha. Wolves rule the canines. There's only one wolf alpha in Vegas and only an alpha can turn at the new moon. Supposedly. Therefore, you're him."

"Logical." He stares at me while nodding. "And partly correct. I am the wolf alpha. I still have no intention of delivering you to Theoden. Especially if you help me."

"Help you? Do I look like I can help myself, let alone you?" I raise both hands, gesturing to the wolves surrounding me. "Besides, you've already betrayed me to Theo once. Why would I trust you?"

He leans closer. "Because Theoden has my niece. My human niece."

CHAPTER 10

A VULNERABLE HOSTAGE. Now the alpha's actions make more sense. "I'm sorry to hear that. But I still don't know how I can help." He'd trade me for his niece in a heartbeat. I can't trust this guy, no matter how sincere he seems.

"I know you don't. But I do, at least to some extent. I know Theoden has kept you in the dark. I can tell you what I know and help you, but only if you're willing to help me. But first, we need to leave. Are you willing to listen? I promise you safe shelter for the coming day."

I suspect this man's word means a lot, but I still don't trust him. "I'll follow in my car."

"Fine." He sweeps his arm to the side, bowing slightly. "Lead on." He turns to the woman behind him. "Follow us."

"Yes, Alpha." The woman curls her lip and glares at me before turning away to climb into the large SUV that pulls up. Two men get into the back seat.

I am fairly certain that same woman drove Theo's limo last night, but I don't ask. I pick up my e-bike and push it back to my Forester. After I open the hatch, the alpha picks up my bike and slides it into the back, then gets in the passenger seat. A piece of paper sticks out from the driver's side door handle. I snatch it, and pretending to tie my shoe, take a glance at it. "Call if you need help. The Badgers." A phone number finishes the message.

Aware that an SUV full of wolves who don't like me much has just pulled up to my bumper, I shove the paper in my waistband, get behind the wheel and start the car. "Where am I going?"

He frowns. "Summit Club Golf Course. You didn't know it's my pack's home?"

I shrug. "I mind my own business." If the chatter and gossip doesn't pertain to me, I don't care. The never-ending stream of inter-pack drama at the bar goes in one ear and out the other. I've probably heard the pack house location at some time or another but have had no reason to retain the information, since I never planned on visiting.

"That is a mistake. You should learn everything you can about everyone around you. And form alliances. Ignorance is dangerous." He scans our surroundings constantly, glancing at me occasionally.

I shoot a glare at the annoying, and very alert man. "Thanks, Captain Obvious. But tell me, who's going to stand against Theo with me? No one can do that, not here."

"You think leaving Vegas will save you from Theoden?" He huffs. "Even if you could, it's not likely. Every major city has someone like him, and they cooperate, when it suits them. Most of them are much more controlling and cruel than Theoden. And they treat other supernaturals even worse. Every one of them would love to get their hands on you. Theoden's influence has actually kept you safe."

"You're kidding me, right?" This has to be part of his game. He's setting me up, softening me for Theo. "Why would any of them want me? I'm a middle-aged nobody. A bartender. I don't belong to Theo, so I can't be used against him. It's ridiculous."

He turns towards me, scowling. "Theo turned you. You took the blood vows. He owns you."

"No. He doesn't. I would have died before swearing to obey him. Or any man. Or woman, for that matter." But I'd wanted to live, so it's hard to say what I would have agreed to at that moment had Theo demanded a price.

His brows rise, and he jolts back in his seat, then recovers his emotionless expression. "Interesting." He nods and returns to his search for threats. "There's rumors of a prophecy—"

I scoff. "Oh, please. I don't believe in destiny, and I'm no chosen one." The idea is ludicrous. Pure fiction. Besides, that role always goes to some clueless kid, eagerly searching for meaning in their life. I don't believe in predetermination or any of that ridiculousness. I believe in hard work and perseverance.

Or stubbornness, most would call it.

"I didn't say I believed in the prophecy, just that there is one. Like most prophecies, what I've seen is very vague and could apply to a large number of people and situations." He waves as if he's brushing away a fly. "But rumors say Theoden believes it. And that the prophecy refers to a woman turned immortal who is free of all chains. I'm sure there are more details that lead Theoden to believe you're that person, and that's why he didn't make you take the vows." The alpha turns towards me again, inspecting me. "I'll help you, but you'd better help me." He snarls. "If you betray me, you'll regret it."

I pull to the side, throw the car in neutral, and glare at him. "Let's get something straight here, buster. If I agree to help you, I will. I appreciate the information you gave me, but I don't owe you for it. Understood?"

"But you owe me for not taking you straight to Theoden and trading you for my niece." He leans in, his face only inches from mine.

Ridiculous man. "Like that would work. You know better. Theo won't let go of anything that puts you and your pack at his beck and call."

"I know that." He snarls again.

I tap him under his sharp jaw the same way I'd tap a misbehaving dog. "Don't take that out on me."

He rears back. "Did you just boop me?"

"Booping is for good dogs. Snarling is bad." I keep my expression blank. "Bad dogs get corrected." His lip curls. I hold up a finger. "Don't make me do that again."

"Do that again and lose your finger." His face morphs, his nose and mouth stretching into a furry wolf's snout, and he snaps his huge teeth less than a quarter inch from my finger. Then his face reforms into his human visage.

Having expected violence, I don't react, but it takes everything I have to stay in place. I hadn't expected a partial shift. Or known that was even possible. Plus, his teeth are huge. "Then don't snarl at me. Threats will get you nowhere, fast. Even Theo learned that much." His shifting control and speed are impressive, especially at the new moon. Or maybe the shifters I've overheard lied about that. It seems that the alpha—I still don't know his name—is right that my ignorance is dangerous.

"Theoden told me that my niece's blood is sweet. I'm going to snarl." It's his turn to be expressionless.

I sigh. "Understood. We're both on edge, so let's try to not antagonize each other."

"Agreed. Let's go." He points towards the windshield. "I'd rather have this discussion in my home. And that puts you closer to a sun-safe shelter."

I check, then pull back onto the road. "I had one that worked fine."

"A bed will be more comfortable." He turns to look behind the vehicle.

"Well, sure." My back is stiff from a day spent on a too thin pad over very hard rock. "But freedom is more important."

"I'd agree. My niece deserves that too."

"And if you get her back, are you seeking revenge? Or going on the offensive to prevent future issues?" Because I don't want to live in a war zone. It never ends well for anyone.

He looks up at the roof of the car. "My pack is well-off, not multi-billionaires. We can't buy the kind of firepower or influence that Theoden can. So no. Even when I get her back, I will not seek revenge. If she's safe. If she's harmed, he's a dead man." He points to the right.

I make the turn. "He's already dead, but his brain doesn't know it. I'm fairly certain vampires are zombies, but without the rotting."

He barks a laugh. "That explains a lot."

"And we want blood instead of brains." I shrug. "Zombies."

"Zombies or not, Theoden is a dead man if my niece is permanently harmed."

I need to redirect this conversation to something useful. "Back to fixing my ignorance. If Theo is killed, what happens to his sworn vampires? Are they free?"

He shakes his head. "You should know these things."

I scowl at the road ahead. "If I knew, I wouldn't ask. I didn't have a normal vampire upbringing, okay? I got out of Theo's tower of terror as soon as possible. He runs his businesses like a human CEO, but other than a few at the top, his vampire community acts like interns competing for a single job without any pesky laws to limit their predatory instincts." I'd been at the bottom, and their abuse was unlimited until I learned how to fight back.

"Interesting. And troubling." He sucks in a noisy breath. "Okay. If Theoden didn't appoint a successor, they'd be free. But I'm sure he did. He'll keep the person's identity secret because they don't have any protection against attack until they take over and inherit those blood vows. But he'd be foolish to leave that position open. It's happened occasionally." He grimaces. "When the vampires are freed, they fight for the lead. Generally, other vampire rulers step in and kill them. They don't usually keep the territory. They seem to have a limit for both square miles and the number of vampires they can rule. But that's a guess based on observation, not a fact I've been told." He shrugs. "But I've also heard there's a vamp taking over multiple territories in California."

He's being generous with his information, but I'm sure there's a reason. "Do you get told a lot of vampire facts?"

He looks out the window. "Sometimes. Under special circumstances."

That pings my curiosity. "And what are those?"

He frowns at me. "None of your business." Blood rushes to his face, and he turns to the window again.

"A lover? That would explain a lot. Not sure why you're embarrassed, though. Vampires are persuasive and, present company excluded, beautiful."

He twists to scowl at me. "You're beautiful."

I scoff. "I'm too old to be beautiful. I'm striking, maybe, or interesting."

"Beauty is more than skin deep. I know you've treated Janice and Troy with respect. And all the other supernaturals who worked for you. You're tough, but fair, and stand up to management. You're good at convincing others to do things your way, without taking away their free will." He reaches out and runs his fingertip along the curve of my jaw. "But you are physically beautiful as well. A few lines don't change that."

I jerk my head away from the seductive glide of his raspy pad. "You're smooth. No wonder a vampire spilled her guts." I pull up to the gate, but it opens before I can stop.

The alpha returns the guard's salute, then directs me through the widespread luxury homes. The fairways are unusually large for Vegas, sprinklers making the grass sparkle in the beautifully designed landscape lighting. "Won't some homeowner report a stranger to Theo?"

"Not if they want to live here." He directs me through the development. We drive west, rising into the foothills. "They're mostly pack members and other supes. The few human residents work for my pack." He points at an immense house. "Drive around back and into the garage."

The gigantic, three-story mansion has the typical Vegas exterior of sandy stucco and red tile roof, but the landscaping is lush with multiple water features. The plants and ponds are low, leaving nothing to hide behind, and the lighting minimizes shadows. Bars cover the windows, including the upper stories, and the door appears to be metal. The overall effect is medieval-style luxury and security on a massive scale.

I drive around the side to the back and pull into the open garage door—one of four. Beyond the house is an iron bar fence, then open, dry land rising into the hills. "Where do you get all the water?"

The alpha smirks. "A water witch owed me a big favor. I wanted pools for my pack members. But it turned out better than I planned because the golf club fees pay for most of the overhead. Humans love exclusivity." He gets out.

"Not just humans." I join him in the garage. Black and white checkerboard coats the floor, and the interior walls are tan, matching the exterior stucco. Dark wood cabinets line the walls, except for a small office area with a desk and chair, and a computer on top. The other four stalls hold the same large black SUVs I've seen behind us.

The alpha leads the way to a door, enters a code into a pad, and puts his hand on a sensor. A glint in the wall above the sensor tells me there's a camera there; probably facial recognition. The pack takes security seriously. A thunk, and the door opens, revealing a large mud room with benches on two sides and hooks above. Clothes hang from a few pegs—perhaps pack members patrolling in wolf form. Except I've been told that changing at the new moon is extremely difficult for most weres. But the badgers invading Theo's office were all in animal form, so maybe that's false.

A second open security door leads to a commercial kitchen, the scent of frying beef hanging in the air, but we take a right, entering a short hallway. At the end, a great room with couches, chairs, and entertainment centers holds at least ten people, but we don't join them. The alpha opens a door on the left and treads down a staircase. I follow him to the basement; it makes sense that any light safe room would be below ground.

At the bottom of the stairs, a smaller seating area with leather couches and a bar on the left-hand wall has a vaguely British Pub scheme. The alpha leads me to another security door and opens it, revealing another hallway with closed, blank doors, all secured with electronic locks. We walk to the door at the very end, and he enters another code and fingerprint. Inside, a large mahogany desk holds three monitors and a fancy-looking chair. The sealed concrete floor in front of the desk is empty, without a rug or a guest chair. To the left of the desk is a leather couch and two club chairs, a photo-realistic forest painting decorating the wall behind the couch. The right-hand wall holds an open door revealing a bathroom; beyond that door is a small bar area. Another secured door is behind the desk to the left. The faint sharpness of vinegar, probably from cleaning, remains in the air, but there's a continual light breeze; most likely from an excellent air filtration system. They'd want to protect their sensitive noses.

"If you'd like to use the facilities, please do so. Would you like anything other than water?" He strides to the bar, pulling glasses off a shelf and filling them from the tap. "We have an excellent filtering system."

"Water is fine. The bathroom would be welcome, thank you." I enter, closing the door behind me and turning on the fan. The alpha's manners remind me of my childhood, and I find myself responding in the same fashion. It doesn't seem likely that he'd be my age—weres, especially wolves and big cats, often die violently. I'll never know unless he tells me; like vampires, weres don't age, and it's rude to ask.

I use the facilities, wash my hands and face, and wipe my body with a washcloth to remove the grit of last night's hideout. Hopefully the light safe room will come with a shower. A comb would be nice, too, but for now, my fingers will do.

After stalling as long as I can, I leave the bathroom. The alpha sprawls in one corner of the couch and tips his glass back. His throat moves as he swallows, the everyday occurrence somehow sensual.

I look at the forest scene behind him. I know better than to let animal magnetism get to me. The man is admittedly sexy; he'd look perfect on a cowboy romance novel cover. His dark, brooding good looks, combined with his confident, but not arrogant attitude and surprisingly good manners, add up to an attractive package. But pretty doesn't equal good. I cross the room and sit in one of the chairs, picking up the glass of water on the low dark wood table between us, and drink. I almost finish the glass before I put it down.

The alpha puts his glass down on a coaster and leans forward. "So, Charlene Flammen, do you want to live?"

CHAPTER II

I keep my seat, but it takes some effort. If he wanted to kill me, it would have been easier to dispose of me in the desert. Although, his house borders the desert, too, so maybe disposing of bodies is easier where they know the territory. "That's why I drink blood now, so yes."

He sits back. "You're a cool customer. Good."

I don't bother holding back my sigh of exasperation. "You can stop testing me any time now. I'm not hiding anything from you. I'm here because you're the lesser of two evils, and fighting you is a waste of time. Plus, freeing your niece means tweaking Theo's nose, which I'm always happy to do. That's why I helped—" I clamp my mouth shut. He might not know about the gargoyle and badger raid, and I won't betray them. "Others."

His thick, dark brown brows rise. "Others?"

I nod once. "Others."

"Those others wouldn't happen to be the man who shot me full of sedatives and a bunch of badgers, would they?" His lip curls. "They made everything worse."

He probably didn't enjoy the knock-out drug hangover. "Worse for them, for you, or everyone? Or Theo? Because if a bunch of badgers made things worse for

Theo, I'm on team badger." I raise my arms like a cheerleader with pom-poms. "Go Badgers!"

He frowns. "Theo wasn't happy, but their actions didn't hurt him, either. He's increased his security, too."

I scoff. "Breaking into Theo's cell block is impossible. Getting out is harder." I spent my first two weeks as a vampire in those cells, learning to control my bloodlust.

"I don't have to break into his cells. My niece is enthralled, living happily trapped in Theo's apartment." His fists clench. "The badgers tried to get her to come with them, and she refused. Got hysterical about it. That's why things are worse."

That explains why the gargoyle had a human-size harness. But in that case, he shouldn't have helped me until the badgers returned. Maybe he knew it was a lost cause. But the alpha has bigger problems. "The longer she's mesmerized, the harder it is to break."

A low growl sounds. "I know that. Fighting it doesn't help, either." A series of pops follows. The alpha has ripped holes into the couch cushions on either side of him with the claws that have appeared in place of his fingernails.

Time to change the subject to something more positive. "Okay, so how can I help? Because I have a few more hours before I pass out for the day." I don't want those long claws used on me.

"How does enthrallment work? And how can I break it?" He leans forward.

I deliberately relax my body and look at the ceiling for a moment. "I wish I knew. After I capture a person's gaze, I think hard at them." I shrug. "I don't have better words, really. I think at someone, telling them they want to please me, make me happy and they'll get their greatest desire in return. It doesn't always work."

"Can you turn it off?"

I'm not doing anything right now, so why is he asking? "I don't do it all the time. It takes effort."

"Are you sure about that? Because it feels like you are." His thick black brows wrinkle, and his eyes squint. But even the squished, skeptical look can't diminish the effect of his rugged good looks—that jawline could cut glass.

"No." I tsk. "If I was trying to mesmerize you, you'd never know." Although I'm not sure I could do anything to an alpha were. Or any were. I've only mesmerized humans, and only when I absolutely have to. "Ask Janet. I've never tried to enthrall her or anyone else who works with me."

He sits back. "I have asked Janet, Troy, Matias and others. They all say you're the best boss they've ever had, and they love working for you." His lip curls up. "But none of them can tell me why they feel that way. They just do. Sound familiar?"

I mirror his position, leaning back against the chair. He's trying to anger me for some reason, and it's not going to work. "I am a good boss. I'm fair, and I protect my people from management's stupidity as much as possible. They may not be able to articulate what I do because I protect them from that, too. It's my job, not theirs." I'm proud of my skills.

"Can you mesmerize someone who's already been mesmerized? Take over from another vampire?"

I scoff. "I don't hang out with other vampires. They're not nice people."

"Including you?"

"Yes." I live by taking from people. Of course I'm not nice. Humans might be near the top of the food chain, but I'm an apex predator.

He leans forward, his elbows on his knees. "If I can get my niece, will you try? Because I'd rather have her in your clutches than Theoden's."

The man's trusting me too much. "You don't know me. I might have a basement full of enthralled humans."

His full lips flatten and he huffs. "I know where you live, where you work, and where you have storage units." I start to object, and he lifts a brow. "Probably not all of them. But enough that I was able to put a tracker on your current vehicle. I hadn't found the one you drove on your original escape. But my point is, you don't have a basement. Or anywhere else to store humans. And you go through a lot of blood boxes."

I want to snarl but hold back. "Were you bribing my neighbors?"

"Didn't take much. You chose poorly."

"I am aware, thank you." Almost everyone who lived in that lousy apartment complex was on the edge of poverty. "Why would you bother?"

He gives me a half-smile. "Because if Theoden's interested, I'm interested. I started tracking you a very long time ago." He shakes his head. "And you should have known that a long time ago, too. Seriously, why do you think Janet's wasting her talents as a cocktail waitress?"

"I thought she liked the money." I take people at their word too much, evidently.

He snorts. "Her tips don't pay for an hour of her salary. She's a financial wizard. My CFO." His lips clamp tight, and he scowls. "Are you sure you're not trying to mesmerize me?"

I hold up both hands, palms out. "Definitely not. But I'm told I'm easy to talk to. One of the reasons I'm a good bartender." I knew Janet was smart, but I don't pry into people's lives.

He shakes his head. "You're a manager, a leader, not simply a bartender. You're holding yourself back. Trying to make a smaller target for Theoden?"

"Yes." It's my turn to clamp my mouth shut. Despite his air of command mixed with danger, he's too easy to talk to.

"Stop. It's not working and it only hurts you. If you want him out of your life, you'll have to get rid of him and take over." His gaze bores into mine. "If Theoden's successor takes over, he'll want you under his control, too. Neither will allow a baby vamp to thumb her nose at their commands. And if he believes in the prophecy, too, he'll want you under his control even more." He jabs his forefinger at me. "Step up. Take charge, and take the fight to Theoden."

I shake my head. "That's a war. What happens to your niece in a war? I'll tell you." I lean forward. "She ends up dead. Collateral damage. War is hard on bystanders."

His mouth twists for a moment. "I'm aware. Fought in several, each one uglier than the last."

A military veteran—his hypervigilance and air of command came from real wartime experience. Several wars also imply he's even older than I thought. But he's kept up with technological advances, too. He's a highly intelligent and motivated man. But I've lived through the mob wars and drug dealer territorial fights, and I've lost friends and colleagues. People in the wrong place at the wrong time, not mobsters or police.

He taps the coffee table once. "My niece isn't living now. Death might be kinder. But regardless, prophecy is a double-edged sword. You can be used, you can use it, or you can actively refute it. Ignoring it won't keep the true believers away, and it makes you more vulnerable to those attempting to use it." He smirks. "I'd bet that group includes Theoden. He's too smart to believe in hokey religions and ancient weapons when he's got so much money on his side."

I can't hold back a laugh. "Are you misquoting Star Wars at me?"

He shrugs. "If the fandom fits..."

"A closet Jedi? That figures." It does. He's a hero for his people, and probably others. But I have to remember he's on the list of people who want to use me. "Back to the current hokey religion. Do you have a copy of this prophecy?"

He grimaces. "Not a complete one. I have a blurry shot pulled from a video. I've had several people and artificial intelligence programs try to reconstruct it, but confidence is low." He pulls out his phone, scrolls, and selects a page. "This is the most likely version."

> ### *The Prophecy of the Unbound Queen*
>
> *When the dusk bleeds into an endless bright,*
> *And battles rage over control of the night,*
> *One shall rise—a queen of shadow's creed,*
> *By choice alone, not by chains decreed.*
> *In mortal flesh, her fierce heart was concealed,*
> *Yet by her will, service for all is now revealed.*
> *With fangs unsheathed, she claims her boundless might,*
> *A sovereign born to rule the endless night.*
> *None who stand in her path shall be redeemed,*
> *For her command reigns supreme.*
> *A tempest fierce, she leads her kin with grace,*
> *The unchained dawn none can hope to replace.*
> *She brings no peace, no mercy to the fray,*
> *Yet freedom fierce as stars keep threat at bay.*
> *The world shall know her rule, unbent, serene,*
> *When black night turns bright and towers turn the desert green.*
> *Behold the rise of the queen freely turned,*
> *Her power flows where hearts and heavens burn.*

I can't hold back a laugh after reading this piece of nonsense. "Why in the world does Theo think this is me? Sure, 'dusk bleeding into endless bright and towers turning the desert green' is Vegas. Mob wars might fit the second line, but there's nothing here that says Charlene Flammen is the chosen one. This could be any woman. Or considering where I work, any man."

The alpha shrugs. "I don't think we've got all of it. Supposedly, there's a whole book, all handwritten."

I chuckle. "Something about a crone with hair of silver?"

A growl rumbles—emphatic enough to feel and hear. "Don't put yourself down. Enough people will do that for you. You might look older than the average vampire, but that doesn't mean you aren't gorgeous." He grimaces. "Looks aren't important anyway. What's important is that Theoden believes you are the Unbound Queen. You are a leader, even if you've never embraced the role. And the only way you're getting out of this alive, and my niece gets free, is if you take over."

"If Theo really believes this thing, why has he let me be all these years? Why push me now?"

"I don't know. I can only speculate that there's more in the prophecy that details the timing. Maybe something about the comet that just appeared?" He shrugs. "Or something else related to the night sky? That's always a popular choice for ancient, hokey religions." His mouth twists.

"Do you know where this prophecy is located? Getting a hold of it might be a good way to start."

He shakes his head. "I don't think that's the place to start. We start with you stepping up to lead your fellow vamps through the endless bright."

"And how am I supposed to do that?" None of them would listen to me, the baby vamp.

He leans forward, with his elbows on his knees. "You stop Theoden's people from rampaging through the humans. Spin it as doing it for their own good, that you are the protector of the people. Lean into the unbound queen myth—lead them down a path of longevity with less excess."

I frown at him. "That's not exactly what this prophecy says. It's more about ruling and might than control."

"It's a prophecy." He chuckles. "You can make it say what you want it to say. I know you've warned Theoden about the Lost in Vegas group, and he ignored it." He tilts his head. "Although, Theoden isn't one of those vampires, generally. He's quite selective and rarely mesmerizes anyone."

I sniff. "Of course he doesn't. He's a billionaire; he's got people falling at his feet constantly. Why work for anything when it's offered freely?"

"True. But he's picky and precise. He used to control his people tightly, too. It's only been in the last five years that they've been allowed this level of freedom over the tourists." He huffs. "Now I understand." He stares at the far side of the room.

"Understand what?"

His gaze meets mine, his brown eyes lightening to an amber glow. "He's waiting for you to take control. He wants the unbound queen to appear. Since you haven't changed, he's making you move." His smile is unsettling. "He's making sure you're free of *every* chain. He knew you'd quit when he bought the Royale, and he knew you'd do anything to stay out of his grasp." He leans towards me. "I'll ask you again. Charlene Flammen, do you want to live?"

CHAPTER 12

I SIT BACK, ROLLING my eyes. Despite the drama, he's got a point. "Ugh. If I have to take over, I don't even know where to start."

His brows wrinkle. "Luckily for you, I do. I've been where you are now."

"Don't you werewolves do the whole fight to the death thing and kill your way up the ladder?" The thought turns my stomach. I don't like Theoden or his people, but I like the idea of killing even less.

"Yes and no." His lip curls. "I have killed those who were unwilling to yield or have betrayed the pack. But I prefer to fight for supremacy and I'm good at it. I can help you." His gaze meets mine again. "But only if you help me."

"I'll help you with your niece, regardless." It's my turn to curl a lip. "But taking over the Vegas vampires? That seems like a lot of work with no reward, just more work."

"Leadership can be difficult, it's true." He points at the ceiling. "My pack is enjoying their normal lives, while I'm in a windowless basement, talking to a blood sucker." He smirks. "But there are benefits, like knowing my people are safer because I'm in charge."

I blink, stunned by his arrogance. "And you know this, how?" I shake my head. "Never mind, it doesn't matter. What matters is that I'm not so certain the Vegas vamps will be better off under my rule."

He taps his chest with his forefinger. "I'm sure. I've seen who you are through my pack. You're thousands of times better than Theoden, let alone those hedonistic idiots lazing around in his tower, making a mess of human lives and hassling us. You will take command and put them to work. That will keep them out of trouble." He growls. "Except Trinity. She's mine."

He doesn't mean that in a positive way, clearly. Trinity must have lured his niece away. "I don't know any of them. Never wanted to know any of them after Reeve almost killed me." Theoden's primary bully boy had starved me, then made me sit in a chair and watch humans run by. If I moved at all, he shocked me, and he kept increasing the voltage. After I stopped reacting at all, he kept shocking me until I passed out. I'd been a man's punching bag and I'd vowed it would never happen again. My only regret was walking away, rather than killing them all. But that would have ended in my death or imprisonment.

He scowled. "I keep tabs on all of them." He taps on his phone. "I'll share my intel with you. Bios, preferences, and backgrounds, although some of them are older than most records. None of it leaves this house in anything but your head, understand?"

I nod. "I agree. I appreciate the help, but I still don't see how I can take over Vegas. Theo's been ruling for decades. He's a billionaire CEO, not some bandit king. He makes decisions impacting thousands of human lives and millions of dollars every minute." I spread my hands. "I mix drinks and talk to people."

He shakes his head. "You lead diverse humans, werewolves, and gargoyles. You regularly manage drunk humans without violence. That's incredibly rare in the vampire world. Theoden leans on technology, avoiding the humans who work for him, because he doesn't have the control to deal with them. Before email became common, a lot more humans died. I'm amazed he sat at your bar for so long without killing anyone."

Back before he turned me, he came in regularly for a week. He'd been in regularly for the last month. Theo's control is better than the alpha believes. Still, not dealing directly with his persistent cloud of disdain and doom is a relief. "I'm amazed I didn't kill him. He's been a black hole, bringing everybody down." My tips were next to nothing, except those he dropped, and I left those for everyone else.

"So why didn't you?" His eyes narrow. "You could have taken care of all your problems with one quick thrust. Plenty of wooden chopsticks on your bar." He mimes stabbing with one hand.

Stake Theoden? In public? No way I'd succeed. "You have greatly exaggerated ideas of my capabilities." Theoden's speed and stealth are terrifying. I can't come close, literally and figuratively.

"I think you underestimate yourself." He shakes his head. "You have plenty of speed, strength, and mental talent. It's confidence, training, and awareness that you lack."

"Oh, just those." I don't hold back my eye roll. "I'll get right on that." Like I haven't been practicing when I can? My opportunities are limited because I trust few.

He leans towards me. "If you want to live free, you can. I will help with the training and awareness. Confidence is all yours, sweetheart."

I huff. I hear enough cute diminutives at the bar. "I'm confident that Theoden can kill me whenever he wants to."

The alpha sighs. "But he doesn't want to, or you'd already be dead. He wants to control you. Don't let him."

I shake my head. "We're going in circles."

A knock at the door interrupts his reply. The alpha rises, strides to the door, and cracks it. He accepts a tablet, then secures the door and returns to his seat. "This contains biographies, likes, dislikes, accomplishments, failures, and suspected strengths and weaknesses. Everything we've been able to gather about Theoden and his vampires over the last forty years. Sixty or more in some cases."

"You've been at this for a while." That's a lot of data.

He nods. "Know your enemy. As I told you, I've got intel on every supernatural and all the important humans in the area, too. Although the human files are shorter, even with scum like your former boss, Ald." He taps on the tablet, then turns it around. "Look into the camera and follow the directions, please."

I take it from him and create a profile, including biometrics. Then I select the file folder labeled vampire. Folders appear, labeled by vampire name. I click on Theoden's, of course.

The alpha—I have to learn his name at some point—taps the edge of the tablet. "Every file contains a summary, with links to the detailed documents. I'd recommend reading all the summaries, then concentrating on weaknesses and strengths. Except Theoden, because you need to know everything about him." He sniffs. "Everything we know, that is. Much of his early years are unknown because he was raised in Russia."

That explained the faint accent when his emotions were high. "Russia? How did he get here?" Perhaps Klaus is his given name, rather than a fake. Northern Russian heritage would explain his ice-blue eyes and blond hair.

He shakes his head. "We don't know for sure, but we think he came over with his creator during the California Gold Rush era. There are no immigration records, but that wasn't uncommon back then, particularly for those who came through Asia. We know that much of his wealth came from gold discovered in California and Nevada. Some supposedly haunted mines weren't—the vampires were living in them. Claim jumpers were a food source."

I wrinkle my nose and I have to clamp down on my thirst. My last meal was too long ago, and I'll have to do something about that soon. Without taking anything from the werewolves. "I suppose that's fair, unless they killed them."

He rises and retreats to the bar, returning with a familiar box and handing it to me. "No, they mostly lived, but with wild stories to tell. Kept all but the most adventuresome away."

He's too perceptive. I stab the straw into the box and suck. After the first restorative pull, I remember my manners. "Thank you."

"You're welcome." He returns to the bar and slides a container into the microwave. "I'm hungry, and I can't eat without offering something to a guest."

I laugh at his smooth handling. "Well, I appreciate your manners. They're rare these days." I scan through the list of vampire files, then the gargoyles, other supernaturals, and the weres—except werewolves.

"True. Some of my people have a lot to learn. Theoden's vamps even more."

"I notice my name isn't on any of these files. Or any werewolves."

The corners of his mouth lift. "I don't gather intel on my pack. They are mine and I know them, inside and out. I have a file on you, and I could probably get a lot from watching you read it, but I try not to betray a trust I'm trying to gain."

He's certainly an alpha—wearing command like a second skin—but an enlightened one. Although, he's gathering intel on me now, so maybe he just hides his inner monarch well. Even without a dossier, I'm fairly certain he's been alpha for a very long time, but it would be rude to ask. "I appreciate the attempt."

He brings a family-sized container to the couch, popping the top and filling a fork with shredded meat.

The hot spice and smoky meat makes me breathe deep. "Carne asada? Smells fabulous." I wish I could have some, but nausea follows my thought.

Smiling with his mouth closed, he nods, then swallows. "It is. Almost too spicy, but it's good training. You never know when you might run into peppery hazards."

I hold back a grimace at his subtle condemnation. I'm not sorry for trying to cover my tracks. "I miss eating tasty food." Sucking at the straw, I force down the bland blood.

"Turning has tradeoffs for any supernatural. There is always a price." He returns to his meal.

"I suppose so." Watching the food disappear, I figure the pack grocery bills must be enormous. I finish the box while I scan the rest of the files. It will take me days to go through all of these—or nights, more accurately. I have about an hour left tonight, so I turn to Theo's file.

Before I get far, the alpha rises, putting his container in the sink and gathering more blood boxes. "Come. I'll show you to your room." He walks to the door behind his desk and enters numbers. "I'm the only one with the code to this room, although there is an emergency entry protocol if I don't log into house security every seventy-two hours." The door beeps, and he opens it, revealing a master suite with a king-size bed, dresser, TV, and a compact, but luxurious bathroom with dark gray solid surface countertops above pale wood cupboards. No bathtub, but the shower has multiple adjustable spray heads and full size toiletries.

"This isn't my room, but I often sleep here when work gets busy. Feel free to use anything you find in here; it's pack property, not mine. The room is completely light-safe; the door seals tight enough to require an independent air filtration system. There are no windows, but there is an emergency hatch in the bathroom that exits into an upstairs safe room. That safe room exits into the mud room or there's an emergency tunnel to the desert behind the fence. Getting out that way requires blowing explosive bolts." He leads me into the bathroom and points at the ceiling above the toilet. "Just turn and yank the toilet paper holder to pop the hatch. Please don't do that unless you really need it. There is no security on the exit above, and it's not accessible from the outside without explosives." He puts the blood boxes on the sink counter.

My previous lair's security is a joke in comparison. "I'd prefer not to use any exit but the usual because that means something has gone terribly wrong." I back out of the small bathroom, uncomfortable with his proximity. "This is very impressive."

He smiles wryly. "When we built this house, we sank every penny we could afford into security. We lived with bare concrete and cinder block for a long time until we could renovate." He follows me out, turning to the door. "I'll lock this from the outside. If you need to get out, just look at the scanner." He points at what I thought was a peephole. "You might have to jump, sorry."

I sigh. "Tall people rule the world."

"I'm not that tall by today's standards, but yes." He opens the door with a quiet hiss as the rubber seals peel apart. "Rest well." The door locks thunk into place and the scanner glows red.

I carefully place the tablet on the bed and take my backpack to the bathroom. I hope the bathroom doesn't have cameras, but the alpha seems justifiably para-noid. Pulling my leggings down, I palm the paper left on my car door, then sit and read it again. After I memorize the phone number, I flush it and get ready for the night.

After a long shower removes some of the knots from my back, I put on the extra clothes in my bag. Then I wash my dirty ones in the sink, wringing them out before hanging them over the shower enclosure. Back at the bed, I put the tablet next to the bed on the floor, then peel back the sheets and climb in. The mattress is firmer than mine but very comfortable.

I attempt my meditation, but the alpha's stare is hard to forget, and Theo's threat even worse. I fret until I fall into darkness.

The next evening, I rise, run through a quick meditation and yoga routine, shower, and suck down a blood box. Then I return to the tablet. I consider letting myself out of the room, but if the alpha is busy, I don't want to bother him. On the other hand, I don't want to make him wait on me, either.

I can read in either place. If he has pack members out there, I'll return to the bedroom. I pack my clean clothes in my bag and wipe the bathroom down with a washcloth. I'd strip the sheets and towels, but it's likely I'll stay here again tonight, so I won't bother. But I also won't risk leaving anything behind.

Rising on my tiptoes, I look at the scanner, and the locking bars thump, the light turning green. I crack the door and peer out. Seeing no one, I leave the door open and enter the office, plopping back on the chair I used the night before.

When the office door beeps, I jump, then shudder. I've been so lost in the files I haven't been paying attention. That could be deadly. I've obviously assumed I'm safe here, and that's a leap of faith I have no business taking, even if the alpha somehow projects safety.

"Good evening, Char." The alpha enters, wearing dark jeans and a long sleeve dark green Henley. He fills out both very nicely; lean, but muscular, just like a true wolf. "I hope you slept well."

"Very well, thank you." I'm alive, so it must be true. As usual, time passes leaving no memories behind. "I haven't gotten much farther with these files."

He hands me a blood box. "And you won't get any farther tonight, I'm afraid. Theoden knows you're here."

CHAPTER 13

I GRIT MY TEETH for a moment. "By the burning daylight, I thought I'd have another day." I place the tablet on his desk. "Thanks for your help, but I don't want to put your people at risk. Is there a discreet way out of here?"

"Several." He shakes his head. "But you won't be taking any of them."

That is ominous. So much for safety. I slide towards the bedroom. "I see. Found a way to retrieve your niece after all, did you?"

"Yes." The corners of his mouth rise, but it isn't a smile. "But it's not what you think. It's time for a conversation with Theoden, rather than a battle. If he really believes the prophecy, he'll want to help."

"In a way that leaves him in charge." I keep moving, even if I have little chance of avoiding the wolf in this confined space.

He nods but doesn't chase me. "Of course. He's a predator, just like me. He won't give up power willingly. If he's not a true believer, but merely hedging his bets, he'll make you work for it. But enough of his people believe in the prophecy that he can't work against you or he'll lose everything. He turned you 'unbound' for a reason. Either there's something in that prophecy that he wants to happen, or enough of his people believe you're the queen that he had no choice."

"He probably considers himself king." Contemplating a personal relationship with Theo turns my stomach. He's a gorgeous man, no doubt of that, but he'd demand complete subservience. I'll never, ever put myself in that position again. "Where are we meeting?"

"At our clubhouse. He's agreed to meet the two of us with a single vampire as backup. My pack will surround the clubhouse. He'll have personnel just outside the club's fence. But with just four of us, we should have mutually ensured destruction."

It's my turn to snarl. "You still have a greatly exaggerated view of my abilities." Confronting Klaus Theoden seems like suicide.

"No." He smirks. "I have an accurate view of my abilities. If I'm not mesmerized, I can easily take out two vampires. Even Theoden."

I have my doubts. "And how do you avoid mesmerization?"

He nods once. "That's your job."

"Again, you have a greatly exaggerated view of my abilities. I've never attempted to mesmerize another vampire. I don't know if I can. Especially one like Theo. All of his vampires have more experience than I do. Theo can move faster than the eye can see, too." He's asking too much of me.

"He's a challenge, but I'm sure I can take him out." The alpha's eyebrows rise. "But I'm also sure about you. I've never felt the kind of...persuasion you emit from any other vampire. Most vamps find me impossible. Theoden's tried, but I've never allowed him to capture my gaze, so I don't know if he can succeed. I highly doubt it. But despite actively avoiding your eyes, I still feel compelled to please you. It's disturbing." He looks away, grimacing.

"I imagine so." This man leads a large werewolf pack and a major company. Being coerced into protecting me, a non-pack member, must be unnerving. "I'm not trying to compel you in any way. I can take care of myself." I can still run and leave Vegas behind. Just because the alpha doesn't think it's possible doesn't mean that's true.

"By running? Won't work." He slashes his hand through the air like a karate chop. "If Theoden doesn't find you, another vamp will. You'll end up fighting, eventually. Do it now, while you're strong, not after you've been on the run and end up starving. Take the fight to Theoden."

He's trying to compel me, and that isn't going to work. But he also has a good point. I sigh. "I'll give it a shot."

"No." He growls. "There is no try, only do." Grimacing, he shakes his head. "Seriously, if you have doubts, you'll fail." He meets my gaze and stalks towards me. If he's willing to risk mesmerization, he's resolute. "You can do this, Charlene Flammen. You absolutely can. But you must believe in yourself and your abilities. If you don't, believe me. I know you can defeat Theoden. I'm positive you can win, and I'm betting my life and my niece's life on that."

I gulp. "No pressure. Just do something you've never done before, perfectly, or a young woman and the pack alpha die. Right." Because I won't survive that disaster. If the vampires don't take me out, the pack will. But the alpha has a point. I've been successful as a vampire because I'm persuasive. I thought it was my natural, somewhat sarcastic charm. But evidently, it's my ability to mesmerize. Which is disturbing on several levels. I should be in control of my efforts and aware of my abilities. Maybe if I'd stayed longer after turning, I'd know more. Or more likely, they'd have fed me more fairy tales, and I'd be firmly under Theoden's control. Perhaps my ability is why Theoden never attempted to enthrall me.

"Char, I'm not joking." The alpha's words bring me out of my whirling thoughts. He meets my gaze. "I know you can do this. The odds are definitely in your favor."

I break his stare, uncomfortable with everything he's saying. "Mixing your fandoms?"

He puts a finger under my chin, pulling me back to his almost glowing eyes. "For a good cause. You just threw off my best attempt at mental persuasion, one that's a hundred percent effective in my pack, and about ninety-eight percent outside of it. I've never tried it on Theoden, but I've compelled other vampires to leave pack members alone." He nods sharply. "Between the two of us, we can do this."

Uncomfortable as it is, I hold his gaze, hoping that his certainty defeats my doubts. Since he's successfully commanded vampires, we have a chance. A decent chance, even. "Okay. We can do this. When are we meeting?"

He spins, not breaking my stare until his neck stops turning. I wince. That looks painful, but I haven't been trying to control him. Maybe he's correct about my abilities because I can't imagine faking that move.

He looks at his watch, a rather massive military-style stainless steel timepiece. "In thirteen minutes." He takes the tablet off the desk, tapping and swiping, then hands it back to me. "That's a diagram of the clubhouse. We're meeting in the ballroom, which is completely empty except for a few decorative tables along the sides. As you can see, there are exit doors on the north side, two doors to the hallway on the south side, an exit on the west, and two doors to the kitchen on the east side. The kitchen has exits on the west and east, plus doors to the lobby, bar, and the dining room. There are exterior exits on the dining room, bar, and lobby, of course." He points at each feature, his words over-enunciated and sharp. "The kitchen has a stairwell to the upper level. That level contains meeting rooms over the dining room and kitchen, with offices over the ballroom. There are several emergency escapes on that level and roof access in the middle and near the east and west sides of the building. Questions about the building?"

"No basement?"

Shaking his head, he sweeps the diagram away. "No. There are escape tunnels. The exits are in the kitchen cleaning closet and behind the bar. Both have hidden, coded key pads, but if you need to use those, we've lost already." He brings up a map of the entire compound. "I've marked escapes from the ballroom. But again, we're going to win, not run."

The alpha is now carefully avoiding my eyes, looking at my forehead or mouth. That should give me confidence, but instead, I feel more alone than ever. He's an ally, not a friend, and once he has his niece back, he might not even be that. If Theoden releases the girl—and I don't know if that's possible—the alpha might turn on me. He seems honorable, but I have to be alert to every possibility. "Okay. We're winning. Do we know what that looks like? Am I taking over the vampires? Theo's business? His tower? I'm a working class vamp, not a CEO." I'd rather not set foot in that place again. But I might have to.

"At least the vampires. The rest, I don't care about." He slashes his hand through the air. "If you take Theoden's entire business, I can help you find your feet."

I sniff. "For a percentage, I assume?"

A wry grin. "Of course. You should never trust people who do everything for free. They're getting a reward somewhere. Usually, a much larger one." He turns towards the door. "Come on. We want to get there early."

I follow him upstairs and into a big black SUV already running outside the garage. He drives efficiently and fast, parking behind the clubhouse and turning towards me. "When you act, move fast with full force and intent. No doubts, no half-measures. Overwhelming force wins battles like these. We'll worry about the war later." He bounds out of the vehicle.

"What war?" Maybe whatever threat worries Theo. But the alpha is correct; nothing but the present matters. Before I've gotten out of the car, he's holding the back door open, a keypad flashing green. He shoves his phone in his back pocket and the SUV key fob dangles from his front right pocket.

Slinging my backpack on, I join him, and we step inside. Four chandeliers sparkle, but bright LEDs on the ceiling light the space. It's probably one hundred and fifty feet long by seventy feet wide, with sandy beige walls above dark wood wainscotting. Wide light wood planks cover the floor, shimmering with a sealant. Small occasional tables flank the room, and logo mats discretely wipe guests' shoes at each door.

We move to the center of the room and face the lobby doors. Rather than wait in silence and let my fears take over, I'll ask questions. "This might be an odd time to ask, but what is your name, anyway? Calling you 'the alpha' takes a lot of time in my head."

He almost barks his laugh. "I didn't realize you didn't know. My mother would have my hide for such poor manners." He turns to face me and bows. "Aleksander Karski at your service, milady. Call me Alek, with a 'k' on the end, not a 'c.'" He pronounces his name with a bit of an accent.

"Lovely to officially meet you, Alek." I hold out my hand, and rather than shaking it, he bows and brushes his lips over my knuckles. A surprising gesture, but one that feels authentic. And hot. But I don't have time for nonsense. "And your niece?"

"Irene Karski. My sister never married Irene's father."

I shrug. That didn't matter. "Does she have a middle name?" Middle-naming a child is a great way to get their attention.

"Ah." His brows rise slightly. "Zivia. Officially, she's Irena Zivia Karski, but we call her Irene."

I nod. "That will help, thank you."

"Of course. But we can experiment with Irene's issues later. Theoden must be your primary concern."

A whoosh of air, the doors bang, and Theo is in front of us. "I'm happy to be Ms. Flammen's primary concern." He practically purrs the words, while attempting to loom over us. Since he's only four or five inches taller than me, it really doesn't work.

"I'm sure you are." I cross my arms and frown at him. "I—"

"Where's my niece?" Alek hovers over both of us quite effectively. "I set this meeting up to get my niece back, healthy and whole."

Alek told me—no, implied—that Theoden found us and insisted on the meeting. Maybe the enemy of my enemy isn't on my side after all.

"You thought I set this up?" Theo ignores the wolf, sniffing while staring down at me. "Hardly. You'll come back eventually, or you'll die."

My frown turns to a scowl. "Let me make something crystal-clear to both of you. You don't own me. I'll walk into the sunrise before either one of you control me."

Theoden's snarl has nothing on Alek's. "You will not."

I put a hand on Alek's chest and shove him back. "I don't answer to you." Turning to Theo, I repeat the same sentiment, but slower. "You don't own me. You may be able to capture me temporarily, but that's all it will ever be. Captivity.

I won't be your plaything, I won't be a figurehead for your religion, and I won't be at your beck and call. Is that clear?"

Theo smiles. "But you will. I made you. I own you." He takes a step back, then another. He meets my gaze. "Come, Charlene Flammen. Now."

At the snapped order, my foot lifts, and I slam it back down. I reinforce my mental refusal. "No. Release Irena, now." I copy his tone.

He leans forward, then scoffs. "No."

"Yes, or your people die." Alek shoves his phone in front of Theo's face. "My pack has every one of your people in cuffs or in the sights of a high-powered rifle. Release my niece, fully, or they all die." He pauses, then growls, "Now."

"You're a dead man." Faster than I can see, Theoden has a hand around Alek's neck.

"So are you." A shot blasts, deafening in the empty room.

Theo and Alek stagger. Theo's hand clenches Alek's neck, and red blooms below Theo's armpit, around the muzzle of the pistol in Alek's hand.

Mutually ensured destruction, indeed. I'm not getting caught in that trap.

I run.

CHAPTER 14

Egotistical idiots! What a waste. I sprint to Alek's SUV. At least the fob was easy to snatch from his pocket. After a pause to open the door, I jump in the vehicle, hammer the gas, and fly through the community, hoping the streets are clear. The front gates are closing, so I put my foot down and ram them.

With a clang and a screeching rip of metal, I'm out of the gated community and speeding through the dark streets of the wealthy neighborhood. I can't keep this car for long; it surely has a tracker, if not a disable feature. But I can get closer to my next storage unit. Except Alek—no, Karski—implied he knows where all of them are. But since his pack is pinning down Theo's vampires, he might not pursue me right away. I can get closer to a daylight safe bolt hole instead. But if I'm on foot, Karski can track me by scent.

If I can get to one of my cars, can I find the tracker before the pack finds me? It's a gamble, but if I avoid my closest storage unit, I might have more time. I drive towards the airport. The busier the area, the easier for me to hide, and the more options I have. I park the SUV on the street near the car rental center, leave the fob inside the gas cap cover, and hop on the airport connector bus. The crowds and accompanying mixture of scents should make me difficult to track even with the plethora of cameras.

At the airport, I find an abandoned makeup case and dump the remaining contents, putting my few belongings inside and ditch my backpack. Karski might have slipped a tracker into my bag and possibly my clothing, too. Outside the airport, I jump in a taxi, giving the driver the address to a drugstore near my closest storage unit. After a quick ride, I pay cash, and in the drugstore, I buy a cheap outfit, including new shoes and a small crossbody bag. I leave and change in a gas station bathroom, scrubbing my body with disposable body cloths and thoroughly wetting my hair in the sink. After drying off on my old leggings, I toss the old clothes in the garbage and twist my hair into a messy bun, tying it with a strip torn from a plastic bag.

With any luck, that will kill all the tracking devices. Striding to the next convenience store, I buy a burner phone. I can keep going on my own and save the badger's escape offer. Or I can take a chance now because I might not be able to call in the future. Leaning against the store's exterior, I dial the number.

"Hello," a woman says. "I'd bet this is Char Flammen, right?"

She's clever. "You would be correct."

"I heard about the confrontation. Need a little help?"

"Yes, but—"

"How do you know it's safe? We owe you. The timing was too close on our escape. You bought us a few critical seconds. It's worth one day of safety, no blood."

I'm an excellent judge of character, usually, and her voice is sincere, without trying too hard. I'll have to negotiate in person to be sure. "How about some information, too?"

"It depends, but talk is cheap. Can you travel?"

"Yes."

"Sending you a geolocation pin. Come here on foot and I'll find you." The call drops, and a text pings. I pull up the location. It isn't far, so I'll walk.

Leaving the store, I jog into a housing development, weaving through the dark streets with the occasional cat, rat, and trash panda for company. I cross a major street, cut through an apartment complex, and walk towards the pin.

"Hey, Char!" A woman waves from the front stoop of a small house. She's about my height but powerfully muscled, and her dark brown hair bears white stripes. A phone glows in her hand.

"Do I know you?" I don't recognize her, and I have an excellent memory for people. But her voice sounds familiar. She must be the badger I'm looking for—the stripes in her hair are a giveaway. I've been running rather than thinking, and that's dangerous.

She shakes her head. "No, but you just called me. Look, I hate owing favors." She holds up both hands. "I offer safety for the next twenty-four hours. We can negotiate additional items. I don't care about vampires, werewolves, or gargoyles. Or the rest of them, except my badgers. And money."

I've been burned several times tonight; adding another seems stupid. On the other hand, an independent party is exactly what I need, and being off the street for the next day seems smart. But I don't move. "How did you find my car?"

She chuckles. "We track the wolves and the vamps. Anything they're interested in, we're interested in." She smirks. "You're important to both, which is intriguing." Putting her hands on her hips, she tilts her head. "So, coming or going?"

She might be a fantastic con artist, but I get a distinct feeling of sarcastic sincerity. "I'll come. Thanks." Having a safe shelter for the coming day is a huge relief. Getting it from someone who successfully invaded Theo's home is even better. Jogging up the sidewalk, I stop outside the door. "I promise mutual defense while I'm here, and I will not prey on you or any household members."

"Good enough. I'm Freddie Schaft." She holds out her hand.

I shake. "Charlene Flammen. Call me Char."

"Hah. Everyone knows who you are, Char." She scans me up and down. "You ditched your old clothes, right?"

"Yes. And my bag. Most of this stuff is new, including the phone."

"Good. Turn the phone off and take the battery out, then I'll store them." She turns and enters the house. "Come in."

I do as she asks, then follow Freddie inside. The small living room holds a worn blue sofa and a fuzzy orange recliner facing a large screen on the wall. A doorway reveals a galley kitchen, and a hallway hints at bedrooms. Cozy and homey; much more my style than the wolves or the vamps' ostentatious abodes.

"We all know how much you hate Klaus Theoden, too. We've got that in common. Can't stand KT or his people." Her lip lifts in a snarl. "Thinks he controls everything and everybody." She huffs. "The wolf isn't much better."

"I'll agree with you there." It seems a common theme. "Did they live?"

Freddie chuckles. "Unfortunately. The vamp holding Irena died, but the rest escaped while the pack got Irena to safety. A couple of the wolves were injured, including Karski, but nothing serious." She sighs. "Unfortunately, they had to sedate Irena. KT didn't release his hold."

I'm not sure he can. Not if she's been mesmerized for a long time, and it's probably worse if they've been intimate in any way, especially blood transfer.

Freddie keeps talking. "They're both looking for you. Dropping the SUV at the airport and ditching your stuff was smart. My doorway detector didn't find any emitters, but let's get you in a shower to change your scent a little." Freddie crooks a finger, leading me to the hall. "Last door on the left. I'll give you some clothes, no obligation there, then we'll head down to the den. If there's anything left on or in you, being underground ought to block the signal."

I stop. "You're awfully well informed about my movements."

She turns back and grins. "I told you we track the wolves and the vamps. Anything they're watching, we're watching. Their internet security isn't as good as they think it is. Come on. Shower. Fast."

"Okay." Knowing they have a basement is a big relief. Making an upstairs room light safe takes a lot of effort; blackout curtains aren't really enough. In the bathroom, I shower, scrubbing hard and thinking harder. I can't afford to relax, so I keep the water lukewarm. One of the badgers must be an expert hacker because both the wolves and Theoden appear to have excellent security. But anything on the internet can be found with enough time and effort. The smallest gap can be exploited. After I leave, I'll leave my burner phone behind and change clothes again.

The door opens. "It's just me. Clothes on the counter. Use anything in here."

"Thanks." After toweling off, I search the skinny jeans and t-shirt for anything solid, pressing hard on the seams, but I don't find anything. That only means the tracker is expensive and sophisticated. The cotton will be more comfortable, so I dress, run her comb through my wet hair, and stuff my drugstore buys into my bag. Both are a little loose; Freddie's got a lot more muscle than I do.

Freddie leans against the wall outside the bathroom. "Sorry it's all black, but I'm a stage hand. That's all I wear."

"They're perfect. I appreciate it and the shower." That's absolutely true. "I'm happy to pay for both."

She pushes off the wall, crooking a finger. "Nah, it's part of the shelter. You being tracked does us no good. Come on." She opens the middle door on the right side of the hallway and bounces down the stairway.

I follow, more sedately. The stair emerges into an unfinished concrete basement. A long, dark brown, L-shaped couch takes up one corner, with a couple of worn blue recliners nearby and a large screen hanging on the bare wall studs. Game controllers sit on a scarred coffee table between the furniture and the screen. Behind the stairwell, the gym matting covers the concrete. Weights are racked along one wall, with a treadmill and a rowing machine on the other. We cross the gym to a vault door with a keypad.

Freddie shields the pad with her hand, enters a code. The pad beeps, locks thunk, and she hauls the door open with a hiss of seals. "This is our armory, but it will make a good vampire hideout. You can leave your stuff in here."

Inside, a tall table holding perfectly organized gun cleaning equipment takes up the middle of the room, my phone and battery sitting on top. Two large safes stand along the left-hand wall, and shelves line the other two walls, full of drab olive military ammunition containers. The labels reveal a variety of calibers. The strong scent of solvents and oil makes my nose wrinkle. "Nice set up. Do you moonlight as a mercenary?" Their guns must be stored in the safes, or they'd never allow me inside. I put my bag down on the floor.

She laughs. "No. Bodyguard occasionally. Quick reaction force sometimes. But these are mostly end-of-the-world as we know it supplies. I've got a blowup bed and blanket for you. You can secure this from the inside with this bar; even I can't get through it without drilling or explosives." She shows me where to place the padlocks on the locking bars. "So don't die for real tomorrow because breaking in here is a pain."

I chuckle. "I'll do my best."

"Leave it open for now. We can hang out on the couch until I go to bed." She flops into the corner and sweeps a finger across her phone. "Looks like all the wolves will live. One of the vamps is iffy, but Trinity is true dead." Her lip lifts for a moment. "No loss. Klaus should have put her down a long time ago."

I shrug. "I didn't know her." But Karski seems to agree with Freddie's assessment.

One corner of her mouth lifts. "I'm sure KT kept her far away from you. She had delusions of ruling Vegas. If she'd ever met you, you'd be dead."

I frown. "I wasn't hiding all these years. KT knew exactly where I was." I like her nickname better than mine.

She shakes her head. "Trinity was old. Really old. She didn't understand technology at all. Couldn't stand watching TV or movies. She liked streaming music once she learned to use voice-activated devices. She'd have never figured out how to find you. Plus, KT kept her on a very short leash. Mostly in the tower so she wouldn't kill too many people. She didn't have much control. Or maybe a better way to describe her attitude is that she didn't care about control. She enjoys killing." Freddie shrugs. "Personally, I think that after centuries of living, the fast changes of the last century drove her insane."

"I've heard of that happening." But I'd thought it was a fairy tale, made up by hopeful humans. Karski says I'm dangerously ignorant, and at this point, I believe him. "You said we'd negotiate for anything more than shelter. What are you thinking?"

Freddie shrugs. "What do you need?" She smiles grimly. "I like favors and information more than money."

I chuckle. "Then I'm not sure what I need matters because I don't know much." But maybe I know enough, because she might not know why the vamps and wolves want me.

"Oh, it matters." She wags her forefinger at me. "I'll go easy on you because you'll make it easier for me in the future. If you survive."

"I'll live. I'm pretty sure of that." Whether I'll be free is the question. "I'm guessing you'd like to know exactly why KT and the alpha want me, right?"

She smirks. "We know about the prophecy. If the wolves have it, we've got it."

"Well, then you know it's ridiculous." I shrug.

"Sure, all prophecy is." She squints. "Until it isn't. It's important to the believers. KT's not a true believer, but some of his vamps are, so he wants you, but not enough to risk damaging you."

I scoff. "More like he wants to use me, like he uses everyone else."

"True." She nods. "But I think there might be more to it. I don't think he likes working so hard. He does it to stay alive and in command. But what I want to know is if you think the prophecy is true and if it's about you." She grimaces. "Ugh. Rhyming."

I don't hold back my chuckle. "I just read it. It might be true, but it's so general it could apply to just about anyone and anything." I pin her with my gaze. "Do you have more of the prophecy?"

Freddie opens her mouth, then slams it shut. "No blood, no mesmerizing. Got it?" She glares.

"Wasn't trying." I hold up both hands. "Seriously. I hate using that. It's creepy." I shiver.

"Hmm. Maybe I understand why they think you're the unbound queen, then." She taps a finger against her chin. "You're seriously convincing. If you can do that without trying, I also understand how you kept Fantastique running. I hear things aren't going so well now that you're gone." She laughs.

"That's too bad. They're a nice bunch of folks. I enjoyed working with them most of the time. But with KT in charge? No thanks."

She flops back, seemingly boneless. "If he really believes you're the unbound queen of prophecy, he's been giving you a lot of freedom. Why change now?"

"I'd like to know that, too." I shrug. "Karski thought maybe there was an astrological event tied into the prophecy, like a comet or alignment or something. Or maybe KT just got tired of waiting."

"Or his big ego got popped because he never expected you to succeed without his help." Freddie huffs. "Most vamps need a lot more care and feeding, it seems like. You? You're made, and boom, you leave KT's tower to make it on your own."

"Yeah, but if he was going to get mad about that, it should have happened a long time ago. I've been on my own for decades." I'm not sure I really want to ask, but Freddie isn't stupid. "Do you have a copy of the full prophecy?"

"No." She shakes her head. "We've never found it online. Supposedly, it's stored in a secret temple in KT's tower. We looked for it during our raid, but no luck. Lots of locked doors we couldn't get through without explosives. We didn't have enough time to use what we brought, other than making a mess." She grins. "I'd have loved to see KT's face when he saw his bedroom, but he doesn't have any cameras in there."

I can't help smiling. "What did you do?" He's dished out enough pain; consequences are due.

"Let's just say that things went boom." Her laughter turns to a growl. "He deserved that and more for taking the alpha's niece. Humans are used enough. Kids shouldn't be pull toys. I'm so angry we couldn't get her to leave."

"So she really is a kid?" Anger rushes through me. I will kill Theoden myself. I bet Freddie would loan me a high-powered rifle. With enough bullets, even he'd go down.

She holds up her hand and tips it back and forth. "Seventeen. Far too young and naive for him. She wasn't exactly sheltered, but no one's prepared for that." She shudders. "We'd have jumped from KT's tower without parachutes before enduring that." She spits the last word.

I nod, feeling the same way. "When things calm down, I'll try to help her." I shrug. "No idea if I can." If I can't help her, I'll find a way to make Theoden let her go.

"If anyone could, it would be you." Her brows rise. "Figure out what you want to ask, yet? Because you've only got a few minutes before this girl passes out. I'm a night owl, but we're getting to my bedtime." She yawns.

"Got any ideas on how to take on KT?"

She snort-laughs. "Right. No. You want an object? I'll get it. Want someone taken out? I might do it, if it's justified. I'll definitely scare someone straight. But I'm not a planner." Her lips clamp together for a moment. "You know who is?"

My lip curls. "Karski."

She smiles, grimly. "Karski." One shoulder rises, then drops when she sighs. "Even KT can't out-think Karski long-term. Especially when KT is more predictable every year. The only time he's impulsive is when it concerns you." She scowls. "There's got to be a reason he's making his move now. You haven't made any changes lately, have you?"

I shake my head. "No. I'm terribly boring. Work, die the day away, work some more. Save money to get out of here. Find places to hide."

Her mouth opens for a moment, then snaps shut. "That's it. I'd bet he's been waiting for you to make a move, then make you stop and grab control. When he got tired of waiting on you, he made you jump. There's something in that prophecy about running, I'd bet."

"Either that, or a true believer pushed him. Is there a religious leader of some sort? Priest, priestess, avatar, someone like that?" If that's the case, maybe I can get that vampire on my side.

Her mouth twists. "Maybe. We know there is a temple. That implies there's a leader or a caretaker. Or maybe someone who keeps the prophecy safe, like a guardian." She nods several times. "That's an intriguing idea, Char. I'll look into it." A snort bursts from her. "Maybe that's why KT kept Trinity around. She's the guardian. Or was. If so, we'll have to figure out who took her place."

Having no clue, I shrug. "I didn't stick around KT's tower long enough to hear any origin stories or religious mantras. I learned to control myself around humans, then I left. KT's actually not all that bad, if you don't mind doing everything his way." It's my turn to snort. "Which I do. But his people are horrible. Nothing but bullies. Physical and mental abuse galore. I didn't survive a mob war to put up with that."

"Preach, sister. They're even worse to non-vamps. They consider everyone prey." She shrugs. "Which, to be fair, we kind of are. None of us can withstand a full-court press from a mature vampire. Not alone. That's why even the most solitary of us weres work in packs. And honestly, we use humans, too. Blending in lets us hide more effectively." She smirks. "I've been told badger blood has a sharp flavor, and it's a last resort." Her lip curls. "Not that it stops vamps like Trinity. She didn't care. Alive and running was her favorite flavor." She yawns again. "Anyway, I'll look into the religious leader idea tomorrow." She stands and stretches. "My house is yours, except the bedrooms. Stay out of those. And stay off the internet and phone, please. They know where I live, but I'd like to remain unconnected to you."

"Sure. I'll stay here, then go to bed. I won't put you at risk." That would be a poor repayment for her hospitality.

Freddie bounces up the stairs. A door closes, then water runs.

I grab a blood box from my bag and suck it down. Sourcing more is my first question for Freddie tomorrow. Next, I need a way to find the trackers Karski put on my stuff. If I work with him again, it has to be on my terms, not because he treed me like the cougar I'm not. I need a way to safely talk to Theoden, too. He obviously isn't giving up, but neither am I. We have to come to an understanding or one of us will end up true dead. Probably me.

I also need a long-term lair; somewhere I can come and go from without interference. Getting rid of the trackers will help with that. But they might have tracked me every step of my searches, and knowing both men—and Freddie—they'll have it all mapped out. Since I ran, they might have put sensors on every one of my potential hideouts. I need someplace safe to spend my day.

I'm not asking much, am I? I pad back to the vault. I'll blow up the bed and get set for the day. Maybe I'll have a brilliant revelation tomorrow.

CHAPTER 15

I open my eyes; a metal ceiling gleams above me. I'm safe in Freddie's vault. Rising, I stretch, then quietly slide the padlocks from the hasps and open the air valve on the bed. Just in case she has visitors, I'll wait for Freddie to open the vault. After I fold the bed and blanket, I pace circles around the bench. Too bad she doesn't have a gun for me to clean; I'd be happier doing something useful.

The vault lock spins and the locking arms retract. Freddie swings open the door, frowning. That doesn't seem like a good sign. As the door opens, it reveals three more women, all wearing striped hair and scowls.

I don't sigh or tense, but I'm ready to run. "Let me guess. Your sisters?"

Freddie nods, her gaze on my chin. "Yeah. They wanted to make sure you didn't mesmerize me. I told them you were strong but hadn't deliberately tried."

I hold up both hands. "I swear I did not try to mesmerize Freddie, nor will I try to mesmerize you unless you're a threat to me. Is that good enough?"

The scowls remain, but heads nod. So they believe my words but don't trust me.

Hopefully, a quick explanation will lead to a clean escape. "Great. Thanks. Look, I don't know why KT chose this moment to try and control me or what he thinks is going to happen. I'm clueless here, and I'd really like to understand. And I'd also like someplace to hide and a way to find the trackers on my stuff, and a hundred blood boxes while I'm dreaming." I shrug. "But I'm not likely to find any of that here, so I'll just go. Thanks for your help, Freddie. I appreciate it." I grab my bag and pick up the pieces of my phone.

"You're welcome." Freddie nods. "I asked around about the priestess idea. If they have one, nobody but the vampires knows who they are. We"—she motions towards her sisters—"don't think it was Trinity. She wasn't stable enough to do anything but hunt. We think KT wanted an easy way to put her down without getting blamed. The weres did it for him." She shrugs. "Why else would you leave a hostage with Trinity?" She shudders. "Anyway, I can help you with one item on your list." She pushes past me into the vault, then comes back out, holding a small device. "This is a bug detector. All it does is find typical transmission frequencies. So don't point it at a radio or pretty much any modern car because they're all connected to WiFi these days." She tilts it to show me the top. "The lights indicate the strength of the signal, five being strongest. Good luck, Char." She places the device in my hand without touching me.

"Thanks, Freddie. Let me know if you need help with anything. I'll keep this phone as long as I can." I hold up the cheap smart phone. "But I'll probably turn it off a lot. Text or leave a voicemail. I truly appreciate the help you've given me, and I wish you luck." I mean every word. Having a safe place to spend the day gave me hope that I desperately needed.

"Same, girl. I'll keep checking on the priestess thing. And I'll talk to the wolf." She sighs. "He's such a stick in the mud. But if anyone can figure out how to deal with this whole thing, it's him. Now that his niece is back, he might be more reasonable. Might." She smirks. "Still going to be a control freak alpha, I'm sure. Take care. Stay alive. I like you." She winks.

"Be careful. I like you, too." Sighing, I leave Freddie's house and jog to the nearest drugstore. After buying a new set of clothes, I change in the bathroom. I hate to ditch Freddie's comfy jeans, but I don't fully trust her. Bundling the clothes and the bug detector into the plastic drugstore bag, I jog a meandering mile through neighborhoods. Then I slide the bundle into a crack between two concrete brick walls. I'm fairly certain I can download an app to my burner phone that will let me check for transmissions. Although, Freddie had my burner phone in her hands. She might have bugged or cloned it. I'll hang on to it for now, but I'll leave it off and the battery out.

I wander farther westward through the dark streets for about an hour, but I know that without taking a cab or a bus, I'll never make it to my natural hideouts in time. Taking any public transportation means the possibility of showing up on a camera. If I stick to rundown neighborhoods off the main streets, I have a better chance of avoiding anything but doorbell cameras. Plus, I'd previously spotted a rundown church in this area and always meant to check it out. While I walk, I slide the phone into an empty diet soda can to block any remaining signal powered by the backup battery.

Two hours later, I reach the church and saunter around the old building. It doesn't appear entirely abandoned, but it's old and the stucco is flaking. The doors are locked and all the windows are about twenty feet above my head, but there don't appear to be any cameras. One of the windows, near the altar end, is cracked. The worn brick and stucco walls give me plenty of hand and footholds, and it isn't long before I reach the window ledge. Pulling the cracked glass from the frame is easy. I stack the pieces on the wide outer ledge and raise one foot, then hesitate.

The rumors say vampires entering consecrated ground burst into flames or get struck by lightning. Or melt like the Wicked Witch of the West. But I'm running out of time and, therefore, options.

Swallowing hard, I clamp my jaws together and slide my foot into the opening, feeling for the windowsill. My foot doesn't burn, so I climb inside, but I face an entirely different problem.

I teeter on the narrow windowsill, two stories above the empty, hard church floor, with no way to climb down the smooth wall or anything below to cushion my fall. Well, I have a lot of speed; maybe that can make up for gravity. Cautiously turning, I crouch and put my fingers on the edge of the sill just outside my feet. Before I can overthink, I slide my feet and legs over the side, flattening the soles of my shoes against the wall to slow my fall.

Hanging by my fingertips, I let go and try to run back up the wall like a cartoon character. I don't succeed. I hit the floor, letting my knees and hips collapse, and roll to my side, then get back on my feet. Ouch. My soles smart, and my joints ache, but I've survived. I explore the space, searching for a basement door or crawl space, but find neither. What I do find, though, is a door to a choir loft.

Climbing the stairs, I step gingerly across the dusty, creaking floor, grateful I am small. On the far side, a door leads to a closet. But a hole in the ceiling dashes my dwindling dreams of a hideout.

Returning downstairs, I explore the area again. At the back of the church, three doors in a row create the outer wall of a confessional. The priest would sit in the middle, while penitents knelt in the tiny rooms on either side, speaking to the priest through a small, screened hole. My best bet is securing the priest's cubby. I find an old board to block one speaking hole. The bottom of a broken chair blocks the other hole. Shoving a ladder-back chair under the doorknob will close off access to the priest's room. It isn't exactly secure, but it's the best I can do for now.

Leaving the confessional, I tie the church's main double door handles together with scraps of cloth and rope and hope today isn't the day the owner tears the place down. I also hope Freddie successfully negotiates with Karski because I'd much rather die the day away in a comfortable bed. Returning to the confessional, I finish securing the space. Then I sit on the floor, leaning against the back wall, and wait to pass out. I hope the wolf is reasonable because mere survival takes way too much time and energy for a working class vamp. In hindsight, all my preparations were too little, too late. They've depended on way too much luck and not enough planning for emergencies.

In short, I've been an idiot.

My best remaining hope—and it is hope, not planning or certainty—is the wolf. He'll be justifiably angry that I left him struggling with KT, but on the other hand, I'm useless during an armed fight. KT would have focused on Karski, and anything I did physically or psychically would be a pinprick in comparison. I have a bargaining chip—my potential influence over the hold KT has on Karski's niece.

So much hope, so little certainty. True death seems more and more likely. The world will probably be better off with one less vampire, anyway.

*

I wake still secure in the priest's confessional—a minor miracle. My back cracks and pops as I stand, and my rear end aches from sitting on concrete all night, but I'm still here and free. Undoing all my security measures, I scatter them, then leave through the back door, which I lock behind me. I keep moving west through neighborhoods, the houses getting larger and nicer as I walk. Near a major street, I take a chance and buy another cheap burner phone in a gas station, disabling the location services immediately. Then I call Freddie, while walking to a neighborhood across the street.

"Hello?" She answers in a neutral tone, with an odd echo.

Relief I have no business feeling sweeps through me. She's a business associate, not a friend. "Hey, it's Char."

"You're alive. Awesome." A huffing laugh. "Smart of you to ditch the electronics, even if it's expensive."

I'm burning through my emergency funds too fast, and hunger rides me hard. I'll have to mesmerize another human or find a blood box source. Both are perilous, one for my body, the other for my soul. If I still have one. "You found them?"

"I know where they are. I didn't go anywhere near them because the wolf and the vamp are watching my house. I'm routing this call through a series of services, so the chances of tracing it are low, but we should wrap this quickly. If you call the wolf, be ready to ditch that phone and run because he's not happy."

"So I shouldn't bother." Even though I already knew that, my spirits sink. I'll have to spend most of tonight finding a safe lair rather than planning my next move.

"Eh. I didn't say that. He's still your best chance of a decent plan. Personally, I'd just get some guns and walk into KT's tower. Demand your birthright as the Queen Unbound, and make them all kneel. But that also seems suicidal, so maybe my advice isn't so good." She sputters laughter.

I join her. "Yeah, I don't see me going all Rambo. Maybe you and your sisters can get away with that, but I'm one working class vamp, not a commando or a mobster." I need a strategy.

"But more seriously, it might actually work." Freddie's tone is sober. "The guns get you past the human security, and you can take on KT in the privacy of his tower."

"Where his vampires will jump me, knock me out, drug me, and use me as a puppet. No thanks." Even though Freddie successfully entered KT's tower, she admitted they hadn't gotten far. If KT and most of his vamps hadn't been in the mall dealing with the smash and grab, the badgers might have found themselves in a whole lot of trouble. KT may have even anticipated an attempt to retrieve the alpha's niece and let them in deliberately, to prove it was useless. But he probably thought he'd be dealing with the logical, practical wolves, not the chaotic, troublemaking badgers. And the gargoyles. They don't seem to fit into the picture. "Why are the gargoyles involved?"

"Hmph. They have reasons, but they're not sharing." She sighs. "You could contact them, but dealing with them is tricky. They're all lawyers, fulfilling the letter of the contract but not caring about the intent."

"Interesting." That doesn't entirely jive with my experience working with Matias at the drag bar. He's been helpful to me beyond his employment terms. But perhaps that's my mesmerizing ability, as the wolf claims. "At this point, I need any allies I can get."

"You do. I talked to my sisters. We'll support you, but eventually, we'll need some return favors."

I chuckle. "To be specified later and I can't turn them down? I'm not sure I need help like that." I'm not committing to open-ended contracts.

"We're not stupid enough to back you into a corner. The thing is, we know Vegas would be better off with you in charge. KT's getting more and more out of touch. He understands business and powerful people, but he doesn't understand that when enough regular people band together, the results can be catastrophic.

And while he's charismatic on a small scale, he'll have a hard time with a mob. That kind of destruction is bad for all of us."

"That's probably why he wants me. He thinks I can stop a mob. Even if I can, I won't. I'm not doing that to thousands of humans who just want to have a little fun without losing their lives along with their money." I'd warned him, and he'd laughed. He deserves the consequences.

"Maybe he wants you to take on the legal authorities. I'm sure he can control one or two, or maybe more when he's present, but he's looking for more complete protection."

Freddie is probably right. Controlling the people in charge is more KT's style. Dealing with the little people who do the real work, like me, is beneath him. His lack of respect towards me isn't just my "baby vamp" status; it's because my working-class life satisfies me. He probably believed the Unbound Queen would roll over everyone and rule the world with enthusiasm. He doesn't understand me or real leadership. Despite the poor example of recent politicians, I know real leaders serve their people, rather than the other way around. "I'm not doing that."

She snorts. "That's why I'm willing to support you. I know that more and more people will find out about supernaturals. With the increasing surveillance everywhere and all the scientific advances humans have made, our secrecy is a thing of the past. We need someone who can act as an intermediary, someone who understands regular humans and those in power. Someone persuasive, but not selfish. Someone to smooth the way into the mainstream. Someone who's not foolish enough to believe a prophecy can become word-for-word reality."

"People join cults for a reason." We've stayed a secret this long because our numbers are relatively low, and we avoid publicity. Klaus Theoden shattered that rule and expects me to use my power to enforce his position. I have no reason to help him, especially after he's pushed me so hard. Until he quit controlling his vamps, the supernatural community had been smoothing the way for a long time. Books, movies, and TV have celebrated and reviled us, but more and more, we're portrayed as regular people with some extra talents and different weaknesses, both good and bad. Still, when we're revealed, probably through DNA, there will be a lot of fear. I suspect that currently, the DNA differences look like unknown mutations or corrupted samples, but that can't last. Humans will be rightfully scared, and even the whole community of supernaturals can't prevail against the armies of the world.

"That's the risk we're taking. With your power, you could easily become a cult leader over millions, including us. We're counting on you staying true to your working-class roots, Char." Freddie's warning is clear.

"I'm assuming you've got plans if I don't." Probably one of those sisters and a high-powered sniper rifle, which is a smart way to go.

"Yep." She pops the end "p."

"Good. No one should have unrestricted power. Why haven't you taken out KT?"

"We've been talking too long. I'll text you Karski's number and the gargoyle's. Later." The call clicks off. Thirty seconds later, a text chimes. I'll find a scrap of paper and write both down, but for now, I need to move because Freddie is right. We've been talking too long, and I need to find safety for the coming day. I power off the phone, remove the battery, and stick the phone in a flattened beer can, my nose wrinkling at the smell.

Returning to the main street, I flag down a taxi. "Airport, please. Cash tip if you keep me off camera and get there quick."

The man grins. "You got it, honey." He sticks a piece of blue tape over the lens of the camera in the ceiling and flips the meter on.

I get in and relax. It might not be the only surveillance, but whatever else he has is probably his, not his company's. I'm done with running on foot. I'll retrieve my next car, more funds, search for transmitters, and get closer to my next hideout. Then I'll find a food donor and figure out a plan. I have a badger girl-gang; I don't need the wolves or gargoyles. Maybe.

CHAPTER 16

THE NEXT EVENING, I wake up on an air mattress in the back seat of my ancient Oldsmobile. The blackout structure is all in place; a good sign. Taking shelter at one of my possibly known locations is risky, but I'd made special arrangements for this particular studio space. The owner believes I'm a flight attendant with little time to work on my car art, and when I do, I work all night. I leave the door open. Everyone can see there's little in here except the carcass of a rusty automobile body with dented body panels stacked against the walls. I've sweetened the deal by allowing the others to use my welder when I'm not here. No one asks any questions, and I've never seen an attempt to enter my space; none of my telltales have been broken.

When I show up, I fire up my welder, make a seam or two on an extra fender, grind it apart, and start over. From what I've seen, doing something over and over isn't uncommon in the art world, and quirky behavior is standard. I've also installed excellent locks and light proof seals for the garage door and the door to the inner common area. But still, staying here all day is a risk I've taken only a few times. I usually depart an hour before sunrise.

I don't know if the wolves or KT have found this location. They might be waiting right outside. But I think it's less risky than the rest because I was extra careful setting up the persona and cryptocurrency-based payment system. I've used a completely fake name with no ID, so I have some hope.

I climb out of the light-safe cocoon I've constructed inside the car, letting the air out of the mattress so the whole thing collapses. After slinging my fully stocked go-bag over my shoulders, I unlock the common area door and peer out. Light shines from a single cracked door, but the common area is empty. I use the facilities, cleaning up the best I can, and stuff my distinctive hair under a black wrap. Then I climb the stairs to the roof of the building, surveying the exterior and streets surrounding the former warehouse south of the airport. No big black SUVs or other inhabited vehicles linger nearby, so I return to my studio.

Slipping black riding leathers over my clothes, I pop a plain black helmet on my head and armored gloves on my hands. After putting my backpack on again, I yank the miscellaneous vehicle body panels away from the wall, uncovering my last best hope for a clean escape.

Grasping the handlebars of my ancient Honda motorcycle, I roll it out the door into the common area. After securing my door and reinstalling the telltales made of hair and a little clear tape, I push the machine out the front door. Then I mount and flip the switches, hoping it starts. I've kept a battery tender on it and started it once a year, but motorcycles can be finicky. Despite my concern, it fires immediately. I let it warm up, then ride towards the glitzy lights of Las Vegas.

I'm not going to do anything foolish, like ride by KT's tower, the wolves' den, or my old bar, but I need information. I'll retrieve the cell phone I stashed that first night and call Karski. Dread tightens my back muscles, but after contemplating the questions for too long, I've determined that Freddie is right. I need the wolf's information, and maybe his plan. Help would be better, but I won't count on it.

Plus, I really want to free his niece. No one should desperately desire that evil, old, nasty vampire, let alone a seventeen-year-old girl. If an adult chooses to believe the snake oil he's selling, that's on them, but even then, taking away their freedom to choose is horrific.

I should know; I'm guilty too.

My only solace is knowing I do it out of necessity, not joy, and release my victims immediately. And while I'm thinking about necessity, I need blood, now. It's still early evening, but I can find a gang-banger easily. The motorcycle makes hunting easy and my quick reactions help me survive the city's wild traffic.

I head to West Las Vegas, one of the most dangerous parts of the city, and cruise a few back streets. It isn't long before a group of men try to pull me off my bike. I bash a scrawny guy in the temple with the back of my armored fist and pull him onto the bike in front of me, then speed away, twisting and turning through the dark streets. When he struggles in my grip, I pull over in an alley and check for cameras. Seeing nothing, I mesmerize him, then feed.

I take a little more than I normally would, grimacing at the bitter traces of drugs and alcohol, probably from the night before. I prop him against the side of a building. Before I leave, I crouch in front of him. "Find a better line of work. Something you can be proud of, or I might come back." I lick my lips, watching the man's eyes widen, then hop on my bike and ride towards southwest Las Vegas.

I retrieve my bag of stuff with the phone, ride a few streets away, and then dial the wolf before I can think too much about it.

"Karski," he snaps.

I smirk, knowing he'll hear the smile in my voice. "Your ego didn't kill you after all. Surprising."

"Thanks for nothing, Flammen," he snarls.

I huff. "Neither of you was paying attention to me. The only thing I could do was catch a stray bullet, so I ran away to fight another day. That's the smart bet."

"The coward's bet."

I shrug the pain of his accusation away. I was right, whether he thinks so or not. "Coward, smart, whatever. I'm alive, free of bullet holes and bites. I doubt you can say the same. Sadly, KT will already be healthy." His legions of human followers will have provided more than enough blood to heal him.

He growls. "Maybe if you'd stuck around to help, I might have won, rather than fighting to a draw."

"Not likely. But that's not why I'm calling."

"Do I care?" He bites off the words.

"I want to help your niece." Hopefully, he can hear my sincerity because it's true.

He blows out a long breath. It isn't a sigh or exasperation; I'm fairly certain he's attempting to control his anger. Along with some fear. "And what do you want in return?" His voice is calm and even.

"Nothing." I grimace. "That's not quite true. I want a truce. While I attempt to free your niece, I get safety from outside threats and your pack, including a safe place to sleep during the day and an adequate number of blood boxes. I make no guarantees that I can free her, but I will try my best."

"Curse you, Charlene Flammen, for finding the one thing I can't turn down. And now I'll owe you."

"You owe me nothing. No one deserves to have their free will taken." Even that gangbanger who tried to pull me off my bike deserves free will, even if he also deserves prison for assault and attempted robbery. "While I'm there, I'd like to keep reading your intelligence summaries, but I'm doing this for your niece and for me, not for you." Helping her might make up for some of the damage I've done over the decades.

"I see." After a long pause, he speaks again. "I can send a car for you."

"No need. I have transportation. That's safe too. No taking away or damaging my transportation." If I don't succeed, I can't count on a clean escape. Even if I do succeed, some of his pack members despise vampires. They'll take any opportunity to get rid of me.

"I guarantee your safety and the safety of your possessions while you attempt to release my niece. I also guarantee safe passage in and out, including a full twenty-four hours after you leave. By then, tempers should have cooled. Especially if you're successful."

Great. So if I fail, I'll have not only the vampires on my back, but offended pack members. All the more reason to leave Las Vegas forever. "Agreed."

"Give me thirty minutes before you show up at the gate. What are you driving?"

"Honda motorcycle. Black helmet and leathers."

"You have a death wish." He snorts. "Thirty minutes." The line goes dead.

Hopefully he's referring to the motorcycle rather than my actions in general, but there's no telling. He and his pack can certainly be the death of me. I kick the bike into gear and weave through the quiet streets.

I roll through the pack's open gate and through the empty community. No one makes a move, but I can feel the hostile gazes. I park between the garage and the house, then walk to the back door.

It opens less than halfway, the woman who drove KT's limo blocking the entrance. She snarls.

I grimace, knowing she can't see my face behind the mirrored face shield. "Hard to free the girl if I can't get to her."

"Take off the helmet. I must confirm your identity."

I raise the face shield instead. "No thanks. I'd prefer to avoid brain damage when I accidentally fall down the stairs."

Her body jolts, like she's shocked. "You've been promised safety. I will not violate that agreement."

"I'm sure." I push past her, then turn halfway back. I'm not leaving this woman at my back. "Is the girl downstairs?"

"Yes." The woman returns the favor, slamming her shoulder into me as she passes. I expect the maneuver, so I turn with her, and she stumbles forward from the unexpected momentum. She continues, leading the way to the stairs I used previously and opening the door. "Down there."

I nod. "Thanks." Keeping my eyes on her, I sidle down the first five stairs, then turn away. If she comes after me, I'll hear her, even through the helmet.

At the bottom, Karski waits. His expression and body language are neutral, but I can almost feel his hostility. I deliberately avoid his gaze; I have no reason to make him angrier. He turns on his heel and strides to the open bedroom door behind his desk.

A young white girl with long, dark brown hair shifts restlessly on a gurney next to the bed, pulling against the restraints at her wrists, waist, and ankles. Karski stands next to her, his lips compressed. "She kept trying to leave, pounding on the door and kicking it, injuring herself. Even sedation isn't helping much." He looks at the wall behind the girl, his jaw working.

No wonder he's furious. I hope I can break Theoden's enchantment. I walk to the other side of the gurney and look at the girl. She's too thin and her skin is sallow, with dark circles under her closed eyes. I pull off my helmet. Moving slowly to not alarm the wolf, I place my hand on the girl's cheek, then push my will towards her. "Irena Zivia Karski, wake."

Irena's eyes pop open, and she struggles against her bonds, her body twisting and her head tossing. "Theoden!" She wails his name over and over.

Karski moves to the head of the gurney and holds her shoulders down. I cup her face between my hands. "Irena Zivia Karski, look at me. Now!"

Her gaze snaps to mine. "Theoden. Take me to Theoden!"

What now? She's looking at me but still wants him. I can't tell her he's evil; she won't respond to logic, not in her current state. He's forced a bond. I'll have to mesmerize her, then let her go, not that I'm sure how to do that. I push my will towards her, demanding her submission. "Irena Zivia Karski, you will obey me, and only me. I am the only person who matters. Do you understand?"

"No, I want Theoden." She tries to pull away from my hold, but her voice and movements grow weaker.

I repeat my demands, and eventually, she stops asking for Theo. By that point, my hunger roars. "Irena, you are safe here. You will stay here in this house. You can act normally. You will care for your body properly. Use the bathroom, then eat if you are hungry. Sleep when you are tired. Pay attention to how you feel and tell me or your uncle if you are uncomfortable or need something. You will obey your uncle. Take care of yourself. Do you understand?"

"Yes. I will obey you. I will take care of myself. I will obey Uncle Alek." She nods, her gaze on mine.

I break her stare, and she whimpers. Closing my eyes, I turn away and sit on the bed, hunger driving me to attack the girl and the man. I grip the comforter. "Let her go. Where are the blood boxes?"

Karski sprints out of the room, then returns, dropping three boxes on the bed next to me. I grab the first, stabbing the opening with my fingernail and upending it into my mouth. While I gulp the thick, lukewarm fluid, Velcro rips.

"Irene?" Karski's voice is the softest I've ever heard. "Do you need help to get to the bathroom?"

"I can do it, Uncle Alek." Fabric rustles, then soft footsteps cross the room.

I grab the next box, taking the time to stab the straw into it but sucking it down fast. The third, I drink slower, my hunger fading, but my head throbbing. When I open my eyes, Alek Karski looms over me.

"Thank you. She hasn't said anyone's name but his since she returned. It's been horrible." He nods and takes a step back.

"You're welcome. I need rest before I can do anything else." I flop back on the bed, the pounding in my head increasing. Despite my hunger being slaked, I still want his blood. I close my eyes.

"Do you need aspirin or something?"

"It won't help. Take your niece and go. Leave me a couple more boxes, and I'll figure out how to release her tomorrow." I put a hand over my full stomach, still longing for more blood—his, specifically, fresh. Gripping the comforter tight, I keep my eyes shut. I will not attack the man protecting me. I will not break the truce.

He remains in place, staring at me, while I struggle to remain on the bed. The bathroom door clicks, and he finally moves. "Come on, kiddo. Let's get you some food. Then you can take a shower and sleep, okay?"

"Yes, Uncle Alek." Their footsteps move away, then the door to the bedroom suite closes and locks.

I open my eyes and sit up, releasing the comforter. That was too close. My head still throbs, but with the human and wolf gone, I can think. I look at the stack of blood boxes on the nightstand but decide I want a shower worse.

Taking my go-bag into the bathroom, I withdraw a pair of loose gray silk pants and a shirt, then strip off my riding leathers and clothes. The hot water and lightly scented bath products help, but my temples still throb.

When I step out of the bathroom, I stop. Karski sits on the bed, and my hunger rages. I lock my gaze on the stack of blood boxes on the nightstand, even though the thought of drinking another box makes me slightly nauseous.

"You don't want that, do you?" Karski's voice is certain and compelling.

I swallow, grip the doorjamb to keep myself in place, and keep my eyes on the boxes. I control myself; my needs don't control me. "Not really. You should go."

"You need fresh blood, don't you?" He thinks he knows the answer.

"Need, no. Want, yes. So you should go. Your niece needs you." My head turns despite myself, and I can see his pulse throb in his neck. I want to bite and drink him dry.

"You've done what none of us could do and may be able to do more. I can donate some blood to the cause." He's outwardly relaxed, but his pulse picks up.

I shake my head. "I can't guarantee my control right now. It's a bad idea."

"But you're in pain, and you can't perform well if you're in pain." He holds out his arm. "Drink. Tell me how long, and I'll remove you if I have to."

"You won't be able to. Part of drinking from someone is taking their free will."

"Have you ever tried to drink without enthralling someone?" He leans back on one arm, the other still outstretched.

"No. I don't think it's a painless process. The mesmerization controls the pain." My hunger grows, and I step back towards the bathroom.

He huffs. "I can handle a little pain." He pulls out his phone. "I'll set an alarm. How long?"

I swallow. "Two minutes."

"That's it? It takes about ten minutes to give blood."

He must have looked it up. There's no way a were would take the chance of donating to a human blood bank, and he wouldn't sell to the blood box companies. "Vampires actively suck, and the hole is larger. Which means it's more painful."

"I've been shot, more than once. It can't be worse than that." His mouth twists in a wry smile.

I shrug. "No idea. I've been shot, but I don't remember my initial donation and turning." More like I actively avoid remembering; it's pain and terror that lasts forever, then morphs into my entire body burning. I'm fairly certain I passed out at that point, but even thinking about it makes me shudder.

He sits upright, scowling. "Who shot you?"

I wave his concern away. "Got caught in a mob battle. The people involved are long dead." I snort. "Theo had been dead for a long time even then."

His scowl changes into interest. "That's why you turned?"

"Yeah. I was lying on the sidewalk, bleeding out, and he asked if I wanted to live." I shrug. "Of course I said yes. He didn't say anything else, and I don't remember the rest."

"You don't want to remember the rest." His brows lift. "Can't blame you there. I feel the same." He shakes his head. "But that's not important." He lifts his arm higher. "You're in pain, and I can fix it. Take what you need." He emphasizes the last word.

"And if I take more?" Because my control is thread thin.

His mouth twists. "I won't let you. If necessary, I can knock you out with my other hand. I'd rather not because you don't need additional trauma." He smiles ever so slightly. "But I'm not worried. You have excellent self-control."

I grimace, then swallow because my mouth waters at his offer. "I hope so."

He taps at his phone, then sets it down on his right side and holds his left arm out. "Let's get this done."

I sit next to him on the bed and cradle his arm in my hands. Then I let my fangs drop and lick his inner elbow.

He sucks in a breath. "That packs a punch."

I huff. "Good or bad?"

"A little of both. Keep going." He licks his lips. "Please ignore any bodily reaction. I, too, have iron self-control."

I know my saliva is an anesthetic and helps heal wounds. I hadn't been positive it had other effects, but it makes sense. "I understand." Finding his vein with my tongue, I adjust, then strike.

He takes in another deep breath and his muscles tense, then he relaxes.

I withdraw a little and suck. Hot, rich, earthy blood flows over my tongue, and within seconds, my head stops throbbing. I suck harder, ignoring the wolf's reactions. When a chime dings, I start. I've been lost in the lovely flavor of iron and salt. Despite my instinct and intense desire to continue, I withdraw my fangs completely and lick the wounds to close them.

Before the holes close, he pulls from my grip. "I've got it from here." He yanks tissues from a container on the nightstand and clamps them on his arm. Then he strides to the bathroom and kicks the door shut.

I let myself flop back onto the bed. Alek Karski's blood is the best I've ever tasted, and it seems to be supercharged with everything I need most. I feel renewed, energized even. If they all taste that good, it's amazing vampires haven't wiped werewolves out. In the wild, packs mean mutual survival; for supernaturals, packs must be even more important.

After a long time, the alpha emerges from the bathroom—in wolf form, and I can't help staring. When I saw him before, conditions didn't encourage gawking, and he was mostly lying down. Perhaps purposefully, so I underestimated the threat he posed.

Because he's huge. Wolves are big, but the alpha is at least fifty percent taller and larger than the wolves I've seen at the zoo or on TV. His fur is black and thick, with a longer ruff, and his eyes glow amber. Lean muscles ripple over a heavy frame, conveying an impression of strength, speed, and endurance. A majestic combination that I don't want to get on the wrong side of. "Wow. You're gorgeous."

He tosses his head and lets his jaw drop, displaying long, vicious white teeth. If that's a smile, it's terrifying. He crosses to the door and stands on his back paws, looking at the sensor. The locks release. He pushes the door open, drops to all four feet, then turns and taps the floor with a paw.

"Are you seriously telling me to stay like a good dog?" I chuckle. His blood has energized me enough to continue working with his niece, but maybe it's better if I don't push my luck.

He nods, then backs away. The door closes and locks.

"Okay then. Guess I'll stay here." I pick up the tablet on the nightstand and let it see my face. Theoden's file appears, right where I stopped reading. Interesting; it seems Karski expected me to return.

Both of these men have been playing politics far longer than I have. If I'm not careful, they'll play me, too.

CHAPTER 17

I WAKE THE NEXT evening, energetic and ready for the night. Even remembering I have to release Irena from my grip somehow doesn't faze me; a challenge rather than a dreaded unknown. Maybe my optimism will fade when faced with reality, but I hope for the best.

I want to start now, but since I have a safe place, I meditate instead. When I can't calm my overactive mind, I roll out of bed and do my yoga routine—twice. One way or another, I will maintain my mind-body balance. I push the memory of Karski's delicious blood away. Attacking a wolf will mean my death.

After I finish, I shower, dress, and suck down a blood box. I'm not hungry, but better to face temptation fully sated.

Before I can fret too long, knocking thumps on the bedroom door. I open the door, revealing Karski and Irena. "Good evening, Char. I hope you're feeling well?"

I step back. "Excellent, actually. How are you? And how are you, Irena?"

Karski waves his hand towards Irena. She grimaces. "I feel...kind of weird. Like I was living in a dream, or more like a nightmare, and now I'm not. But I don't feel quite normal, either."

I nod, glancing at Karski. "Alpha, I hope you have trusted counselors. Post-traumatic stress is no joke." I turn to Irena, looking at her chin. "Irena, it will take time to recover. The vampire's link made your own mind betray you, making you do things you'd never do on your own. I'm so sorry." Irena's trauma might keep her from ever feeling normal, but with care, she can recover. Walking to the seating area, I wave my hand at the couch. "Let's sit down."

Irena follows me and sits. Karski hovers next to Irena, shifting restlessly. I don't know if he's worried about the girl, or concerned I'll attack her. Or maybe it's something else, like an outside threat.

I ignore him and lean towards her. "Irena, yesterday I told you to obey me and your uncle because I was trying to break Theoden's hold on you. When I say the name Klaus Theoden, what do you think of?"

She shudders. "A monster."

"He certainly is that." Good, that worked. "The problem is, I don't want you to have to obey me or anyone else. I want you to live a free, normal life, or as normally as you can after such a horrific experience. When I talk to you, what do you feel?"

"She's still obeying me to the letter, if that's what you're asking." Karski scowls.

I glance at him and nod. "Irena, what do you feel?"

She shrugs. "Nothing, really. I don't really know you." She shudders. "But whatever you did let me see that vampire in a different way. When I look back, I don't understand why I allowed him to do that to me without a fight. I didn't want to fight him! All I wanted to do was make him happy, no matter what it took." Her words are wails; protests to the heavens.

She seems traumatized and unsure but not broken. "I'm so sorry. I've been where you are and it's awful. But I got loose, and you can too. If you agree, I'll mesmerize you again and tell you that you are free. I'm not sure that will be sufficient. If you can't stand the thought of being under my spell again, we'll find another way." I look at the ceiling for a moment, needing a break from her scared but still too-trusting expression. "I'll leave you a reinforcement affirmation. I know you can resist vampires, but you must believe it. I'll leave you the seeds of that truth." Looking at her chin, rather than her eyes, I try to prevent influencing her decision further. "You can say yes or no. Do you agree to be mesmerized?"

She looks at Alek, and he nods once. But every muscle in his body is tight. Despite his clenched fists and hostility, I'm attracted to him—and his blood. That dangerous thought makes me return to the traumatized child. "Do you agree?"

Irena squeezes her eyes shut, then nods. "I agree."

I sit on the coffee table in front of her and then hold out my hands. "If you're sure, give me your hands and look into my eyes." I keep my tone neutral; I don't want to force this moment. Of course, I told her to obey me, so she doesn't have a true choice. I hate myself for taking her free will. But better me than Theoden.

Her hands shaking, she reaches out and places her fingers against my palms. Then she looks up into my eyes, deliberately meeting my gaze.

Enfolding her hands in mine, I push my will towards her. "Irena Zivia Karski, you are your own person. You do not have to obey me, your Uncle Alek, or anyone else unless you choose to do so. You have free will to do what is right for you. You are intelligent, wise, and compassionate and will make your own decisions based on your sense of integrity and common sense. You are free of all unwanted ties, compulsions, and connections." I repeat the concepts of free will and push my belief towards her, imagining the girl free and happy and gradually pulling my will back. When my connection to Irena has thinned to a gossamer whisper, I remember the prophecy. "Irena, picture this with me. A force shield surrounds you, a sphere of sheer will, shining bright. Can you see it? Glowing and strong, the light shines all around you, keeping others from forcing their will on you, cutting all unwanted exterior ties. It allows only what you want, like love, to penetrate, and only when you want it. Do you see it?"

"I am surrounded by a wall of light, unbroken. I am free." Irena raises her chin, smiling triumphantly, but doesn't break my gaze.

The words come to me without thought. "I release you from all bonds of obedience. You are unbound." Keeping her gaze, I imagine the shield surrounding her closing, cutting the connection between us. An arrow pierces my heart, and I clamp my hand over my chest, groaning. Then I slam my mouth shut, holding the pain inside. I won't create additional trauma.

Irena collapses on the sofa, fainting like a girl in a horror film. Which, in many ways, she is. Karski snarls and shoves me off the coffee table, away from his niece. I hit the floor, but look up to see him cradle the girl in his arms.

I scramble to my feet and back towards the bedroom door, ready to run. If she's done more than faint, I'm forever dead. But my problems will be over, at least on the earthly plane, and I'll have the satisfaction of knowing Irena is free—I can hear her heart beating.

Karski checks her pulse. "Alive." He arranges her on the couch, his movements slow and deliberate.

His tenuous control obvious, I retreat to the bedroom, leaving the door barely cracked. Then I grab a blood box, sucking it down slowly. I'll give the wolf time to settle. I'm not as hungry as last night, but I definitely need the nourishment. The door to Karski's office opens, a man and a woman talk to Karski, then the outer door shuts. As I finish a second box, the wolf taps on the bedroom door. "Char, you okay?"

"I'm fine. Irena's okay?" I can't hear her heart anymore.

The man pokes his head inside, his eyes glowing like the wolf's. "She seems to be sleeping. Are you okay?" He grimaces. "I can't—"

I hold up my hand. "I'm not asking. Today was much easier." No headache, no raging hunger; I'm fine with a box. Or three.

"I'll be back later. I'd recommend you stay here." He backs out, and the door shuts.

I'm not stupid enough to stroll through his pack home without his escort. I take his tablet off the nightstand and return to reading about Theoden.

But less than a minute later, the bedroom door opens, and Karski enters, a smirk on his face. He taps his phone.

A man roars, "He's dead to the world! Not responding at all!"

The corners of Karski's mouth turn up. "And he said Char's name before he dropped?"

"Yes. What did she do?"

I grin. "I cut off his connection to the alpha's niece. Pedofiles who steal under-age girls get smacked. I'll do it to you too." I put a snarl into the last line.

"You did this? You're a dead woman."

Finally, I recognize the man's voice. Reeve—Theo's primary bully-boy. I huff. "Have been for decades." But I see a way to solve several problems all at once. "Rather than yelling at me, why don't you take advantage of the opportunity I've given you, Reeve?" I make sure he hears my hatred.

Karski grins. "Yes, why don't you, Reeve? Then I'll throw you a party. A hanging party." He growls the last phrase.

Reeve swears, and the line clicks off.

"Too bad. I was hoping to hear a sword." Karski shakes his head.

"Me too, but I'd bet Reeve isn't alone. Now they're arguing over who's in charge, and Theo will wake soon."

"When will Theo wake, Char?" Karski meets my gaze, then looks away.

"Now. And he's furious." The foreign emotion cuts off. "That's interesting. We must be connected."

"He turned you, so it makes sense." He quirks a brow. "Can you still feel him?"

I shake my head. "No. I only got a flash. I bet he's got very strong mental shields."

"Do you? Or can he feel your emotions?"

I suck in a breath. "I don't know. If I'm the 'Queen Unbound,' then no. But like you said, he turned me, so it's likely." I hold up my hand. "Give me a few moments." Ignoring his looming presence, I clear my mind. Using the same imagery I gave Irena, I imagine a sphere of light surrounding me and close it tight. I can almost feel the severing of my connection with Theoden. The question is, how does that affect him and can I hold it? I have no way to know.

Karski's phone buzzes then shuts off before he can accept the call. One corner of his mouth lifts. "What do you bet that Theoden passed out again?"

"No bet." I smile. "I just cut him off. But I don't know if I can keep him out."

He nods. "I wonder. If Theoden gets killed, will your bond pass to his successor? Or is it a bond at all, Unbound Queen?"

"I don't know. But I do know that I desperately want a copy of that prophecy." I don't believe in predictions of the future, but that document might tell me a lot about my abilities. Because I'm fairly certain I have many I haven't discovered, yet.

"Then let's find a way inside." Karski points at me. "And a way for you to take over, for good. Because that's the only way this ends well for you." His brows lift. "And me."

"Pack not happy with you?" I bet they aren't. With one of his humans taken hostage, he's been forced to submit to Theo, and that weakens him.

"No, they're not. But it's more than that. I have a long history with Theoden's vampires. While Theoden and I have, until he took my niece, kept a careful truce, the same can't be said about his people." He scowls. "We've had trouble with all of them. Theoden always had excuses and paid for damages, but that doesn't revive or bring back the people I've lost."

I'd bet that Karski doesn't make excuses for his people. "Par for the course. Theoden's big on authority and privilege, but not the associated responsibility. But we've had this discussion. Time to talk to the badgers."

"Why?" His revulsion is crystal clear. "Undisciplined, unorganized, mean, nasty—"

I've had enough. "Quit with the prejudice. One, they've gotten into Theo's tower. Two, you're wrong. They may not be planners, but they are organized, and more importantly, they're determined." I smile at him. "Did you know they can turn without a moon?"

He growls. "Of course. Badgers don't follow the rules."

I can't hold back a smirk. "Poor baby. Can't deal with the rebels, huh? Well, those rebels will save our asses because it's their disregard for the rules that will let us win." I hold up a finger. "You were a soldier. Planning is important, but plans never survive first contact with the enemy, right? So how do you win?"

"Adapt, improvise, overcome. If you can't get over it, go under or around." He snorts. "Okay, you're right. Badgers are great at that." He can't be more grumpy about that admission. "This won't help me with my pack."

"Not my problem." For once. "But a successful raid will help, correct?"

"Only if heads roll. Because taking my niece was a declaration of war, and making me a herd dog only added to it." He glowers.

I nod. "Understandable." I huff a laugh. "Well, let's get some, then. Because evidently, that's the only way I survive, too." I wish Reeve had taken his opportunity at command because the mere thought of killing Theoden makes me nauseous and elated. It's rather like the immortals in the movie Highlander. If I kill my rival, it's going to hurt. I suspect the pain will be mental, physical and intense, because everything associated with vampirism is painful. I'd rather make him submit to my will, but that seems impossible.

Every action has a reaction, and every decision brings consequences. That's life. I'd rather face the consequences on Earth than carry them over to my next life—if there is an afterlife for vampires. I pick up my phone.

"That won't work down here." Karski hands me his phone. "WiFi calling."

I nod my thanks and dial Freddie's number. "Hey, it's Char. Got a few?"

"For you, always. Where and when?"

"I know you won't like it, but can you come to the wolves? We'll meet at the clubhouse." I lift my brows at Karski. His lip lifts, but he nods.

"No problem. We've been expecting your call, and we're bringing friends. In an hour or so?"

"That's great. Thanks." The line clicks off. I force a smile. "In an hour. The badgers are bringing friends, so make sure your people don't attack on sight, please."

A rumble underlays his words. "Worry about your problems. My people are under control."

"I hope so." I grab a notepad and a pen. Planning to kill someone, even Theoden, is awful, but it's the only way ahead. "Our goals are to capture a copy or the original of the prophecy and to control Theoden. Is that correct?"

Karski jolts, then he smiles. "Yes, that's goal two and three. Goal one is putting you in command. Therefore, our operational priority is neutralizing Theoden. If you can't get him to submit, he's got to die. Agreed?"

I write the words, despite my misgivings. "I don't see another way ahead. He's too set in his ways, too stuck in the past, too driven by his ego, not logic, and too dependent on allowing his people to prey on others. He's got to go." I can't see how I can possibly take over, but I have to, at least for the short term. Even if I know it will be disastrous. But fewer innocents will die.

"He's not just allowing his people to prey on others. He's doing it too. But he's good at making the evidence disappear and convincing those around him that he's the good guy. All that money makes a big difference. Especially when he uses his money to make life better for his supporters. Those people forget about the minorities, the poor, and the downtrodden."

I grimace. "The golden rule: those with the gold, rule. I may be a predator, but I'd like to see the real golden rule revived."

Karski smiles. "I think many of us would like to see that." He grimaces. "But getting there will be painful for everyone. You're going to make mistakes. Your people, my people, and humans will suffer along the way. The difference is, you're not playing people against each other to make more money to spend on things that don't matter."

I snort. "Oh, I'll make a ton of mistakes; there's no doubt about that. And everyone will point fingers at me. We'll have to keep the human cops off my back, too."

"You can leave that to me. I've got dirt on the District Attorney, and I have an excellent relationship with the local police chief. And a lot of the national office representatives, like the FBI and DEA. Many people who support Theoden are getting paid off, or he's financing their elections. A lot of them will support you once the money's gone." Karski seems overly optimistic.

"I hope so because I'm not playing that game. Call me naive, but I believe in free elections that aren't unduly influenced by the rich just trying to get richer for no reason. And local politics should remain local."

"It's a great ideal." He shakes his head. "Suck down another box and let's get going. We've got too many things to do and not enough time to do them in."

CHAPTER 18

I watch the military-style preparations surrounding me with despair. Karski is in his element, born to be a general and doing it well. The badgers just want to tear things apart. The rest of the shifters agree but want a plan. The gargoyles are present but not engaging other than to answer direct questions.

All I can see is a lot of people dying, including a lot of bystanders. There has to be a better way.

"You don't look happy, Char." Freddie's voice comes from behind me.

I spin and frown at her. "Thanks for startling me. Like I don't have enough trouble now."

Freddie smirks. "You've got a ton of it here, for sure. Theoden's got excellent air attack defenses on his tower, so we can't parachute a small team in anymore." She puts her hand out flat, twisting and turning it in a descending spiral. "Even gargoyles can't glide in. He's got big caliber automatic weapons on the roof, and they'll eventually chip the gargoyles to pieces. Those pieces will fall on the streets below. His big elaborate war plan is doomed to fail, with a ton of collateral damage."

"Tell me something I don't know." That's why the alpha is planning a suicidal frontal assault with shoulder-fired rockets.

She smirks. "Theoden and his buddies aren't in his tower anymore. They've relocated to a secret underground vault in the mountains. It's built into an old mine, and the only way in will take a huge amount of shaped charges to blow through. Or maybe a nuke." She smiles slowly. "Unless you know about the emergency escape tunnel. Then, it just takes a single shaped charge or the combination, plus some stealth and a little luck."

I roll my eyes. "Let me guess. You know where the emergency escape is, and you want me to get the shaped charges."

"You're smart, Char." She winks.

"Or Theoden paid you a lot of money to bring me in, and this is the easiest way to do that." Freddie told me that money is her driving force.

She puts a hand over her heart and glares. "Ouch. Why would you ever believe I'd work with that guy? I hate him."

She does, that much is obvious. But exactly why is the mystery. "You might hate him, but you love money, and once you're bought, you stay bought. You told me that." I scan the room and stare at Matias, the Fantastique's security manager. He's always had my back, and I'm fairly certain he won't let me down now. Plus, trying to extract Karski quietly from the middle of his shifters will never happen; the gargoyle is a better bet.

"It's true. But I'd never willingly work with KT." Her lip curls. "He's scum."

Karski didn't want to work with Theoden either, but he has, and for good reason. I'll never forget his nose shoved against me, pushing me into Theo's car. Matias glances at me, then meets my gaze. I widen my eyes, and he barely nods. While I reply to Freddie, I look at the ballroom ceiling, then return to Karski at the war table. Matias's gaze follows mine, then he looks away. "Let's talk upstairs. You can tell me what you're thinking." I leave the ballroom and trot up the stairs to one of the club meeting rooms. Freddie is on my heels. Even though I can't hear them, I'd be willing to bet her sisters aren't far behind. I hate not trusting friends, but that's the only reason I've survived so far. Of course, I'm trusting a gargoyle who isn't even a friend, just an ex-coworker, and a wolf with his own agenda.

With his niece free, I trust Karski more than the rest of them, though. At the top of the stairs, I walk down the hallway and enter a conference room, striding to the far end of the table. Freddie probably thinks she has me trapped. They don't know that I'm fast enough to go through the window or across the table, straight through them.

Freddie stands behind the chair to my right, and as I expect, the rest of the badger girls run in, two of them firing tasers at me. I sweep my arm down and across the wires before the barbs embed in my body, ducking and pulling the wires under the end of the conference table. More projectiles sail over my head, smacking into the wall behind me.

I pick up the chair in front of me and stand, swinging hard and bashing Freddie in the head. I catch her sister with the backswing and throw the chair at the third. By the time I reach the far end of the table, Matias blocks the door, the fourth badger's throat in his hand.

I run back to Freddie and copy Matias's move, grasping her throat. Her pulse pounds under my thumb and forefinger, and I can't help licking my lips. "Such a bad, bad badger. Did you think I'd trust you?" I force her to meet my gaze. "Tell me everything about this attempt to take me. Start with the initial contact." I mesmerize her without remorse; she's brought this on herself.

But it isn't working. Her jaw clamps and her pulse and breathing rate rise. I push my will on hers harder, surrounding her with the same spherical shield I used on Irena. Words pour out of my mouth. "The Unbound Queen frees you from all other binds. Speak truth, now!" I slam the sphere shut, enclosing the two of us.

She gasps in pain, then her eyes pop wide. "KT. He got me. He got all of us." Gasping the words, she pants in between phrases.

I loosen my grip and do a quick sweep of the room. Matias and Karski restrain the other three badgers, struggling in the iron grip of their captors. I'll have to unbind them, too. "How did it start?" I capture her gaze again.

"Normal contact from a human on our portal for a snatch and grab. The woman assured us it was an abduction for child support leverage, not a killing, so we agreed to meet. As soon as we got there, KT's vamps surrounded us, and he mesmerized all of us." She shudders. "It was horrible. I owe you for getting me free."

"You do. In blood, Freddie. Because cutting people loose is hard." I hunger, but it isn't raging—yet.

She shivers but nods. "I understand. Can you free my sisters, please?"

I nod. "Same deal. They owe me blood." The women in Matias's and Karski's hands fight harder.

"Agreed." Freddie swallows hard and holds out her wrist.

"Not yet. Sit. Stay." I push past her and capture the gaze of the next badger, surrounding and freeing her, then the next, and the last. Each one is easier, but by the time I finish, I'm ravenous. Not looking away from the last badger, I speak to Matias. "Are you willing to run a timer for me? Two minutes."

"Yes." He pulls out a cell phone and taps on it. "Go."

I lick and drink from the badger. Her blood has a strange flavor, but it isn't unpleasant; it's similar to eating sharp cheese. Power sweeps through me. Not as good as the wolf, but better than a human. When the phone chimes, I pull away and lick the wounds shut.

"That's so weird," the girl says. "It hurt, then it didn't, and then it felt good. I really don't like vampires." She shudders.

I laugh. "I don't like them either. We're all horrible."

Freddie shakes her head. "Not really. Taking someone's free will is awful, but other than that, I don't see much of a difference between you and me. You're a specialized carnivore rather than an omnivorous predator. Plus, you're not drinking people dead or mesmerizing for fun and sex. That's the difference."

"Let's focus on the current situation." Karski sits on the table in front of Freddie. "What do you know about Theoden? Where is he now? What's his plan?"

"I told the truth before, just not all of it." She shrugs one shoulder. "He and his buddies are in their super-secure hideout, inside an old mine in the mountains. Going through the front door would take a couple of anti-tank rounds, and the back escape hatch is the same. The plan was to bring Char to the escape hatch, and then the vampires would surround us. They'd overwhelm her with numbers in the narrow space."

An idea rumbles in the back of my mind, but it isn't quite ready for prime time. "Have you been there?"

She grimaces. "Only the outside. One of KT's minions showed me the entrance to the back escape. You wind through a big stack of broken-off hoodoos and boulders, then the tunnel starts. The vault hatch is supposedly about fifty yards down the tunnel."

"And what about the main vault door?"

She shrugs. "You can't see it from the mine entrance. I don't know how far down you have to go. The mine entrance is fenced off, and there are cameras everywhere."

I turn to Karski. "Why didn't we know they left? And can we find out who they took with them and who was left behind?"

Matias breaks in. "We knew they left. We watch that tower closely."

Karski shoots a glare at him. "That would have been useful information." He grimaces. "There are limos in and out of Theoden's tower constantly, and they all have dark windows. We do what we can, but that's not much. Every time we hack the cameras, we're in for five to ten minutes, if we're lucky, then they kick us out. He's got excellent network security."

"You know who normally lives in the tower, though, right? Can you get a list of those missing? I want to know if any of the vampires are still in the tower and which humans are gone. Because I think there might be an easy solution to the entire problem."

Karski frowns, then his lips turn up as he catches my meaning. "It might be a cat's solution, but I think we can make it work."

Three days later, I have answers, but I'm not happy about most of them. Theo, all his vampires, and all his humans have literally gone underground. If the humans were all willing donors, I'd have buried them alive in their litter box and let them prey on each other. But there are too many innocents involved. Theoden isn't stupid. He knows I won't cause that much collateral damage.

The gargoyles report he sends vampires in and out of his tower every night. Usually, they transport boxes and bags to the mine and envelopes out—a mail run. Karski's people uncover a copy of a commercial delivery contract for food, liquor, and other comfort items three times a week for the next month. Vampires aren't fans of roughing it.

During the day, Karski's foxes and coyotes search a five-mile diameter around the mine and find two more escape tunnels. They also map the Starlink antennas, cameras, tripwires, and other sensors and evade multiple drones running surveillance patterns. Three of them get hit with tranquilizer darts. Since they work in groups, they rescue the fallen before the vamps' security can snatch them.

One of Karski's wolves runs a major construction company and, after winning a poker game against a competitor, gets a look at the mine blueprints. The facility has multiple air intakes with excellent filtration that automatically shut down if foreign substances are detected, like tear gas. If I'm willing to kill everyone, we can get enough poison inside, but I'm trying to save the innocents.

Karski pounds his fist on the table. "There's got to be a way to get the humans out."

"I don't think there is." Matias shakes his head. "Theoden's not stupid."

We've been over this before. Maybe it's time to look at where we can go, rather than where we can't. "Let's go with our first plan and break into Theoden's tower. I bet we'll find some interesting things, even with the vampires gone."

"I'm sure he's set traps." Karski grimaces. "I would."

I nod. "I know, but I still think we should look, especially at the temple. I'm sure they took the book of prophecy, but we might find some clues."

"You may find more than that, Char." Matias's thick brows almost meet, an unusual display of emotion for the normally stoic gargoyle. "We're talking about a religion with centuries of worship. That can create a deity. If there is a temple, it might be dangerous."

I'm not the true believer type. Becoming a mindless priestess or an empty vessel for a minor god is a terrifying thought.

Karski tilts his head, his amber eyes glowing brighter. "That might have been Theoden's plan all along. Leave, draw us into the tower, take us out with traps, and sucker Char into the temple where whatever they've hatched can take over."

Freddie inspects her fingernails. "I don't think so. KT's been stalking Char for a long time. He's tried courting, he's tried manipulation, he's tried forcing a business relationship, and he's tried abduction. It's not just the thrill of the hunt. He wants her to join him willingly, but he's lost patience. Whatever he has planned now, it's not going the way he wants."

Matias nods. "I think you're partially correct, Freddie. Theoden lives for the chase, but he's adapted to modern times and done very well chasing money rather than prey. I think he applied that same method to Char. His sudden escalation says two things to me. One, whatever he wants Char for, it will work better if she does it willingly, under his leadership. Two, he's being pushed by outside pressures. He's not one to give up easily. He enjoys challenges, and Char has provided decades of entertainment. But I've watched the ballroom video, and that's an unhappy man who's no longer one hundred percent certain he can win."

"He's lucky he kept his life." Karski finishes with a growl.

Matias shakes his head. "You're lucky too. If you hadn't shot right away with the correct placement, you might be under his control. Next time, don't let him touch you, especially not skin to skin. That strengthens his abilities. Wear long sleeves, a hat, and gloves. Plus armor, preferably."

"I appreciate that information very much." Karski nods. "You're partially right. My humanity almost fell, but my wolf was still free. I was about to shift when he ran. If we invade any of Theoden's abodes, the pack will be in wolf form, which limits our usefulness with modern weaponry."

Now he tells us? But Karski can change partway, so maybe he can use a weapon. I won't ask with all these non-pack members around.

"That's why we went in badger form," Freddie says. "Took forever to force the change, but it was the only way we could be sure."

I doubt she's absolutely certain even in badger form. Although, if any animal could withstand an ancient vamp, it would be a badger.

Freddie continues, "Whatever we're going to do, we need to do something soon. All this sitting around talking is getting us nowhere fast."

"Failure to plan is planning to fail." Karski frowns at her.

"Staying in place makes us sitting ducks for an attack." Freddie motions at the second-floor conference room, the blinds drawn and ultrasonic vibrators—to prevent long-distance listening devices—mounted on the glass. "I know you've got people out watching, but every minute we spend here increases the chance of them coming after us."

He growls for a moment. "I know that. That's one of the reasons we didn't meet yesterday. I'd planned on making a final decision today, regardless."

I spent yesterday going over the intelligence Karski gathered on Theoden and his vampires. His lieutenants aren't simple bully boys, after all. Looking back at my time in the tower, I suspect they tried to force a reaction from me. It doesn't excuse their behavior because the issue could have been resolved if they'd simply listened to what I had to say. But they're too set in their ways, too certain that a new vampire couldn't control her emotions and reactions the way I did. They attempted to make me snap, but I learned to control myself in a much harsher environment than KT's luxurious rooms. I also learned that running keeps me alive, so I have. KT probably forced Cerise to contact and shelter me, supposedly to keep me from slaughtering every human in my vicinity. When I didn't go blood-crazy, he was finally forced to admit that I could survive on my own. Then he modified his approach. That still leaves me wondering why he forced the issue now. "You know, Theo's organization didn't listen to me. Maybe I need to talk to him."

"No." Karski slashes his hand through the air in front of his body. "Way too dangerous. Besides, he's made it clear. He wants complete surrender or nothing."

Freddie backhands his shoulder. "They have these things called phones, genius. She doesn't have to get close to him. My sister can even route the call to mask the location."

I push the corner of Karski's phone, making it spin on the table in front of him. "He knows we're here. Just call."

"I don't think this will work." But he taps, and the call rings through.

After five rings, a voice finally answers. "What do you want, Karski?" It's Theoden's voice, unusually impatient.

"Nothing, Theoden. But Flammen wants to talk to you. I recommend you listen and discuss, but that's your decision." Karski's tone is flat, but I can hear the exasperation.

Theoden probably can, too. "Charlene," he practically purrs. "I'm listening."

My lip curls, but I control my immediate revulsion. "What exactly do you want with me, Theoden? We can fight, but it's a waste of people, time, and money. If you keep forcing me to submit, we will have a war. I don't belong to anyone, especially you. So what is the problem you're trying to use me to solve?"

"I'm not talking about this over the phone." He snaps the words.

"Then I guess we'll fight because I'm not wasting lives trying to meet with you in person. You can't be trusted. You've proven that."

"How dare you doubt my word!" Something thuds in the background; probably his fist on a desk or a wall.

I snort. "You broke your word by attacking Karski."

"He broke first. He threatened my people."

I can't hold back a sigh. "You had his human niece, doorknob. And your people were armed. Of course he threatened them. Let's return to the subject, which is talking about whatever issue you've got. You said there was a threat coming, a threat to all of us. What is that threat, and why is it my problem?"

"I will not share my secrets with animals. Charlene Flammen, come here to me, now."

I can hear the command in his voice even over my team's protests, but it rolls over me without effect. "No. I won't. That doesn't work on me, Theo. Not even in person. And you're not going to seduce me, either. Stop trying. It's annoying." He might be physically attractive, but his personality negates that entirely.

"I will talk to you and you alone about this, Charlene. Meet me at Arrolime in an hour. I will drop a pin and text it to Karski. My people and yours will remain at the bottom of the hill while we meet at the top. No listening devices, no sniper rifles."

Karski shakes his head. "How do we know it's not already trapped?"

"Make a counter-offer." Theoden speaks without emotion.

"Send your pin."

A text pops up on Karski's phone, and he displays the location on the large screen in the conference room. The location is at the top of a hill, one of several near Highway 91. Karski zooms out, then into a facility nearby. He mutes the phone's microphone. "I'll tell him the open area behind the fireworks company where they test and build displays." He doesn't wait for agreement but taps the middle of the open area, then sends that pin to Theoden.

"Stand by." I count to thirty-three, then Theoden speaks. "Agreed. One hour. Our people remain outside the field. Charlene and I meet in the middle."

I hold up my hand when Karski opens his mouth. "Agreed." I tap the phone, ending the call. "You can yell at me or get ready."

"Born ready, Char." Freddie winks, then faces Karski. "Snipers on the warehouse?"

Karski nods. "Of course." He stands and crosses to the map display.

I'll leave him to plan because I have more important work to do.

CHAPTER 19

THIRTY MINUTES LATER, I ride in the back seat of a large SUV. Karski drives. A coyote in human form sits next to him, carrying a small semi-automatic rifle. A wolf sits next to me, and two more pant behind me despite the air conditioner going full blast. Our vehicle is in the middle of a long line of dark-colored SUVs. I know Karski sent a couple of motorcycles ahead to scout the area, and more pack members are setting up sniper positions. The badgers and gargoyles have taken Karski's communication devices but haven't promised to stick to his plan.

That's fine by me. Unpredictability might save the day, or me, maybe. But I can't count on anyone but myself. If Theoden gave his people kill orders, I'll be dead. If he doesn't, then he'll try to take me over. The best thing I can do is shore up my defenses. Knowing I'll need the energy, I've taken blood from two more of the badgers, leaving Freddie's contribution for after the confrontation. My body almost hums with power.

But Theoden will do the same or worse. I meditate, imagining a shield surrounding me, powered by my adamant will. I will triumph and save all of us. When we make a sharp turn, I open my eyes, knowing I'm ready. The bullet resistant vest, a helmet, and tactical clothing don't hurt, either, although none of it will save me from a high-powered rifle round.

"We're almost there," Karski says. "We've cleared a path so we can drive straight to the meeting point where we'll drop you. Our perimeter is solid, but the vampires have one too. We haven't confronted any of them, but they're all under surveillance."

Theoden will do the same. "And yours are in the same boat?"

Karski nods. "Yes. My people are being watched, mostly through high-powered rifle scopes and armed drones. We're targeting Theoden's people with the same, plus the pack in animal form."

Great; we have mutually assured destruction again, just on a larger scale. "And if it looks like I've given into Theoden?"

He glances over his shoulder. "You won't."

I smile, but I know it looks grim. "I won't. But I might do something that looks like I have, so don't let your people kill me." Sometimes, the best way to success is from the inside.

"Char, you're not going to fall under his spell. I know that. But as much as I want to protect you, you are not pack. I won't start a war for you if you lose."

No sane person would, nor do I want that, even if the betrayed child inside of me wails in protest. I know the voice of my emotional trauma. I'm an adult and capable of reason, rather than reaction. "Good. Don't."

"I will, however, defend my pack against all outsiders, including you, if necessary." His tone is grim.

"Understood." And I do. I'm not his responsibility. I've made that clear; he's making sure I understand all the ramifications. Getting Theoden to understand will be harder. Despite his centuries of life, KT is a privileged toddler used to getting his way and throwing tantrums when he doesn't. But he has plenty of power, money, and people to throw. I hope we can have a simple conversation, but I'm not betting on it.

At the very least, I'll have to fight off mental control attempts right away. I have a few advantages—very few. Theoden is used to success. He hasn't had to fight on his own for a very long time. Which makes me wonder what traps he's already planned and who he's involved. Probably the representative of the religion spawned by the prophecy and his highest lieutenants. There might be a way for those people to join Theoden's mental efforts against me, and they'll plan on getting close enough to overwhelm me with numbers.

I must strike hard and fast. Karski pulls to a stop in the middle of a huge barren area, the ground covered with odd markings from the fireworks testing. I wait for the dust to settle, then open the door.

Karski turns, his eyes glowing amber. "We're all pulling for you, Char. Go get him."

"Thanks." As the vehicle pulls away, I don't look back. I'm on my own; I've refused to wear a microphone or earpiece. Theoden will overhear anything they say, and I don't need the wolf overreacting to Theoden's words. He will do his best to get a rise out of me.

Within seconds, another vehicle appears—a limousine, of course. Theoden is undoubtedly sipping blood wine, ready for a quick escape with the prize.

I reinforce my mental shield but leave a small "window" to push my thoughts through. As the long black car stops twenty feet from me, I can feel Theoden, the driver, and three others in the car. The driver gets out and opens the back door.

I project disdain through my shield. "Alone, Theoden. That was the deal. You agreed."

Theoden gracefully exits the vehicle. "That will be all until I call." The driver gets back in and drives away.

Theoden wears a perfectly fitted black suit with a blood red tie, and his mind pummels mine. His hair has grown and flops in the wind, his face is dark with taken blood, and his fangs extend halfway down his chin. He holds out his hand. "Come, Charlene Flammen. Now!"

I thrust his pitiful attempts to control me away. I lower my tone and volume, shoving the thoughts of pleasure and favor to him, while keeping my revulsion hidden. "Come to me, Theoden Klaus. Come here." I lift the corners of my mouth in a seductive expression.

He takes one step forward and clenches his hand. "No. You will come to me!"

Using my hard-won bartender-to-the-ugly skills, I smile and shake my head slowly, while employing every bit of mesmerization I've learned. "You want to come. Join me, Klaus Theoden."

His body shaking, he thrusts both arms skyward. "Now!"

Rifles boom, making me jump and fumble my connection to Theoden. I set my feet and reinforce my desires. I can't outrun a bullet, so I won't try. Theoden will come to heel.

Vampires sprint across the open ground almost faster than the eye can see, but the fusillade of rifle rounds keeps them away from the two of us. The sand in front of each vampire fountains under the impact of automatic fire, forcing them back in a twisting, turning dance.

My attention remains on Klaus. "I name you oath-breaker, Theoden Klaus." The old-fashioned words rise unbidden. My arms rise, my hands stretching towards Theo. "Who are you to bind the Unbound Queen?" I hiss, my fangs dropping. "My book, now." I shove my will at him. I don't know where the words are coming from, but I can't spare the time to worry about it. Especially when it's working.

Theoden reaches into his jacket, withdraws a slim, black rectangle, and tosses it at my feet. Then he appears in front of me, clamping his hand around my neck. He releases me, screeching.

I grab his wrist, keeping his burned hand close. The gargoyle glamor worked—Theo hadn't noticed the silver-clad leather neck guard I wear. "You are mine." I put my other hand on his cheek and stare into his eyes, forcing him to submit.

"No!" He jerks away, then stoops.

I jab my knee into his chin, knocking him away from the book of prophecy, sending him sprawling on the sand. I scoop the book up and hold it to my chest. "Mine."

Theoden runs, his vampires following. He almost flies, reaching his limo and diving inside, leaving his people to follow on foot. The car speeds away, dust rising in its wake, scraping through a hole cut in the fence. His vampires reach the fence and climb into a fleet of SUVs.

Two bodies sprawl headless on the plain, black blood oozing from shattered spines. My people, their second life wasted by that selfish man. I stare at the true dead, mourning.

A black SUV rolls towards me, slowing and stopping a few steps away. Karski lowers the window. "Char, are you okay?"

Char. Char is my name. I shiver, shoving back the presence that put words in my mouth and forced my body to act. "I'm not sure."

"Is that the prophecy?" He nods at the greasy leather notebook in my hands. "Are you getting in or standing there?"

The sun will rise before I can return to a safe spot. Going with Karski is wise. "I'm coming." I walk towards the door behind him.

He frowns. "Get in the passenger seat."

I walk around the SUV and climb inside, then put the book on my lap. Keeping one hand on the leather, I buckle in. "Go."

Karski's head jolts, and he leans away from me. "Are you okay, Char?"

"Yes. Go. We must reach safety before the sun rises." I feel disconnected from my body, and a sense of mortal danger lingers.

He puts the vehicle in drive and follows the path the fleeing vampires took. "Before you ask, the two vampires who died are known for preying on children. They've been marked for death by the supernatural community, excluding the vampires, of course. Neither has been seen for years."

"A year is a blink in the life of a vampire." I stare at Karski, hunger rising. "Hold out your arm."

Karski's arm rises, then his hand clamps around the steering wheel. Yanking the wheel, he pulls off the road, slamming us against the seatbelts. "You aren't Char." He unbuckles, turns towards me, and snarls, his head morphing to the wolf's.

I hiss at him, my fangs dropping, then I retract them so fast it hurts. The pain shocks me, and I drop the book on the floor. "Whoa. Sorry." I reinforce my personal shield and nudge the booklet away with my booted toe. "I don't think I should touch that." Anger and need pummel my mind, but I close it out. It's still there, though.

Karski gets out of the SUV and runs to the back, raising the tailgate. He comes around to my door and opens it. "May I?" His hand is covered in a thick leather glove.

I nod, frantically. "Yes, please. But don't throw it away. I'm pretty sure we'll need it."

He pinches a corner of the slim volume between his forefinger and thumb, the book falling open. He growls and runs to the back of the SUV. I follow, watching him toss the book into a metal container. "Hopefully, the ammo can will shield you from the effects until we can get back to the house." He closes the can and slams the tailgate shut. "But I don't want anyone else carrying it. Too risky."

Anger burns through me. I grit my teeth and back away, hardening my mind against the book. "Yeah. It's not happy now." I return to the front seat, forcing my dragging feet forward.

Karski hooks his arm into mine. "Come along, Char, just a few more steps." We reach the seat. He shoves me in, then closes the door.

Concentrating on my shield, I fasten my belt and roll my shoulders, then pay attention to my breathing, grounding myself. This is my body, flaws and all. My mind, my heart, my soul. I am me.

Karski gets in, belts, and pulls out. He clicks a button on the steering wheel. "Call Virginia."

"Calling Virginia. Please stand by," the pleasant female voice says.

"Yeah, boss?" A woman's voice; Theo's previous limo driver.

"I need a containment vessel. Lead-lined preferably. Big enough for that book I was holding. Can you get one?"

"We don't have one, but I'm sure we can come up with something. I'll get on that when we get back. Are you okay? Need someone else to drive?"

"I'm fine. Not a problem now." He clicks the button and disconnects the call. "Are you doing any better, Char?"

"Yeah." I feel in control again, but the anger simmers and pushes at my shield. I shove it away. "That thing is gonna be a problem."

"Yes, it is." He glances at me. "Not only did that thing try to burn me, but I couldn't read a word of it."

My gut sinks. I haven't even tried—yet.

CHAPTER 20

We pull into Karski's garage, and I retrieve the ammo can, pinching the handle between my thumb and forefinger and holding it at arm's length. Being controlled by an ancient prophecy or deity spawned by the belief of nasty vampires creeps me out. But I can't forget that the prophecy book helped me win against Theo. Honestly, help is too weak a word, though. Rather, it used me like a puppet. The effort and willpower were mine, but the targeted refinement of that willpower was beyond me.

Whatever this thing is, it can manipulate my thoughts and feelings. I'll have to guard against it and fight it or find a way to work with it. Or burn it.

Anger floods me again, and I drop the ammo can. It smacks against the floor, shattering a tile. "Sorry, I'll pay for the damages."

"Don't worry about it." Karski huffs. "Wolf claws chew up tile. We replace them regularly."

I regard the can, swallowing my revulsion. That...thing enabled me to fight off Theoden. I can't afford to turn down an advantage. But it has to provide more than it takes, and I won't be a puppet. Revulsion wars against need. I retrieve the ammo can, still holding it at arm's length, and trot down the stairs.

Karski lets me into his sanctuary and strides to the bedroom beyond. "I hope my people can find a containment vessel quickly. Until then, we need to keep it as far from my pack as possible. I'll find another shelter for you." He opens the door, holding it open for me.

"I understand." After I enter, I turn back to face Karski. "There's no telling if lead will work. It might take silver or gold, or maybe nothing will work."

"That's a good point." Karski's mouth twists. "I'll find some silver and gold foil. We can use multiple layers." He pushes the door, then catches it before it closes. He stares at my chin. "And Char? I don't want to, but if I come down here tomorrow and you're that...thing again, I'll kill you true dead myself." His eyes flash gold, then the door slams shut.

Fury batters me, but I really can't blame Karski. That thing wanted me to drain him dry as we drove, which could have killed both of us. I take the ammo can to the bathroom and put it in the tub, directly under the faucet. Then I pop the can open and thin my mental shield. "Here's the deal, book. I'll work with you, but if you attempt to take me over, I'll drown you. I'd bet your ink isn't waterproof. I am the Unbound Queen, and I will not be bound by you. Understood?"

Hatred batters me, but I keep my hand on the faucet handle, ready to slam my shields closed and turn the water on. The slim volume is about four inches wide and six inches tall; the cover shimmers like an oil slick on swampy water. No writing mars the slightly pebbled surface. I want to read it, but I'm not touching it until we come to an understanding or I have protective gear. Since it burned Karski through a heavy leather glove, I'm not sure anything can shield me from the effects.

Dull thuds come from the bedroom door. I close the can, compartmentalize the book's anger, and renew my shields. Crossing to the door, I peer at the sensor. Matias stands there with Karski. I open it to let them in. "The sun rises soon."

"I know." Matias enters, Karski closing the door and standing with his back to it. "Where is it?"

"You can't have it." The book is mine!

Matias holds up his hands, palm out. "I don't want it. Trust me, I don't even want to talk about it. But I'm the one who's here, so I have to." He folds his arms across his massive chest. "And unless you want to go full Gollum 'my precious'"—he hisses the quote—"I suggest you listen."

I strengthen my shields again. "Sorry. I'm trying to keep it out of my head, but it's tenacious."

"Powerful immortals revered that book for thousands of years." Matias spreads his hands wide. "We don't think they intended to create a deity, but we believe they did."

"Who's we?" I have no trouble believing his words, but his motivations are unclear. "And why do you want to help?"

"We are the Gargoyle Guardians." He smirks. "Yes, I'm aware of the alliteration." Returning to his normal blank expression, he continues. "The Gargoyle Guardians protect the magic the supernatural community relies on. We call it the 'Pool of Life.' You use it for your talents, and to stay hidden. But as technology improves, it's become almost impossible to cover up your presence and you use more and more. The supernatural community must change their ways if they wish to remain a secret and keep their magic. The Council has created guidelines, but we know most of the community won't follow them. They're too arrogant, too ignorant of scientific and technological advances."

"I tried to warn Theoden that he was playing with fire, but he wouldn't listen." I can't see his bully boys giving up their petty amusements.

Matias grimaces. "Believe it or not, he's made some progress with his people. Vampires like Trinity were kept close. But Theoden feels threatened, and I'm not sure he's wrong."

"What can threaten him?" Karski snaps the question before I can.

Matias turns to face Karski. "Vampire rulers have remained in their territories for centuries, both through agreement and magical limitations. We're not entirely sure how, but they seem to be tethered to the area they were turned in. With enough power, that tie can be broken. The threat to Theoden's creator was so immense that he escaped, but even though he was ancient and immensely powerful, his efforts broke him. He never recovered, and Theoden had to kill him." Matias focuses on me. "Vampire leaders around the world have been waiting for the

Unbound Queen. They believe the Unbound will free them from all constraints, including their place ties. If she does, the vampires will war for dominance. Theoden is relatively young. He inherited the prophecy, but he doesn't have the power to hang on to his territory if the older vamps attack. Vegas is valuable and the prophecy even more so."

Theoden's efforts to control me now make sense. "So if he controls me, then I keep him safe." I don't hold back my eye roll. "Ridiculous man. If he'd shared his concerns, I would have told him I have no interest in freeing the vampires to war on each other. The carnage would kill too many innocents."

"It would also irrevocably reveal supernaturals to the world." Karski frowns. "But Theoden, for all his business sense, is still a product of his times. One, he can't handle the thought of a woman in charge. Two, humans are food. And three, he believes altruism is weak."

Matias nods. "That's only part of it. One of the reasons Theoden hasn't forced you to take the crown, Char, is because he didn't want to bring attention to you. When you were turned, the Council felt the impact in the Pool of Life. They didn't know what the shock was, only that it occurred, and in the Vegas area. It took years of research to figure out what caused that reverberation and the possible repercussions. Once they discovered you'd been turned free because of an ancient prophecy, they set watchers on you."

He nods at my unspoken question about his employment at Fantastique. "In addition, the oldest vampires felt your turning. They were furious because they were all positive Theoden didn't have the experience or age to know who the right person was to fulfill the prophecy."

I snort. "I'm pretty sure they were right." Why anyone would pick me is a mystery. Uneducated, poor, and middle-aged—none of that screams royalty or chosen one.

Matias shakes his head. "They were wrong. The prophecy picked you. The Council summoned Theoden to an audience here in Vegas. No one can withstand the power of the gathered council, and they dragged the story of your turning out of Theoden. After Theoden killed his creator, the prophecy told him about you through dreams. It didn't know what you looked like, but it knew the measure of your soul. After you were born, the dreams became more specific. Then you moved here, and the prophecy felt your proximity. Theoden's vampires searched for you, and they found a woman they couldn't mesmerize. Nor could Theoden, no matter how hard he tried. He finally brought the book with him when he was trying to take you over at the bar. When it didn't work, the book told him it wanted you. He suspects the book created the mob confrontation that killed you."

"Are you kidding me?" I glare at the book right through the walls. "Now I really hate that thing. If Theoden had told me what I'd be doing to survive, I'd have told him to let me die." At least I think I would. In that moment's cold, I might have begged for my life, regardless.

Matias's head tilts. "He did not fully inform you? What did he say?"

"No." I don't like remembering that time, but some things are permanently etched in my mind. "I was lying in a pool of my own blood. Dying. He asked me if I wanted to live. I said yes. He said, 'If I keep you alive, it will hurt. It will create the worst pain you've ever endured. But you will have a life. Do you agree?' And I said yes." I remember drinking his blood, then fire running through my entire body. The rest I try to block out.

"That is not true consent." His head shakes ponderously.

I shrug off his concerns and the memories. "Doesn't really matter. I'm here, I've been living with the least amount of negative impact I can, and I'm apparently the Unbound Queen." I can't hold back a huff at the ridiculous statement.

"It is indeed a rock already thrown." Matias sighs. "However, Theoden did not tell the Council about this, which makes me suspect he lied by omission more than once. That is the nature of vampires."

Karski huffs. "That's the nature of most supernaturals. Don't share."

"I'll share the rest, but Theoden may not have been telling the whole truth." Matias meets my gaze. "One, the oldest vampires believe the Unbound Queen can also free them from other constraints, such as burning in the sun and the need for blood. Two, Theoden and other vampires can read part of the prophecy, but not all of it. Theoden told the Council what he knew."

When Karski makes a scoffing sound, Matias holds up his hand. "Or claimed to know; he certainly held information back. Three, if you are killed, the prophecy will search for the next Unbound Queen. Many vampires are unhappy with Theoden's choice, but they don't want to wait for centuries for the next chosen one to appear. We believe that's why Theoden pushed you—more than one vampire threatened to have you assassinated unless you manifested as the Unbound Queen. Tonight, the vampires recorded your confrontation with Theoden from multiple locations. He wore a camera, too. We don't know if that demonstration will placate them or not." He grimaces.

Just what I need. A price on my head that I can't pay, and even if I could, I won't. I'm not freeing a bunch of ancient vampires to war on each other, even if that means they no longer need blood.

"Char, the Gargoyle Guardians Council wants to know if you've read the prophecy." Matias points at the bathroom. "Whether you have or not, they require your attendance. Immediately." He crosses his arms, blocking the door quite effectively.

My life is so weird. Only I'd get stuck between a rock, a wolf, and an angry magical book. "I haven't read it yet. Last time I picked it up, it almost took me over. I've devised a way to hold it off for now, but I really don't want to touch that thing." I shudder.

Matias shakes his head. "You must. The Council will compel you if necessary."

My fangs drop, and I hiss. "I am the Unbound Queen! I do not answer to them."

CHAPTER 21

Sunburned book! I turn away from Matias and strengthen my mental shields again. "Sorry. Occupational hazard, I guess." I'm not positive I can completely block the prophecy.

Matias, who seemed to grow taller and wider at my hiss, returned to his normal size. "Understood. I recommend you wear gloves and spend as little time touching it as necessary. Does it seem sentient?"

I shrug. "It's certainly blasting me with anger. It keeps trying to take me over, control me, make me into a puppet. But I will not let that happen." I will not be owned. Especially by an object.

"In that case, I recommend that you treat it as a living being and explain your boundaries in simple terms. Think in pictures while you speak, if you have that ability. The prophecy chose you as the Unbound Queen for a reason, so it should not be shocked that it can't control you. But you could accept guidance, with the understanding that attempts at binding will be met with fire." One corner of his mouth rises in a half-smirk.

I glance at the bedroom door behind me. "I told it I'd drown it if it kept trying to take me over, but fire might be more effective." I turn to Karski. "Got a flamethrower?"

He shrugs. "Maybe. But you can't use it inside." He glances at his watch. "It's almost sunrise. If you could secure that...thing in the can, I'd appreciate it. I'll keep my pack out of the basement today, and we'll find a better place for your days."

"I can provide that," Matias says. "The Council's chambers are deep below the earth, and we have human quarters in the complex. You are not a physical threat to us, and we will protect you, both night and day. We also have magic experts who can help you. Do you agree?"

I trust Matias, but there's always a catch. "What will it cost me?"

Matias nods. "First, mutual defense. Second, you must be open with the Council. They want to know the extent of your abilities, and they expect you to keep the vampire community here under control, if that is possible. Third, if you attempt to take over the entire world, bring all the vampire leaders together, reveal the supernatural community to humans, or any other similar authoritarian action, you will truly die."

I snort. "I don't want to do any of that. I don't want new abilities or to work with that book-thing, but I'm guessing that if I don't, I'm as good as dead anyway." Other options are nonexistent. "I accept your offer, but unless you've got a magic carpet, I'm not going anywhere right now." Ruling the Vegas vampires isn't on my bucket list, but I'll do a lot to keep humanity safe. They have enough problems without being treated like cattle. Or worse.

Matias nods. "Agreed. I will guard your day, Charlene Flammen." He turns slightly towards Karski. "If the prophecy calls them, I will keep your pack away, Alpha." He swings back to face me. "And if the prophecy makes you day-walk, I will prevent you from going anywhere."

"Are you kidding me?" That isn't terrifying at all.

His head swings ponderously from side to side. "No. If you can help other vampires day-walk, why couldn't you do it yourself? Whether your mind would be awake is unknown. That's the primary reason I'm staying."

"Thank you." I have no desire to go wandering around at the whim of the prophecy. Especially if I'm not conscious. I could end up doing something truly awful, like draining someone. I'm hungry now, so I back towards the bedroom door. "I appreciate your help. I'm going to drink a blood box and sleep."

"I'll make sure you have a fresh supply, Char." Karski leaves, closing and locking the door behind him before I can thank him.

Matias leans against Karski's desk. It creaks but holds. "Good day, Char. I'll see you tomorrow evening."

I nod. Certainly, I feel safer with Matias outside, and I believe he'll keep everyone else in the compound safe, too. "See you then." I secure the door, then trot to the bathroom, snagging a blood box on the way. After sucking down the thick, cool liquid while resisting the prophecy's demand for hot, living blood, I sit on the tub's rim and open the ammo can.

The pressure on my shields doesn't increase noticeably, so the metal can is probably useless. But as promised, I'll keep the book in there. "Look, book." I feel silly talking to an object, but Matias has always given me good advice. "Stop trying to take me over. I'm the Unbound Queen and you are not." The prophecy stops battering me, so I guess it's paying attention. "I will work with you to fulfill the goals I decide are reasonable, but first, I need to read them and agree. I don't think you understand the world today. Your worshippers have created a false sense of security. I cannot create an empire built to subdue all humans because that will get me, and all the other vampires, true dead. Fast."

Fury at lesser creatures spews from the volume, so I sigh. "I'll talk when you're done, unless I fall asleep." I slide to the floor, putting my back against the wall next to the tub, just in case my timing is off. Then I concentrate on my breathing, reaching for serenity. Gradually, the book calms. Maybe it's ready to listen. "There are over eight billion humans in the world. They have weapons of mass destruction." I picture scenes from US rallies and religious pilgrimages around the world. Then I think about a picture of the aftermath of the atomic bombs that fell on Nagasaki and Hiroshima. "Those bombs are weak in comparison to what we have now." I picture horrible scenes from the latest wars in the middle east. "World militaries can easily destroy us. Or a single suicide bomber. If you force my actions, you will get me killed, and you'll be destroyed by fire. Is that really what you want?" I think about Theoden's life experience. "The last vampire who carried you was too optimistic. He doesn't understand the power of infuriated humanity because he's been insulated by wealth."

I climb to my feet and remove the uncomfortable body armor, then the clothing, and put on sweatpants and a t-shirt. "The masses can overcome us if we aren't subtle. But we can create a solution that works for the vampires, the other supernaturals, and the humans. You think about that while I rest." I close the can lid, retreat to the bedroom, and climb into bed.

Blanking my mind, I concentrate on my breath while waiting for the sunrise. The time comes and goes, but I remain awake. I continue meditating, acknowledging my shock and letting it go. Gradually, I become sleepy, then I fade into darkness.

I wake with nightfall, still in bed. From the pressure on my bladder, if I got up during the day, I didn't do anything logical. Rising, I enter the bathroom, take care of business, and get in the shower. "Good morning, prophecy. Thank you for letting me rest. Did you contemplate my thoughts?"

Images flood my mind. Mobs, wars, political rallies, lynchings, the Holocaust, and then, the lights of Vegas from Theoden's penthouse. The feeling of hot blood in my mouth, the joy of feeding. Puzzlement over sharing resources rather than ruling. Image after image from my memories, along with those from earlier times; probably from Theoden and his vampires.

When I shake off the book's visions, water cascades over my body. Under the prophecy's deluge, I've curled into a ball on the tile floor. Concentrating on each step, I get up, finish my shower, and don't say a word or think about anything else until I'm dressed and my bag packed. I strap the body armor and helmet to the outside of my backpack. "Okay. Obviously, you learned some things. I'm guessing you got all that by rummaging around in my brain and your worshipper's brains."

A picture of my ex-husband comes to me, along with anger and a need to drain the man. I laugh. "He's long dead. When he got the flu and couldn't get out of bed, his second wife took the telephone and ran. I sent her some money, and she lives quietly in a town far away." They didn't have trauma counseling for partner abuse survivors back then, but much like me, she decided that man wouldn't take anything more from her. She became a school librarian and volunteered at the local women's shelter. I wish I could do the same, but that isn't the life I created.

Or been drafted into. "I'm taking you with me to the Gargoyles Council." Wariness comes from the book. "They won't take you from me, and they will help me lead the vampires into a better balance with humans. I want to work with you, not against you. We can create a better world, and eventually, we can find a way to openly exist among humans because we won't stay hidden much longer."

A double helix and a feeling of confusion come to me. "Yes. Genetic testing isn't good enough yet, but it will be soon. If we emerge as predators, we will be destroyed." The book sends a picture of wolf skins hanging from a long line. "Exactly. There are too many humans to fight off. If we convince a few key leaders that working with us is smart, then we can live in harmony." Anticipating anger, I strengthen my mental shield slightly. "I will probably have to destroy some vampires."

Anger flashes but is quickly followed by a feeling of righteousness. "It's my duty to control my people?" The righteousness strengthens. That isn't exactly the result I was hoping for, but I'll take progress. Hard to overcome thousands of years of arrogant worship in a single day. "Okay, then." I pick up the can and carry it and my bag to the door, opening it to reveal Matias and Karski. "Good evening. I have come to an understanding with the prophecy—for now. Matias, if you can guarantee they won't try to take the prophecy from me or kill me, I'll take the Council's offer of shelter and training."

Matias nods. "Excellent. The Council doesn't want to kill you or take the prophecy, but they will defend themselves, their home, and the Pool of Life. Understood and agreed?"

I return his solemn nod. I don't know what the "Pool of Life" is, but with that title, it seems logical. "Understood and agreed." I focus on Karski's chin. Trying to influence him, even subconsciously, would be a poor way to repay his assistance. "Thank you for your help and hospitality. I appreciate it."

"You are welcome. Work fast, Char. Theoden is sending a lot of encrypted messages, both electronic and hard copy." He moves to the side, clearing the doorway.

I cross his office, chuckling. "Did you check with the badgers?"

A low growl rumbles behind me. Matias says, "A useful suggestion, Char. I'll do that on the drive."

Before I open the office door, I turn. "I'm taking my motorcycle."

Matias nods. "I anticipated your need for independence. We'll escort you. We'll make a lot of twists and turns through town, and we may send you alone through a few alleys because we don't want to be followed."

Karski's head tilts, and he frowns at Matias. "There are only so many ways out of town."

"Ah, but that's where magic comes in." The corners of his mouth rise. "I hope you didn't waste resources putting trackers on Char's bike."

Karski's lip curls. "Of course we did." His expression clears, and he gestures at the door. "I'd appreciate it if you kept me in the loop."

I have no reason not to. "If you do the same." I return to the bedroom and put on my riding clothes, then speed up the stairs and outside, joining Matias and Karski. My bike remains near the garage where I parked it. Four massive white pickup trucks idle in the driveway beyond.

A mirrored window rolls down on the nearest truck and an arm holds out a headset. Matias takes it and hands it to me, so I slide it into place, then put my helmet on. The pressure is a little uncomfortable and will get worse over time, but I'll deal with it in exchange for the security.

"Grease Spot, Stone One, comms check." Matias taps his ear.

I snort-laugh. I guess they don't think much of my mode of transportation. "Stone One, Grease Spot hears you loud and clear." I strap the ammo can on the back of my motorcycle.

Before I can mount, Matias holds out his hand. "I can take your backpack. Leave your microphone enabled and stay behind Stone Two until directed otherwise."

I hadn't considered turning the mic off. "Of course." About to throw my leg over the bike, I look at the ammo can and the relatively flimsy net holding it in place. If I have to make tight turns, the whole thing could go flying. I remove the contraption and tuck the prophecy into the inside pocket of my jacket. Keeping the seemingly sentient book that close isn't comfortable, but the thought of losing it is worse.

"Thanks for waiting." I jump on the bike, start it with a roar, and wait for it to warm up. After putting the bike in half-choke, I roll into place behind the second pickup. "Grease Spot is ready." Without another word, we drive away, idling through the gated community, then speed up on the streets beyond. Winding through residential areas, the convoy travels gradually east and south and into industrial areas. I close the choke and follow Matias's directions, occasionally riding alone through narrow passages, then reconnecting with the convoy.

When the city becomes empty desert, we pull off the highway and stop behind a berm. Matias gets out of the lead pickup and slashes his hand across his neck, indicating I should turn the bike off. After I do, two more large men—I assume they're gargoyles, too—get out of the second pickup and join Matias in front of my bike.

Matias crooks his fingers in a beckoning motion. "Char, if you'll join me, we'll load your motorcycle, then continue after we obscure our vehicles." He cracks a small smile. "And kill the trackers on your machine."

I put the kickstand down and dismount. "Understood and agreed. Thanks for understanding." I can't allow myself to be stranded.

While the two men pick up my bike and secure it in the back of the second pickup—with strength like that, they don't need a ramp—Matias leads me to the first pickup and opens the back door for me. After he gets into the passenger seat, he speaks over his shoulder. "We understand the need for an emergency escape. Rock can be broken."

"Or worn away." The driver's words have the tone of a rote reply.

Matias nods. "If you could shield yourself, that would help."

I don't hold back my huff of uncertainty. "I'm not trained in any of this, but I'll do my best." I used a shield of light to cut the badgers free, so I picture that. The prophecy shoves into my brain, and I push back, hissing. The book grows hot in my pocket, and I unzip my jacket and yank it out. "Listen here, book. Quit trying to take over. You want to tell me something, show me."

Anger floods me, but I don't let it wash me away. I hold firm, picturing myself with my hand in a stop position. Eventually, the anger fades, and acceptance takes over. A picture of a bulbous structure comes to me, like a round water tank on a tall stem. Power flows up and down the stem sunk into the ground, while the tank forms into a structure that looks like a geodesic dome combined with a toy Hoberman sphere. Each panel thins or solidifies as needed, independent of the structure's size. "I understand, thank you."

Using the prophecy's instructions, I implement the suggested shield, then lessen the power flow from the grounding stem to a trickle. My shield glows rather than burns, and the connection lets me draw power from outside, rather than draining me.

"We can work with that." Matias turns to face forward, and low rumbles emit from him like rocks grinding against each other. It must be their native tongue. The sound makes sense, since gargoyles are supposedly living rock.

I doubt any human could speak their language; it might not even be possible for humans to understand it. Is their natural form a crouching, winged animal form like those on cathedrals or something else entirely?

Eventually, the rumbling stops. Looking out the window, I don't see anything different, but perhaps their magic isn't visible to me. The driver puts the truck in gear, and we get back on the highway.

Matias turns in his seat again, handing me a scarf. "Please put that around your eyes."

I take the cloth from him. "Sure, I get it." Hiding their location will help keep them safe. After I wrap the scarf around my head, I relax against the seatback and meditate. If I don't, anxiety will make me jittery.

The rumbling diesel engine and tires humming on asphalt enhance my trance. I rouse when we turn and the ride roughens, gravel pinging off the truck's undercarriage. We bounce along, slowing and speeding as the road conditions allow, then finally stop, the rumble of the motor ceasing.

"You can take the blindfold off now," Matias says. Truck door latches click and dry, dusty air flows. I remove the scarf and grab my helmet. My door opens, Matias holding it and my backpack. "You can leave your helmet with the motorcycle. It will be safe here." He points behind me. The same two large men lift my motorcycle from the back of their pickup, then roll it to the side of the parking lot.

I follow across the gigantic rock cavern. Our convoy's pickup trucks are the last row of a fleet of large vehicles parked in orderly lines. Bright lights above illuminate the orange and beige walls and ceiling and the slightly sandy floor I tread. Immense doors, like those on an airplane hangar but much sturdier, block the cavern's exit. Human-sized doors on both ends of the cavern's opening allow foot traffic in and out.

Or, in my case, a motorcycle. I hang my helmet on my handlebars and return to Matias. The rest of the convoy's inhabitants are already moving to a tunnel beyond the parked vehicles. Another hangar-style door, about fifty feet tall and a hundred feet wide, blocks the entrance, with smaller doors on each side.

Matias nods once. "Welcome to Council Shield, Charlene Flammen. We offer sanctuary, but only if you swear to harm none within and assist with mutual defense." His heavy brows rise slightly. "Do you so swear?"

CHAPTER 22

I FROWN AT MATIAS. "I swear to harm none unless they attack me first. I will defend your home, but I will not protect a criminal from prosecution."

Matias scowls back. "You do not know us, so I will let the insults go. So agreed." He turns and walks away.

I follow. "I didn't intend insult, only precision. Every species with intelligence and free will has those who flout the law." I'm matching Matias's slightly formal speech.

"Gargoyles don't have free will. We cannot last long on this world without magic, so we are bound at a young age. For us to become criminals, we must break from the magic. Then we die."

That's both amazing and disturbing. And after my escape from Theo's tower, unlikely. Those gargoyles were definitely breaking the law. But that's human law; perhaps gargoyles don't care about that. I trot downhill beside him, the round tunnel narrowing slightly. It's still fifty feet in diameter, which seems exceedingly large even though Matias is bigger than the average man. The temperature drops as we walk, becoming cool, but still pleasant. "You aren't native to our planet?"

"No." He shakes his head. "We come from another plane. Physically, our world was very different from this one, but we have much in common. We abused the abundance we were given. We ruined our planet and all the others in our system.

Our researchers found a way to leave, but powering the gate required blowing up our sun. Since we had nothing left to stay for, we did just that. We created a passage but left a hole in our souls." He stops and moves to the side of the empty tunnel. "Then, the magic on this side of our gate caught us completely by surprise. We were scientists. It took many years of study and experimentation before we could thrive here. We must bind to the magic, or we slowly turn to rock and crumble to dust. Exposure to sunlight, including the reflection of the sun on the moon, hastens that death."

Interesting that he's sharing so much about his species without asking anything in return. And while magically binding your people might be a survival tactic, there's always a way to get around the rules. I'll remain cautious and start with simple questions. "So the appearance of gargoyles on gothic structures wasn't an accident?" I'm not sure of the timeline, but many medieval cathedrals bear the winged forms as waterspouts or decorations.

Matias huffs with a small smile. "We were desperately searching for a way to survive during your Gothic period. Our young flew the night skies, spying on the scientists, priests, and magicians of the time. What we found, however, were the vampires and weres. They understood the magic better than the humans because they too depend on it. But not in the same way we do." He moves away from the wall and continues downward.

"Thanks for telling me that. I'm kind of surprised you did." The tunnel remains a gigantic hole in the earth, with smooth redish rock walls, a slightly sandy floor, and bright overhead lights. I wonder how far down we'll go before it changes—if it does.

"We learned the basics of magic from the vampires. If you had stayed in Theoden's tower, I suspect you would have been taught eventually." He holds up one hand. "Not that I blame you for leaving. I realize conditions there were far from ideal. Quite frankly, we will do a better job of teaching you. We approach magic as scientists, so we understand the rules and limitations. We also understand that our lack of self-control led to the destruction of our planet and solar system.

When we bound ourselves to the magic, we also promised to protect this planet's resources."

I smirk. "Which allow you to continue living."

Matias nods. "Enlightened self-interest. The rapid changes of the last century are dismaying but we hope that we can help control the damage. If not, we can create another gate, but we don't want to leave another destroyed system behind us, especially when we may not survive the next destination." He shrugs. "We might not survive the destruction of this sun, depending on what it does to the magic."

His use of "we" makes me assume he's speaking of gargoyle survival only. "I'm guessing none of us Earthlings would survive your gates?"

He shakes his head. "Unlikely. The forces during transition are extreme. You might come up with a transport enclosure, but you'd probably have to create one for each person, and there aren't enough resources on the planet for that now. But that doesn't matter because we're staying. We will protect the magic."

"Understood." I'll have to find out the lengths they would go to and what they consider a crime, since home invasion and stealing isn't. And if all supernaturals and/or humans also fall under their justice system. That would be problematic, to say the least.

Near the end of the tunnel, massive airplane hangar doors again block our way. We stride to a smaller opening on the left. Sliding doors whoosh aside as we near, and we enter a much smaller tunnel, exiting through another set of sliding doors twenty feet later.

The other side, a football field-sized cavern, is an entirely different world. Unlike the plain rock parking structure, the walls of this cave bear beautiful, elaborate carvings, enhanced with swirls of color. Green plants surround fantastical water features along each side of the massive space. The cool air is laden with the scents of flowers and herbs. Matias tugs my arm, moving me away from the doorway where I've stopped, staring at the amazing surroundings. "Wow. This is gorgeous."

And overwhelming. A row of gorgeous, stately buildings are carved into the cavern's rock wall on the far side. The floor level of each building is an open patio, with doors at the back, presumably leading to more rooms. Graceful balconies decorate the upper stories. A walkway meanders in front of the houses, fountains and containers of plants lining both sides. The nearer side of the cavern holds similar carved buildings, walkways, and decorations, but these seem to be businesses, not living spaces. The cavern's ceiling is light blue with white, fluffy clouds, mimicking the sky, with a glowing light suspended in the center. Smaller lights dot the space surrounding the center, mimicking the light of a full moon. Fans turn slowly above the suspended lights, creating a light breeze. People walk in and out of the houses and businesses, some carrying bags. They all appear male.

I turn to Matias. "Do you live here?"

He nods. "Yes, although I share a residence in Las Vegas, too." He sweeps his arm in front of his body, indicating the cavern. "Outer Shield residents interact with the world often. We are also Council Shield's first line of defense, if the automated defenses are defeated." He points at the far end of the cavern. "You see the next set of hangar doors down there? Those lead to the next community, called Inner Shield. Those residents don't travel as often to the surface but still need access. Many of them work remotely. Beyond that are more communities and, finally, the Council chambers." Curling his fingertips, he beckons me to follow, and we cross the cavern.

Small kiosks and carts stand in neat rows at the far end of the cave, selling clothing, sunglasses, games, and oddly, rocks, gemstones, and precious metals. Although I can only see about thirty people, all in male human form, gargoyle voices rumble like heavy snowmelt in a mountain stream.

Walking along the path, he leads me to the third house in the row. The carvings remind me of Petra, Jordan, where they filmed the exterior of the Holy Grail scenes in *Indiana Jones and the Last Crusade*. He points at the stone benches on each side of the open patio. "These are our human accommodations. Please wait here while I make sure your quarters are ready."

The entry lounge is ten feet square, and the walls are carved in gorgeous Moorish patterns. Tiny, brightly colored mosaic tiles lighten the heaviness of the rock. The floor is the same slightly sandy pinkish rock as the outer cavern. Large planters hold flowering plants, adding more color to the space. Water features tinkle, providing a high note to the rumble of gargoyle voices and adding moisture to the dry, cool desert air.

After exploring the small space, I'm about to sit when Matias reappears. He crooks the fingers on one hand in a beckoning motion. "Come. I'll show you to your room. You can leave your backpack there. Then I will take you to the Council."

I follow Matias through the door, entering a tall, wide hallway with evenly spaced, decorated doors blending into more beautiful wall mosaics. The third door on the right, the last in the row, is open. We turn into a room about ten feet square, the walls covered in restful shades of green and blue mosaic tile. A full-size bed with a forest green cover takes up one corner, a lounge chair in a deep brown next to it, and a door opens to a small, human-standard bathroom on my left. I drop my bag at the end of the bed. "Perfect, thank you."

"You are welcome." He points at the entry door. "Note the door seals, ensuring no light can penetrate, even underground. Also note there are no emergency escapes. If you cannot get through the door, we recommend remaining in the bathroom until you are rescued. Earthquakes are rare, but the bathroom ceilings are reinforced to withstand even major quakes."

I nod. "Understood. Let me use the facilities, and I'll be right with you." The idea of being trapped under so much rock is a bit terrifying, but I assume that a species that can carve rock so beautifully can also cut through it quickly.

Matias withdraws, closing the sealed door behind him. I enter the bathroom, use the toilet, and wash my face and hands. I'm rather casually dressed to meet important people, but better the motorcycle leathers than sweatpants and a t-shirt. Opening my mind to the prophecy, still in my inner jacket pocket, I get nothing back from it. So I join Matias in the entryway lounge.

He leads me along the gently curving walkway in front of the houses. Men stand around small, high tables in the center of the cavern. They rumble what I assume are greetings in the grinding gargoyle language. I don't see any women, but I'm not sure gargoyles have genders, and I have no idea if it's rude to ask. But I can always plead ignorance. "Hey, Matias, I don't want to offend you, but I'm assuming human forms aren't your natural form, right?"

He shakes his head. "No, they aren't. Our natural forms aren't possible on this planet unless we risk volcano diving. The human form is comfortable enough most of the time, and it takes effort to change." He shrugs. "We can easily add wings for gliding, or four legs for running, or other attributes. But much like the weres, we change shape when threatened. That's where the monsters perched on churches come from. It's easier to change form when you're young; the watchers were probably too immature for the job." He sniffs. "Like me. I've learned better survival techniques since then."

We stop in front of the smaller door at the end of the cavern. Matias turns towards me. "Please ensure your shields are secure. As we get closer to the Council chambers, we'll pass through areas with younger members. We must protect them from outside influences, especially emotions. That which you carry holds much anger."

The prophecy has been eerily silent since entering the cavern, but I agree. My shield seems solid, but I run through the building process the book taught me, ensuring every panel is tight and the structure fed by a tiny trickle of power from below me. "Okay. I think I'm ready."

Matias scans me from my head to my toes. "Agreed. If you need to stop to reinforce the shield, please do so."

"Because I'm new to this, or you expect me to be shocked?"

He huffs. "Eventually, both. You've done well for an untrained practitioner, but be on guard." He walks to the door, and it slides aside, revealing another tunnel curving to the left, away from the main hangar doors. As we walk, the tunnel curves back to the right, forming a semicircle.

The sliding door on the far end opens into a cavern similar to Outer Shield. It's the same size and has the same lighting and fans but with houses on both sides, all of them elaborately carved and decorated. Even the walkways are tiled with colorful patterns. Delicate rock screens break up the main cavern floor into what appear to be sports fields. Closest to me, men play a ball game that looks similar to baseball or cricket. Beyond that, more men stand around high tables, playing games with rectangular tokens like dominos or mah jong. The gargoyles vary in height from a little shorter than me to about eight feet tall, with shoulders that are too wide and legs too short to be human.

Matias continues to our left, along a walkway tiled in swirling patterns of yellow, changing gradually to orange, then red. Looking ahead, the end is purple—the colors of the rainbow. Are all the women in houses? Or do they have women? "Everyone out here mimics the male form. Is there a reason?"

He grimaces. "Yes, we all take the male form. First, because males are traditionally leaders in your world. It's an outward appearance and has nothing to do with procreation or our thought processes. We can look female just as easily, but conservation of mass is a law of physics. As females, our size makes us stand out even more."

"I can understand that." All these large men don't make me particularly comfortable, even though the numbers are low for such a gigantic space. I'd guess there are maybe a hundred or so people in this cavern.

He slows slightly. "I'm sorry if it makes you uncomfortable. I intellectually understand why, although I can never fully sympathize. There is little on this planet that can physically threaten us."

I look at my small hands. "I certainly can't."

Matias stops and turns towards me. "Not right now. But when you master the magic, you could be a real threat. I warn you now—do not lie to the Council. Even a partial truth is dangerous." He huffs. "I like you, so I'll tell you this as well. If necessary, speed is your greatest asset. Use your magic and run."

I force a chuckle. "That's my favorite tactic. Fast feet for survival." But his warning makes this journey to the center of the earth seem even more perilous.

He nods, then turns and continues. "Exactly."

I tread the path next to him, watching the shifting colors below my feet and the matching change on the carved walls of the cavern. At the end, another set of hangar doors blocks the way, with the same sliding doors to a side passage.

Matias stops again, scanning me. "Are your shields holding?"

I check; they appear solid. "Yes."

"I hope so." With that ominous sentence, Matias turns and passes through the sliding doors.

Swallowing hard, I follow.

CHAPTER 23

WE TREAD THE GENTLY curving tunnel, the temperature rising as we walk, and stop in front of a door with a dark-colored wheel in the middle, made of iron perhaps. Matias grasps the wheel and turns it, a scraping noise coming from the door, then he swings it open. The door is thick rock, with long locking bars attached to a matching wheel on the far side. We pass through the doorway and into another gigantic cavern. Hot air roasts me and dries my mouth. As Matias secures the door, I move to the side and take off my jacket but I can't stop staring. And blinking, trying to wet my eyes.

Rather than houses along the sides, ten-foot diameter tunnels roar with flame. Massive gargoyles in their traditional four-leg, horned head beast form blast fire from their mouths, while two more in human form shovel black rock—possibly coal—into the tunnels. The human form gargoyles are giants—easily nine feet tall—but their legs are short in comparison to their wide, muscular torsos. None of them wear clothing, which makes sense because it would be burned away.

"Stay here." Matias walks away from me. "I'll be right back." He disappears into an opening in the wall.

I unzip my leather motorcycle pants. I'll be meeting the Council in leggings and a t-shirt after all. But I doubt what I wear matters to gargoyles.

Matias returns and hands me a metal water bottle. "Drink all you need. I can refill it." He raises his volume so I can hear him over the fire-blasting gargoyles.

"If it stays this hot, I'll need a lot." The cavern seems hotter than Death Valley and swirls with even fiercer currents as the blast furnaces war for dominance. It even smells hot.

"I should have warned you, but I don't feel the difference unless I walk into one of those." He points at the furnace.

"Is this your heating system for the caverns? Seems like a lot of work." Solar panels and electric heaters would be easier.

Matias rumbles, interrupting my thoughts. "No. We are forging new gargoyles. It is a very long, difficult process and not always successful."

"Oh." Forged, not born. He's sharing a lot of information with a stranger. Will I ever leave these caverns? Despite my fear, I can hear the sorrow in his tone. "I'm sorry it's not easier."

"Come." Matias walks away.

I roll my leathers into a bundle and follow. While Matias moves at an even pace, I sprint across the furnace openings and slow between them. Sweat pours out of me, evaporating immediately and leaving my skin tight and dry.

At the end of the cavern, I wait for Matias to open the lock bars, then scamper into the tunnel beyond. The air isn't much cooler, but it's better than being dry-roasted in a furnace. I drink the bottle dry and hold it out to Matias after he secures the door. "More, please."

He shakes his head. "In the next cavern. Come."

We continue along another identical, gently curved rock tunnel, then Matias cracks the next vault door and points a finger, indicating I should go through. The cavern beyond the door is just as large as Outer Shield, but the carvings and tile work are on a much larger scale. The gargoyles, in human and traditional form, vary from giants of twenty feet to almost human size. Some carve the walls, while others add to the mosaics, the tiles looking miniscule in their massive hands. Others plod across the cavern. Some slump or crouch against dark gray mounds sticking out from the walls. The mounds are shaped vaguely like crouched gargoyles that have eroded over centuries of wind and rain, but there's no sign of weather down here. While it's still hot, I no longer feel like a pig on a spit.

Matias takes my bottle and fills it at a towering fountain with a wide pool at the bottom, then leads me across the space, winding around the slow-moving giants. "This is Forger's Rest. All of these people have completed a full forging cycle. They stay here until they are ready to move on. Approximately half return to forging. About a quarter of them shed size and power and rejoin the Inner Shield community. Another quarter join working groups for the Council and, eventually, the Council itself. Rarely, they remain here and gradually return to dust." He points at the mounded backrests at the sides of the immense cavern.

"Those mounds are people?" My immediate reaction is horror, but I shouldn't judge them by human or vampire standards. I hold up my right hand. "Wait, I'm sorry. I shouldn't have said that."

Matias nods once. "I understand. It doesn't seem right to a biologically grown species. But we are literally forged from carbon, one of the main elements of Earth, so to carbon we return. Forging new life is strenuous, both physically and mentally. Once they give their all to a new life, some can no longer hold on to theirs, particularly if the forging was unsuccessful. It's not common, but it happens. We don't know exactly when the soul lets go, so we hope that by leaning against what remains, we bring comfort and ease to their passing."

I close my eyes, trying to comprehend the pain and compassion. "That's beautiful and tragic."

Matias continues walking. "It is. But less tragic than before we figured out how to bind to this world's magic. When we arrived, we lost so many. All over the European continent, the remains of our people return to dust, deep in closed mines. Only a few hundred of us survived the gate and the early transition. Even now, we are only a few thousand, split between the Americas, Europe, and Asia. But any more would be too great a burden on your world."

"Would any of the other planets in our solar system be better?" I wait for Matias to open the vault door.

He turns the wheel. "The temperature of Venus would be better, but there's too much sulfuric acid in the atmosphere. We'd disappear like human tears in the rain. The pressure on Jupiter is too great and the rest of the planets are too cold. We've adapted to this one quite well, and we have a fulfilling role."

"I suppose." While aliens saving humans is popular in fiction, I'm more likely to believe they're invaders, lulling our suspicions. Certainly, few humans are truly altruistic. If they aren't getting an obvious reward, then they're taking a larger one, secretly. But gargoyles aren't humans. "Just how much of Earth's magic does it take to sustain your species?"

He shakes his head and motions for me to walk through the opening. "I don't know. You'll have to ask the Council. But I don't think it's excessive. And we offer an important service in return."

We traverse the now-familiar semi-circular tunnel and stop at the next vault door. Matias opens it and we enter another massive cavern. While still too warm for me, it's cooler than the last. But that doesn't matter in comparison to the gigantic gargoyles in front of me. They wear bipedal forms, but without the details that let their smaller members appear human, and stand in groups of three to ten. The smallest gargoyle is probably ten feet tall, with a five-foot wide torso; the largest at least thirty feet tall. They're linked, either by holding hands, a hand on a shoulder, or leaning against each other. "I guess that explains the hangar doors."

"Yes." Matias points at my water bottle. "Don't forget to drink."

As we walk, I sip water and Matias explains. "These are working groups for the Council. They monitor the magic by geographic region. The more magic users in an area, the more people it takes."

Nearing the far wall, I notice our footsteps are loud in the silence. Before opening the next door, Matias takes my water bottle and fills it at another fountain with an even larger pool at the bottom, then cracks the next vault door. Rather than a tunnel, we step directly into another cavern, about half the size of the previous spaces. Seven gargoyles in their traditional forms crouch in a circle, the smallest at least thirty feet tall, the largest almost brushing the suspended lights.

Matias points at the group. "The Gargoyle Guardians Council. Since their voices would deafen you, I'll interpret. Come. I have to touch them."

I grimace. I'm tiny next to these behemoths, and I really don't want to get stepped on.

Matias chuckles. "Don't worry. They don't usually move fast. And before you ask, yes, we use a form of telepathy, but it requires contact."

But the Council members aren't touching—except they are. Each has two tails, linking them together. "Before we interrupt them, I'm assuming you grow larger with age?"

"Yes. That's another reason for the split between Inner and Outer Shield. Outer Shield people can pass for human. Inner Shield are too large but not strong enough to join the forgers, or they are newly forged and learning."

This is all too easy. "You're sharing an awful lot about your species with someone you hardly know. Why?"

Matias cracks a smile. "But I do know you. I've worked with you for years." He holds up a hand. "It's not the same as being friends, but in some ways, it's better. I've seen how you treat others, how you manage difficult people, and your leadership abilities. We can trust you." He turns and walks towards the Council. "But if you betray us, we'll crush you like a gnat and throw your prophecy into a forge."

Anger floods from the prophecy, but it's tinged with fear. The book must be vulnerable to magical fire, if not mundane flames. "I don't break my word. But I won't make a blind promise, either. I need to know what your help costs." Karski is right—my ignorance is dangerous. I don't know how to use magic, other than my instincts or what the prophecy teaches me. I don't know what the prophecy says or the extent of its abilities. Or what it means to the other vampires in the world, all of them with more knowledge and skill than I have.

In short, I might be safe for now, but I still have a lot of trouble waiting. The gargoyles might help, but I have to know why and how much they expect from me. And I want to know what kind of burden they add to our planet. Are they protectors or a protection racket? "Civilized" invaders rarely benefit the natives.

However, my choice right now is simple. I can leave and die or listen to the gargoyles and possibly survive. I follow Matias towards the looming danger of the Gargoyle Guardians Council.

CHAPTER 24

By the time I join Matias, he's already placed his hand on the nearest, and smallest, gargoyle. Then he hugs the gargoyle's leg. Perhaps more contact eases communication?

A grinding noise draws my attention upward. All the massive gargoyles stare at me with shiny, solid black eyes, unblinking. I almost take a step back but stop. If I move, I'll run. Besides, between their size, the alien eyes, the giant beaks, and the claws, I don't stand a chance. They could shred me to bits before I take three steps.

"The Gargoyle Guardian Council welcomes the Unbound Queen of the Vampires." Matias releases his grip on the gargoyle's leg and turns towards me but keeps one hand on the giant. "They look forward to discussing a mutually beneficial way ahead. They've empowered me and a sub-council of Outer and Inner Shield members to discuss the details with you and offer you training. There is no obligation connected to the training because it benefits everyone, especially the Pool of Life. You burn bright."

I nod to them, then look at Matias. "Please thank all of them for me. I look forward to hearing any insights they have on the prophecy I carry and any they might have on how to fulfill my duties and obligations." Screwing up my courage, I look upward to meet their eyes again. "However, I must know how much your people take from my planet and how you balance those scales. While it is true that Earth's inhabitants haven't done well with the bounty given us, we are natives. You are not."

Matias tilts his head, then turns away to clench the Council member's leg again. After a few moments, he completely releases the gargoyle's leg and points at the door. "The Council acknowledges your question is fair. They aren't sure our expenditure can be measured. They believe that our work to protect and balance the magic more than makes up for what we use because much like water on Earth, magic is recycled. When our souls leave our bodies, the magic used to sustain us returns to the Pool of Life. The Pool hasn't significantly diminished since our arrival." He opens the vault door, holding it for me.

I slip through and wait until he secures the locking bars. "But it has gotten smaller."

"It's impossible to scale. They say it's lost some...power. But not enough that any magic user on Earth would notice. They believe that if every gargoyle on Earth passed on to the next life, the pool would grow because we brought energy with us from our system." He snorts. "Not that it's easy to kill us."

"I imagine not. I have no desire to kill any of you, but if you were taking far more than you returned, conservation would be critical." It would be smart for Earth inhabitants, too.

He opens the vault door, we slip into Forger's Rest, and he secures the door. Then he refills my water bottle again. "As we learn more about Earth's magic, we do our best to sustain it. We admit that when we arrived, we weren't careful. We were trying to survive. That's probably why the Pool of Life is somewhat diminished. But watching humans move west across America and repeating our mistakes made us more conservative. We've done our best to reduce our load on the Pool and on Earth's material goods, too. For example, we supported research creating synthetic diamonds and other gemstones. They're an important energy source for us, but we don't want to pay for human conflict."

I stop. "You eat diamonds." Why this seems more shocking than the other revelations is a mystery.

Matias turns towards me. "Yes. Compressed carbon is an excellent source of energy." He continues walking, moving around the recovering forgers. "We don't eat the way you do, but the term for absorbing energy is close enough. We need water, too, but don't actually drink. It soaks into us. That's why we have fountains rather than faucets." He opens the door. "And yes, we have to get rid of waste. Your room is one of several set up for human visitors. We recycle all waste products."

That answers a few questions. I have so many more, but we're nearing the forging cavern again. I'll wait until we reach the cooler tunnel on the far side. Matias unlatches the door, lets me through, and secures it again. The heat of the forges blasts me, and I give up on looking professional. I alternate sprinting and speed walking until I reach the far side. Striding steadily, Matias keeps up with me, and he opens the door.

As we walk through the tunnel, the temperature drops, and even though it's still quite warm, a shiver runs down my spine. The entire experience is unsettling, particularly realizing that someone I've considered a colleague is far more alien than I've realized.

However, even if he were a purple, tentacled monster, he's a sentient, which means he's a person. He's proven reliable and clever in the years he's worked for me. I suspect he's hidden some of his intelligence to stay in his position as Fantastique's security manager. "When I left the casino, why did you say you needed the job? Weren't you there to watch me?"

"I couldn't tell you that, could I?" He shrugs. "Besides, we were watching Theoden more than you. He was the bigger threat. Staying at the casino let me keep a close eye on him. Except he abandoned his responsibilities to go after you, and then he took his people and hid." Matias opens the next door and we enter Inner Shield. "Take your time crossing. Explore the public areas, or return to your room if you want. It will probably take me half an hour to collect people, then we'll meet in Outer Shield. I won't have everyone the Council specified, but you'll meet most of them tonight and the rest tomorrow." He tilts his head. "Sound good?"

I nod. "Yes, thanks." Wanting to see as much as possible, I cross to the path on the opposite side of the cavern. It follows the same rainbow pattern, using entirely different but equally beautiful patterns. I know laying mosaic tile takes a long time for humans, but perhaps gargoyles are faster? Or maybe their lives are so long that they think nothing of spending months or years enhancing their spaces. Matias implies that he was young when he arrived from their original home, and gargoyles have appeared on churches since the fifteen hundreds, so he could easily be a thousand years old or more. They may have moved to the Americas long before Europeans did, or maybe they crossed the ocean at the same time.

However long it's been, the caverns are gorgeous, despite being deep below the surface. I stop to watch each different game. The sports have human patterns, like baseball and soccer, but they move slower and use much larger balls. The tile games are played standing—I haven't seen a chair anywhere but the human house. Gargoyles stand, crouch, or recline, but they don't seem to sit, even in human form. I guess there's no need for physical rest when you're made of rock. Or carbon with a rock-like appearance.

I meander along the gentle curves of the walkway, enjoying the tinkle of fountains and scents of the flowers and herbs. Despite what I assume are lounge areas at the front of each house, I don't see any gargoyles there. Perhaps they prefer the common areas when they're awake. If they even sleep. These structures imply they need time separate from the larger community, but that might be a poor assumption, too.

I reach the far end of the cavern and pass through the sliding doors, sauntering along the connecting tunnel and through the next opening. Since I still have time to kill, I wander through the market kiosks and booths. Most offer clothing in a variety of styles, along with hats, shoes, sunglasses and accessories like messenger bags. Two booths display men's suits in dark shades—no flashy plaids or pastels for these guys. Gargoyles work at sewing machines in the back. Finding suits off the rack for such massive shapes would be challenging, so having tailors makes sense. I reach the sparkling kiosks offering precious metals and gems.

Matias catches up with me. "Come. We're meeting at the fountain near the front door to Outer Shield." He points towards the hangar doors. "You have the prophecy?" He walks away.

I catch up with him, wondering why he doesn't want me near their food merchants. Or maybe the timing is just chance. "Yes, I have the prophecy."

"Good. Along with council representatives, we have experts in many written languages. If you can't read the book, it's likely we have someone who can."

I stop. "I haven't had time to even crack it open." I've been so busy surviving and then the prophecy seemed to talk to me, so there was no reason to try reading it. But no matter what, I'm not handing it over to anyone else.

Matias keeps moving. "You can take a look before the meeting starts."

But there's no time like now. The walkway is wide and empty, so I take the book out of my jacket pocket and open it up. The first page contains beautiful script—the kind you'd see in old Bibles, with pictures and all—but I can't read a word of it. As I flip through the book, the writing style changes, but I still can't understand any of it. The pictures disappear, and the script becomes plain, and then on the very last pages, I finally find some English. Old style English, with the odd letter substitutions, but readable.

The first page in English holds the prophecy; the version Karski showed me.

The Prophecy of the Unbound Queen

When the dusk bleeds into an endless bright,

And battles rage over control of the night,

One shall rise—a queen of shadow's creed,

By choice alone, not by chains decreed.

In mortal flesh, her fierce heart was concealed,

Yet by her will, service for all is now revealed.

With fangs unsheathed, she claims her boundless might,

A sovereign born to rule the endless night.

None who stand in her path shall be redeemed,

For her command reigns supreme.

A tempest fierce, she leads her kin with grace,

The unchained dawn none can hope to replace.

She brings no peace, no mercy to the fray,

Yet freedom fierce as stars keep threat at bay.

The world shall know her rule, unbent, serene,

When black night turns bright and towers turn the desert green.

Behold the rise of the queen freely turned,

Her power flows where hearts and heavens burn.

Still the same ridiculous proclamation that could apply to almost anyone. Hoping for enlightenment, I turn the page. It's English but seems to be an introduction, rather than a continuation of the prophecy.

> *In this year of 1852, by the sacrifice of our Dear Leader, Ivan Sereda, we have relocated to safety in the Americas. At the order of our new Dear Leader, Klaus Theoden, and with the agreement of our High Priestess, I, Trinity, assume duties as keeper of the sacred records.*

> *We await the Unbound Queen's arrival, knowing our patience will be rewarded. Under her gracious rule, our fetters will fall away, and all shall offer their life's blood to us under the tamed sun. We shall revel in the day and the night, bathing in the blood of our enemies and drinking their children down.*

Dropping the book with a splat, I choke, trying to hold my revulsion back. No wonder Karski wants Trinity dead—what a revolting ideology. I grip my thighs, leaning over, trying not to throw up.

A shadow falls over me. "Char, are you okay?" Matias asks.

I pick up the prophecy and straighten, even though I want to curl into a ball and avoid the entire world. "Yeah, I'm...well, not okay, but I will be." I shudder. "I can read the last part of the prophecy, but it might take me a while, because it's disgusting."

"I'm sorry. If you want, we can read it for you and find the relevant parts." He holds out his hand.

"No." I hug the book to my chest. "This is my responsibility. After I read the English parts, I'll let your experts take pictures and translate, but I'm not giving anyone the prophecy. It's mine." I meet Matias's gaze and keep it, even when his eyes change into the solid black the Council members display.

"Are you sure it's responsibility, or is the book compelling you?" Leaving his hand outstretched, he raises both brows. "We can shield you from it and then you'll know."

Rage blasts from the prophecy, but I block it. "I'm more than capable of doing that myself. Why are you so determined to take it from me?"

His arm drops and he leans over me. "Because it's influencing you. You changed when you picked it up. You're a different person than you were before."

I raise my chin and rather than stepping away, I lean towards him. He can undoubtedly crush me like a bug, but I'm not backing down. "Oh, so you want the nice girl back? The one who negotiates and placates everyone because she has no power? The one who is easily manipulated? The one who goes along to get along?" I poke his chest with my forefinger. "No. Back off."

He takes a half-step back, then rumbles.

"I don't speak gargoyle. If you're insulting me, I'd prefer to understand it." I turn and stride for the room they've assigned me. The sun rises soon, but I'm not staying with people who threaten me because I've gained a bit of leverage. I'll find a hole in the desert. Wanting to sprint, I hold myself to a steady stride because I might need my speed later. Tucking the book into my inner pocket, I stop before I enter my assigned quarters. While they're light-safe, without an emergency escape, they could be a prison. I spin on my toe—while I'd be more comfortable with my things, I don't need it.

"Char, wait." Matias blocks me. "I'm not insulting or threatening you. We offered you safety and we meant it."

I stare him down. "Safety or captivity? Or maybe your version of safety means treating me like a child? I don't have your years, but I'm not immature or stupid."

He raises both hands, palms out. "If I gave you that impression, I'm sorry. Rather than meeting the rest of us tonight, why don't you read the book, alone. You can meet with us tomorrow night and tell us what you need and want. I promise that you are not trapped here. We guaranteed protection, and we meant it. Besides, it's too close to sunrise for you to leave safely."

"That's my decision, not yours." I'm not going down without a fight.

"Agreed, and I understand your reluctance to remain. My words were rash." He steps towards the house. "I'll get your pack and show you to a safe room in the parking area beyond Outer Shield. It has an emergency escape and rock doors that lock from the inside. While we could collapse the escape tunnel, you could get out. I'm sure the book could teach you several techniques to blast your way free. But truly, we want an ally, not an enemy."

I put my hands on my hips in a power pose, more for me than him. "I want allies, not owners. You cannot force me to do anything." I'm not a pawn or a plaything for anyone.

"Understood. I'd appreciate it if you'd wait." Matias strides into the house.

I might have a better chance to escape with him gone, but a group of gargoyles stand in a tight group near the closest exit. They might be under orders to stop me. Or they might not. The sliding doors are at least seventy-five feet away, maybe farther. The mosaic patterns throw off my sense of distance. If I sprint at my full vampire speed, I can probably make it there before the gargoyles, but I'll need blood after that. My blood boxes are in my pack, and finding a large enough animal to feed from in the desert is difficult.

I've trapped myself, an hour and a half before sunrise.

But if I can get out with my motorcycle, I can find shelter. I put my leathers back on and wait, counting the seconds. Before I reach a minute, Matias emerges, holding out my pack and carrying a large bag in his other hand.

I grab my pack and pull out a blood box, sucking down the fuel. After the first few pulls, I slide the backpack on and walk towards the sliding door, drinking and walking.

Matias walks alongside, grinding out something in gargoyle when we pass the group. "I'm telling them I'll explain when I get back."

At least he doesn't make me ask. The doors slide apart, and we traverse the plain rock tunnel to the exit in silence. The lack of pattern and color is somewhat of a relief; while beautiful, the mosaics are overwhelming. That's kind of a metaphor for gargoyles, period.

We slog up the long tunnel out. On the way in, the slope seems almost undetectable, but leaving, the uphill effort almost makes me pant. The air warms and dries, so I have to drink more water. Exiting the tunnel, Matias leads me towards my motorcycle, but before we reach it, he stops in front of a door I hadn't noticed. It blends into the surrounding stone, and the handle looks like a small fissure in the rock.

He opens the door and leads me down a short hallway to another door. "This is an earthquake shelter." He opens the second door and taps the wall just inside, turning on a light and revealing an empty room that's about ten feet long and tall, and only five feet wide—a roomy tomb. A wheel with locking bars sticks out from the small door on the far end. "The tunnel emerges into the desert just beyond the entrance to the parking area. I can bring your motorcycle in here, but the fuel fumes might be excessive because the ventilation is passive, not active." He spins and points above the door we've just entered. The door to the parking garage also has a locking wheel and bars, and above it is a rock screen that's less than a foot square. A lever sticks out on the right side. "You can close the vent using that."

Except I can't reach it. I'm not sure I can open the rock doors, either.

Matias drops the bag on the ground. "This is a blow-up mattress. You're free to stay and use it or leave. It's up to you." He bows slightly. "We hope you stay so we can discuss a way ahead tomorrow evening." He leaves, leaving the door to the room open but closing the door to the parking area. It also has bars on my side.

Stay or go? We've burned more time, so staying is the smarter thing to do. I spin the wheel on the exterior door, which moves surprisingly easily, then blow up the camping mattress. After that, I secure the inner doors and use a couple of zip ties to warn me if anyone attempts to spin either locking wheel.

Putting my weapons in easy reach—not that they'd do me much good against gargoyles—I sit on the mattress and lean against my pack. Then I retrieve the prophecy.

Before I can think about it too much, I open it wide.

CHAPTER 25

TRYING TO REMAIN UNEMOTIONAL, I scan the English entries below the prophecy. More flowery language yearning for the freedom to hunt humans however and whenever they want, freedom from their constraints, and speculation about the Unbound Queen's powers. As they find gold and purchase luxuries, their desire to rule the entire Earth grows. Dreams of destroying the gargoyle invaders, capturing and caging the "diseased" weres for blood, and hunting humans on ranches are scribed in dark ink. Frustratingly, there isn't anything concrete on what the Unbound Queen can actually do or how to do it.

Occasionally, Trinity adds a note about relocating to a new home and getting better furnishings for the temple. A more relevant entry appears the day I was born.

The High Priestess reported a surge of joy from the prophecy! Worshiping with our Dear Leader, they have discovered the Unbound Queen has manifested in her nascent form! Blessed are we who shall see the prophecy fulfilled in our lifetimes.

From there it devolves into more ranting about hunting, so I skim. Thirty-six years later, they're losing hope. The prophecy can't tell them where I am, only that I've been born and still live. Trinity expresses subtle doubts that the turning will ever happen, then the next paragraph is blacked out. I sniff the paper, then touch it. The paragraph might have been scorched rather than redacted with ink. Whatever was written there must have been blasphemy to risk burning a book. Although, I'm fairly certain the pages aren't paper; they're too thick, with an odd texture.

I turn the page. The handwriting changes, becoming more old-fashioned and slightly spidery, but the writer doesn't identify themselves. Perhaps the priestess writes rather than a secretary, so there's no need for an introduction.

After concentrated devotion, Dear Leader Klaus reports the common form Queen Unbound has entered his territory. All search for the unturned who will free us from our shackles of night so we may rule the world as is proper and right. He will search for an elegant home for the Queen Unbound and the Temple.

Ugh. The same excuse as always—power gives them the right to push everyone else down.

The next entry reports that seven vampires tested a female human and could not mesmerize her, but some doubt the woman's validity as the future Unbound Queen. I don't remember talking to seven weirdos like Theoden, but so many creeps came to the Stardust; they all blend together. I keep reading.

> *The candidate is adamant against our power so far but of low station and even less dignity. She serves rather than commands and is most likely a woman of ill repute among the humans. Our Dear Leader will test her and report.*

> *Our Dear Leader reports the candidate resists his best efforts. If she remains so after seven nights in a row, he will bring her to me. If she can withstand the gathered might of the congregation, Our Dear Leader, and me, she will be turned. All will then hail the Unbound Queen.*

No wonder my turning is contested. I haven't undergone the final tests. I flip the page. Only three lines are scribed, two on the left page, the last in the middle of the right. The words have deeply scored the paper—the priestess used a heavy hand.

> **Klaus Theoden has turned the candidate, untested by me.**

> ***This will not stand.***

> **We wait for the true Unbound Queen.**

As I read the words, the depressions caused by the priestess's hard writing on the last line disappear, and then the words themselves fade. I put the prophecy down on the rock floor and shiver. That isn't creepy at all. Will I ever get used to a sentient book?

I turn the now-blank page.

> *Despite my objections, the failed candidate remains, polluting our tower. I have forbidden her entry into the temple—Klaus Theoden has no power to force my hand. No matter how quickly the untested adapts, it proves nothing. I will not bow to a failure.*

The rest of the pages are empty. I close the book and let my head drop against the stone. I hope for an instruction manual or at least some clue on what I'm really supposed to do, but there's nothing except expectations of a brutal rule over "lesser creatures." No wonder the prophecy tries to steer me towards evil—that's all it has learned.

While I can hope the previous pages contain more, I have a feeling that they don't. Perhaps most of the traditions, religion, or whatever they might be called are passed down orally. Or maybe there isn't anything more to the whole mess. It's the ravings of ancient vampires determined to dominate everyone. Plenty of humans believe in their innate superiority because of a particular physical attribute. Vampires come from humans, so their attitude would only get worse after gaining real power.

I have decisions to make. Apparently, the whole purpose of the prophecy is to find the future Unbound Queen. If I'm that person, then its job is done. However, the prophecy has proven it can teach me certain vampire skills. But those skills might be twisted by the need to dominate all living creatures.

The gargoyles say they can teach me magic and that they're better at it because they approach it scientifically. But they aren't natives; they aren't even from this plane, whatever that means. And I have no way to know if their magic system uses more resources than a native magic user. Plus, while they say they can only have so many new gargoyles, all those furnaces are roaring, and they tried to take the prophecy. Maybe they're sincere in their offer to help me, or maybe they aren't.

The werewolves offered help because they don't want the vampires ruling. The badgers don't want the vampires in charge, either, but they're more interested in making money and causing trouble than helping.

The vampires won't teach me anything. Theoden will put me in a cage and starve or torture me until I obey him. Which means I'll die because I'm not giving in to him or anyone.

Rage burns my soul, and I stare at the prophecy. "Yes, I'm the Queen and he's not. But he has many bound followers, your priestess repudiates my claim, and he's got a lot of money and influence. Can you teach me how to escape a cage? Melt through the bars or unlock a lock? Or short-out an electronic lock?" I try to picture each action in detail, but I'm not a locksmith or electronics expert.

The prophecy's anger lessens. It pushes the picture of the gang member I mesmerized in the alley to me.

"That's a human. Vampires are harder. Especially if I can't touch them. When I was there, his cells had tiny openings to the hallways for blood boxes. Or they'd shove people through fast. I'm sure that these days, those openings are locked and unlocked remotely, along with the doors. They probably have airlock-style entries, too. Shove a blood box, or worse, a human into the airlock, lock the outer door, then open the inner door. A starving vampire won't pass up a meal to escape and it would be practically impossible, anyway."

The prophecy's anger grows, but I get nothing useful from it. I should ask better questions. "What can you teach me?"

It pushes the picture of the shield at me again but shows me shoving a person away with it. "If I can make the shield strong enough, I can physically move objects?" Agreement comes from the book.

That's useful, especially if I can surround myself with a shield like that. Or maybe I can change it to shock someone. But first things first. I call up my shield and find it still active, but thin. Interesting that I've integrated that ability already–it's as natural as breathing. I strengthen the shield and pull it tighter to me, then push at the prophecy still on the floor.

The book doesn't move. I feed more power into the shield, concentrating it near the book, and try again. The book jolts but doesn't move. Trying harder, I shove again, sliding the book a half-inch away.

Then I collapse against the rock wall, panting and hungry, my shield in tatters. "Well, it's possible but not easy." Hopefully, practise will improve my abilities. I grab another blood box out of my backpack. I only have three more left, so I'll have to get more before I do too much. Matias says he can help, but a species that eats diamonds doesn't need blood.

I drink and wonder if I have more skills. I can mesmerize and shield and use the shield physically and mentally. Can I electrically charge the shield? I assume mental shields are to keep other vampires from mesmerizing me, but the gargoyles asked me to use one while they work magic that obscures our trail and burns out electronics. Without my shields, will I be vulnerable to whatever they do? If so, I have to learn their magic to shield against it.

The prophecy's simmering anger increases, along with the feeling of tight, scorched skin. The threat of magical furnaces really bothers the book. Is it ever happy? Immediately, the feeling of satisfied hunger comes to me with thoughts of praise, devotion, and longing for blood from a dozen different minds.

Worship makes it happy. Everything else angers it. "Well, book, you'll have to learn that there is more to life than fury and praise. Or existence, I guess, since I don't think you're exactly alive."

I have other vampire abilities. Speed is the main one, but Theoden is much faster. Some vampires have unusual strength, but I don't. If I'm well fed, I have endurance and a very high pain tolerance. I don't have much education, but I've learned over the years that I'm smarter than the average man drinking at my bar. Plus, even the educated ones become stupid with enough alcohol or sexual distractions.

I'd rather rely on my intelligence than my abilities, especially mental abilities. Those seem to burn through my energy stores much faster than regular thinking.

But, I'll probably have to use my mental abilities against Theoden to survive, let alone take over. Unless I can convince him to support me, which seems unlikely. I also have to convince the High Priestess that I'm the Queen Unbound if I want her support. Having her on my side will make the vampires easier to control, but only until they realize I'm not going to bring them unlimited feasting. Then they'll kill me and wait for the next Unbound Queen.

The book throws anger at me again. "Got it. You like me." But why does it support me when I'm not doing what the vampires want? Arrogant certainty radiates from it. "You don't make mistakes. You picked me, it's a done deal, and their opinions don't matter." If the book could nod, that's what it would be doing.

Probably because centuries of vampires told the prophecy that. It's an infinite loop of reinforcement; a cult. Generally, encouraging critical, independent thought and gently pointing out errors can break people out of group-think, but it takes time. I'll be dead before I can accomplish that and the book doesn't care. "Can you teach me anything else?"

Hot blood pulses into my mouth.

I harden my shield and the phantom fluid disappears. Great. The book wants me to slaughter everyone around me. "Not going to happen." Even if I wanted to do that, it would lead to discovery and humanity hunting us down. Certainly, there's nothing like drinking from a willing human. But unlike fiction, I don't think there's any upside to that for humans. They don't get powers, or a longer life, or special healing, other than the coagulant in our saliva. I'm fairly certain that science already knows how to accelerate that process.

I slide down on the mattress. I'm tired, and the sun is well above the horizon.

Which surprises me. Normally, I'm out cold by this time, but either the book has changed me or it's a side effect of being the Queen. Whatever it is, I'll rest, and maybe a solution will come to me. Or more problems will pop up, which seems more likely. I slide my backpack under my head and meditate on my breathing, hoping for a better tomorrow.

CHAPTER 26

I wake before the sun goes below the horizon, another new side effect of the Unbound Queen designation. If I'm going to leave the gargoyles, now would be the time. But learning more about them seems smart, especially since they claim to guard the magic and can teach me more than the vampires.

I meditate, then deflate the mattress and do some yoga. By then, the sun is down. I turn the locking wheel and slide the bars from the slots in the rock wall. Getting the door open takes a bit of effort, but once I get it moving, it swings easily. Slinging my backpack on, I pick up the mattress and open the exterior door, jumping when Matias materializes next to me. "Your glamor is too good."

He smirks. "It comes in handy, but in this case, I wasn't even trying. If I lean against rock long enough, I naturally blend into it. Staying human-toned takes a bit of effort for most of us." He holds out a hand. "I'll take the mattress."

I give the bag to him. "Thanks. I rested quite well."

He nods. "Have you decided what you want to do?"

"Not going to ask me about the prophecy?" I regard him skeptically.

"It's yours." He shakes his head. "We'd like to help, but you're right—I overstepped and I apologize."

His admission surprises me; it seems like a good sign. Or a way to lull me into complacency. "Thank you. I accept your apology, but I admit I'm torn. I'd like to learn more about your magic, but I feel like we're running out of time." It isn't until I say the words that I realize just how true that is.

"You may be right. Karski called me. The vampires know you're sheltering with us, and they are not happy." He shrugs. "They believe we are invaders and they'd cut us off from the magic if they could."

"They can't?" Curious that the native users don't have a better grasp.

He grimaces. "If they could use it correctly, they might be able to block us. But they don't understand what they're doing. They mesmerize humans and each other. The weres use it for shape shifting. Both are instinctive; rather like breathing. But if you know something about science, you can concentrate oxygen and bottle it. We concentrate magic to forge new gargoyles, shape shift, glamor, and protect the Pool of Life."

"And yourselves?"

He jerks his chin. "Yes. Only in self-defense. We don't use magic offensively. It's too costly to the wielder and the Pool of Life."

Asking species-survival related questions might get me smacked like a bug, but I have a responsibility. "Speaking of that, you said forging more gargoyles used too much magic. But all of your furnaces were in use. So why not forge fewer, since you're practically immortal?"

"The vampires and weres keep turning people. We have to keep up."

I've never understood that argument. "That makes no sense." I hold up my hand to count down my reasons. "One, vampires and weres die. Vamps less often, but we all die. Two, if you can guard the Pool of Life with the numbers you have now, you don't need more. Three, you've admitted forging new gargoyles is a load on the Pool, so by continuing, you're doing more damage than helping."

Matias crosses his arms. "How can you judge our guardianship when you don't even know what we do or how we do it?"

"Then I guess you'd better show me." I notice he isn't denying any of my charges, though.

Turning up his hand, he sweeps his arm towards the vault tunnel. "I am not a Guardian of the Pool. The Council guards the Pool. But we can return there."

I don't want to waste time walking through all those tunnels again. "Why don't you have someone else ask while you teach me what you can about the magic? While we're doing that, I'll let your people look at the prophecy, but I don't think you'll find anything useful. It's just a lot of dreams. Or nightmares, if you're human." I shudder.

We enter the main tunnel and begin the long downward trudge. But before we go more than a few hundred feet, Matias stops. I stop, too. The rock under my feet vibrates, and a roar sounds from below, followed by a crashing sound.

Matias pulls me to the side of the tunnel, then runs back up, towing me by the wrist. "The vampires are attacking!"

"What? Why?" That makes no sense at all.

"They want you."

I stop running. "To see me or take me?"

"Come on. We can't stay here. We'll get trampled." Matias takes off.

A thundering sound, like a huge waterfall, resolves into the crack-thud of rock feet on the tunnel floor. I sprint after him, then zoom past, careening through the door and over to my bike. The chatter of machine guns and boom of explosives are muffled slightly by the outer hangar doors. Lacking body armor, I put my motorcycle leathers on.

Before I finish, Matias joins me. The hangar doors to the tunnel slam open, and gargoyles pour out. First, the Outer Shield residents, then the larger Inner Shield members. They line up on both sides of the outer doors, forming a circle along the outer walls of the parking cavern. As more gargoyles join them, the circle grows, the larger gargoyles joining the circle in front of the outer hangar doors.

"We will join and strengthen our shields. Talk to Theoden!" He hands me a phone, then steps into the line when it reaches us. When they've encircled the entire parking area, they stop and link arms.

My bike and I are outside the protective circle. So much for mutual defense. I tap the phone's screen, which opens without a passcode. Theoden's contact appears, so I hit the call button.

"I warned you, Matias." Klaus Theoden's tone is unusually angry. "I warned you, and you did it anyway. This is what you get."

I scowl. "This is Char, not Matias. I'm a free person, and I'll talk to whoever I want to talk to. Back off!"

"Don't tell me what to do, little vamp." He hisses the words, his venom unchecked.

I hiss back, backed by the prophecy's fury. "I am the Unbound Queen, and you will speak with respect!" The same technique I use to mesmerize, powered by our combined anger, blasts from me. The gargoyles near me waver, like they're dizzy, and the closest drops to his knees.

"Yes, my Queen." Theoden's tone is subservient. "What are your orders?"

By the burning daylight, I've controlled the Night King of Vegas over the phone!

But before I can enjoy the moment too long, the prophecy shoves an image at me. The vision shows a beautiful white woman, with vibrant green eyes, long, curling blonde hair, and camera-ready makeup wearing a bright red, tight formal gown with a diamond tiara. Her long fangs slide over plump blood-red lips. A feeling of disdain mixed with fondness and gratitude comes to me.

I mute the phone and pull the prophecy from my jacket. "Is this the priestess? You think I should talk to her?" Anger spikes, and the image drops to her knees and puts her forehead to the ground.

"She needs to acknowledge me. Got it. Do you think I can do that over the phone?" Doubt rises, then the scene changes, showing me bending over the priestess with my hands on either side of her head. "Understood." I unmute the phone and let my mesmerization powers flow. "Klaus Theoden. You will stop attacking the gargoyles and bring the High Priestess to meet me just outside the doors. You will not attack me, nor allow any other to attack me. Do you understand?"

"I understand, and obey, my Queen." He yells, but the sound is muffled, like he's covered the microphone.

The sounds of assault lessen, then fade into silence. Carrying the phone and the prophecy, I walk to the exit door. If I can make Theoden obey, I can control the priestess, too.

As I reach for the handle, Matias grasps it first. Gargoyles clutch Matias's shoulders—he's pulled the entire circle with him. "We will support you, Charlene Flammen, but please pull the magic from all of us, not just those closest."

The gargoyles near me sagged because I took their power. Not what I intended, but it explains why Theoden gave in. "I'm sorry. I didn't mean to. I'll do my best, but since I don't know how I did it, I'm not sure I'll succeed."

"Understood. We'll balance the pull ourselves." He taps on a keypad, and a clicking noise comes from the handle under his hand. "I recommend you strengthen your personal shields."

I swallow and wish I had time for a blood box. But I've demanded the confrontation—delaying makes me look weak. I feed power to my shields and thicken the panels in front of me. Theoden could be faking, just to get me out there and shoot me to pieces. "Ready."

Matias turns the handle and shoves the door wide.

Swallowing hard, I step out like the queen I'm not, with my head held high. The door closes behind me, and moments later, vampires sprint to me, Theoden leading. The beautiful woman I see in the vision grasps Theoden's arm.

For a split second, I think about running, but Theoden is too fast. He'll catch me for sure. If I really have mesmerized him, I'll look weak to the others. If I haven't, I'll just prove that I'm not a leader. Besides, if Theoden is faking, he wants to take me down personally. Then I can use my power again. I step towards them and pose with my arms crossed, toe tapping, like I'm impatient.

Theoden stops five feet in front of me and drops to one knee. "As you commanded, my Queen, the High Priestess."

If he's faking, I don't have time to check. The priestess hisses and saunters towards me, stopping inside my personal space. "Well, well, well. If it isn't the low-bred girl who would be queen." Her heavy Russian accent almost sounds fake. While she's beautiful at a distance, up close that beauty isn't even skin deep. Makeup plasters her face, and long false eyelashes beat against her flushed cheekbones. Her red lips look like they've had too many filler injections, and she has to suck her bottom lip in to keep her very long fangs from piercing it, giving her voice a breathy tone. And a severe overbite. Elaborately tooled black leather covers her petite body from neck to toe, silver flashing at her neck and over her heart.

I hold back my smile. I've dealt with so many of her type. More money than sense, they follow every pricey medical spa recommendation and end up looking like cartoons rather than real people. These women, just like Theoden, are convinced of their superiority simply because they have money. At the bar, I had to toe the line, using flattery to make them behave. But here, I set the rules. I hold her gaze but don't try to control her. "According to your own prophecy, I am the Unbound Queen."

"You are not! You have not completed the tests, and you will not complete them now." She sneers, which looks hilarious with her features, and spins on her heel.

I catch her arm and yank her close. "If that's the case, don't you want your precious prophecy back?" If I'm wrong, I'm dead. I hold the book high, waving it in my left hand. The prophecy doesn't project anything to me, so I might be making the wrong move, but it's better to know now.

"Mine!" She swipes at the book, her long nails rasping against the cover, and then grabs it with both hands. Screaming, she drops it, pulling her hands to her chest, screeching again when the backs of her hands hit the silver decorations on her jacket.

Leaving the prophecy at my feet, I put my palms against her cheeks. The heavy makeup is slippery, so I thread my fingers through her heavily sprayed hair and capture her gaze, sending the full force of my power into her. "I am the Unbound Queen. You will submit." Energy surges through me and into her.

The priestess sags in my hold, then straightens. "No. I will not give in to a child." Her words emerge slowly, and she trembles.

I push harder. "You will acknowledge me as the Unbound Queen." I shove my will into her, picturing her dropping to her knees.

She holds my gaze and tries to mesmerize me, but her attempts are like a cloud of gnats. Annoying, but easily swept away. "No, no, no!" The last is a wail. Then she drops to her knees.

I keep my grip on her face and hair, bending over her. "I am the Unbound Queen."

She tries to look down, but I don't let her. "You are the Unbound Queen. I will serve you forever, my Queen."

"Unfasten your neck guard." I loosen my grip, letting her slide away, and wipe my greasy hands on her shoulders. The prophecy tells me what to do next. I'm not thrilled but understand the purpose.

"Yes, my Queen." She fumbles at the buckles, which don't seem to be silver. Either that, or she's already been burned so badly by the prophecy that she can't feel it. The neck guard drops to the ground, too close to the book.

I grab the book, returning it to my inner pocket. Then I push her head back and to the side, bend, and sink my fangs into her neck. Warm blood flows sluggishly into my mouth, rich with power but sour from the fear and pain of her victims. I suck her essence into me until I have her completely under control, and power rushes through me. Then I drop her to the sand without trying to close her wounds. Looking up, I crook my finger at the closest vampire. "Tend to her." The vamp leans over her, licking her wounds.

Then I stalk to Theoden, still kneeling, and do the same. His blood isn't as powerful, but it isn't as sour, either. As I drink, I can feel the connection to every vampire he's turned, and their power threatens to overwhelm me. I shut that connection away and concentrate on Theoden. Once I have him under control, I let him go, pointing at the next vampire. "Close his wounds."

I step back from him and face the gathered vampires. "I am the Unbound Queen, and you will obey me!"

Every one of them drops to their knees, weapons clattering as they fall. It seems too easy, but I'm not going to complain about success.

Matias pulls his line of gargoyles closer to me, and the nearest vampires bound to their feet, blocking his approach. I scowl at Matias. "Stop. All of you. Matias, please convey my thanks to the Gargoyle Guardians Council. I will contact you later about a way ahead for the mutual benefit of all our peoples. Please tell the weres the same. Theoden, organize our return to the Tower and put the underground shelter back into caretaker status." I don't want to take over, but if I'm going to, I've got to consolidate my power now.

"Yes, my Queen." Theoden rises and bows, then calls his lieutenants to him, barking orders.

I face Matias. "Thank you. I appreciate your help and I will be in touch soon."

"You are welcome, Charlene Flammen, Unbound Queen of the Vampires. Rule well." He nods his head, then retreats, pulling the linked gargoyles with him.

I hope they'll return my bike, but I have the feeling it will be a while before I get to ride again. A long black limo comes to a stop in front of me.

Theoden opens the door. "My Queen, High Priestess, please enter."

I nod and duck into the car, sliding across and buckling up. The ride across the desert track will be rough. The priestess—I'll have to get her name at some point—gets in and takes a seat on the side-facing bench, then Theoden joins her. Two of his bodyguards take the seat facing me, compact machine guns slung across their laps.

He opens a bottle of blood wine, pouring three glasses and handing the first to me. "My Queen." Then he gives one to the priestess and they both raise theirs. "To the Queen Unbound."

I nod but don't bother drinking. I don't need more blood—power sparks and fizzles in my veins.

Theoden throws the drink back and laughs, letting the glass drop to the carpeted floor of the limo. "Thank you for taking care of that problem for me." He jerks his head towards the priestess. "Now I don't have to worry about her little cult because I've got the Unbound Queen right where I want her."

He's faked his capitulation. Despair sinks into my gut, followed by sheer fury, the prophecy joining me. I knew it was too easy but ignored the signs. Not only will I pay for this, but everyone in Las Vegas and beyond will, too.

CHAPTER 27

Theoden turns towards his henchmen. "Don't look into her eyes. If she tries to touch me or mesmerize me, shoot her in the legs." Then he looks at me. "Did you really think you could take me over, little girl? You're nothing. A low-class, uneducated, stupid call-girl."

His name-calling is designed to infuriate me, make me act rashly, but I've dealt with worse people than him. "I suppose you've got a story already worked out for my injuries? I think I know this story." I look at the limo's roof and tap my chin, then return to Theoden. "The priestess broke away from my control and attacked me. In the rush to defend me, I was injured. I will need time in seclusion to heal. Is that about right?" I harden the part of my shielding facing him and his henchmen, curving it sharply in front of my knees and down below my feet.

Then I open my new connection to Theoden's network of vampires. He's evaded my control, but I can feel every single one of the vampires in his network, so drinking from him has accomplished something. I search for the branches controlling the men in front of me. They've been turned by a vampire that Theoden had turned. I bypass that vampire for the moment and search his line for the essence of these men.

His brow furrows for a moment, then smooths. "Precisely."

"Didn't expect the stupid girl to figure that out, did you?" I smile and find one henchman, then I find the next. I'd rather put both of them under my control and get them to take out Theoden, but I'm not certain I have that kind of precision. So instead, I command both of them to sleep. They immediately sag in their restraints.

Theoden grabs the closest weapon and fires it at my legs. Bullets fly and rebound from my shielding, most of them directed into the limo's floorboards by the curve I've created. One hits the priestess, who screeches and curls into a ball on her seat. Several hit his bodyguards, startling them awake, and one smacks into Theoden's leg. He screams and drops a hand across the wound.

I smirk and raise my voice to penetrate the ringing in my ears. "Didn't expect that, either." Keeping my shields solid, I grasp Theoden's connection to all of his vampires and rip it away.

He screams again, the bellow of rage turning into a high-pitched wail of despair. Dropping his head to his knees, he clamps his hands on his head. "No!" Then he sags in the seat, apparently passed out, but I won't trust it.

"Yes." I hiss the word. "They are all mine, not yours." Turning my attention to my new people, I firm my connection. "Protect me from Theoden. Staunch your wounds, and then care for the priestess."

"Yes, my Queen." Both men bow their heads, then one kneels to push up the other's pant leg, while the wounded vampire aims his weapon at Theoden.

I rise and put my hand on the back of Theoden's neck, then sink my fangs deep again. I drink, pushing my will into the maelstrom of despair and fear he's become, ripping it all away and giving him a worthy goal—to please me. Rooting through his psyche, I ensure every hint of disobedience is gone, then soothe the wound I created by severing him from his progeny. Retreating from his mind, I close his physical wounds. He shifts slightly, waking, and I retreat to my seat. Running roughshod over his mind makes me sick to my stomach, but I can't afford to take chances with this particular vampire. "Klaus Theoden, we will not allow your disobedience. Look at me."

With a jerk, his head comes up and his gaze meets mine. "Yes, my Queen. I will obey your every word."

"And you will never, ever betray me, in thought or deed." I push my will into him, powered by his blood and the vampires under my command.

"I will never betray you, my Queen, in thought or deed. Your wish is my command." Despite his wounded leg, he slides from the seat to his knees, still holding my gaze.

"Excellent. You will continue to run your business network, ensuring we have funds for our rule. But you will treat your employees fairly and compensate them well. If there is a conflict between those goals, you will consult with me. You will tell me your overall strategy tomorrow afternoon." I smile. "And you will remember I'm not stupid or foolish."

"Yes, my Queen, I will. You are both wise and intelligent."

"Very well. You may take a seat. Bind your wound." I drop his gaze, then click the intercom button. The limo has stopped. "Driver, is the vehicle okay?"

"No, my Queen. The engine has stopped. I think the fuel line was hit."

I grimace. "Get us another vehicle, please, and arrange for this one to be towed and fixed."

"Yes, my Queen. The car behind us will take us."

"Thank you." A dark SUV pulls up next to us, and my driver gets out, opening my door. The SUV empties, the vampires spreading out around both vehicles, pointing their weapons out.

I get out, check the SUV's interior, and see no one, so I get in behind the driver. "Theoden, Priestess, join me." They do, sliding into the seat next to me.

My limo driver takes the wheel, and one of my new vampire guards takes the passenger seat. "My Queen, it is approximately forty minutes to the tower."

"Thank you. What is your name?" I'm not Theo, treating people like interchangeable, disposable pieces.

"George, my Queen. Tom is your bodyguard."

"Thank you, George and Tom. I appreciate your care. Please let me know if you need anything to make your job easier. Tom, do you need anything to heal your wounds?"

George says, "Yes, my Queen."

Tom continues scanning our surroundings. "No, my Queen. I will feed when we arrive at the tower."

Then I turn to the priestess next to me and Theoden. "Buckle in. It's going to be a bumpy ride." I laugh and fasten my belt. The future will indeed be a bumpy ride.

EPILOGUE

I NOD TO TOM, and he opens my office door. I'm still uncomfortable with all the formality, but a bodyguard is sadly necessary. No one has attacked me—yet—but some of my vampires have become obsessed with the Queen Unbound, and their devotion can be rather unhinged. I can, and occasionally do, control them or mentally punish them, but I prefer using positive reinforcement. Tom is good at physical restraint and enjoys it—a win-win situation.

Theoden enters and bows. "Good evening, my Queen. As you directed"—his lip curls—"I have purchased your old apartment complex and we are gathering renovation bids. I do not think this is a wise use of our funds, when we have more than enough room in our secure tower for our loyal employees."

I stare him down. In the month since I took over, we've had this conversation twice, and I've had enough. I need to address his not-so-subtle undermining of my leadership through his partial claim to ownership, but it can wait for another day. For now, it suits my purposes. I tap my chest. "But this way, we provide a safe, inexpensive solution for those who don't want to be under our thumb. And eventually, they'll give me loyalty. I won't have to command it or expect undying gratitude for some small thing. That breeds contempt."

I maintain eye contact until Theo bows. The prophecy doesn't attempt to force my hand, either. It doesn't like the idea of benevolent leadership but no longer tries to make me behave like a despot. It knows I'll slap it down, hard. During my confrontation with Theo, it successfully influenced me, but wasn't able to take command. Now, the prophecy can't stand against the power of my many vampires. However, controlling the massed might of my people is exhausting, so coming to an understanding has been critical. I've smacked it a few times, and now, the prophecy keeps any objection to a low wail, rather than a screaming fit accompanied by crushing, tearing pain until I shut it out. Progress is good.

"Yes, my Queen." He straightens, keeping his gaze pointed at the floor. "All other businesses are progressing according to plan, and Fantastique has exceeded expectations. Your previous employment there carries weight with the lesser supernaturals." He sneers. "It's become a tourist attraction. Like a carnival."

I chuckle at his disgust. "It's always been a carnival. I can't wait to take our vampire visitors there, even if it's over a video feed." The senior vampire leaders—or more accurately, rulers—still don't believe I'm the real Unbound Queen. But being tied to their places of origin makes it difficult for them to challenge me directly. They prefer to send overly-formal, vaguely threatening hand-written letters sealed in blood.

They aren't completely out of touch. Conventional spying and network attacks have increased. The spies are usually human, but we've caught weres and witches, too. Fortunately, they're only watching, not acting, and leave after we confront them. Eventually, we'll convince the leaders to meet over video, despite their distaste for technology. Or their people will attempt violence and find out how badly that will end.

Theo's chin rises, and he looks down his nose at me. "They wouldn't lower themselves to those depths. They have cultured tastes."

I'm over Theo's high-brow sneering. But better that than the arrogant misogynist I've fought to a standstill for the last month. "No wonder you came here. None of them wanted Vegas, did they? Not back when it was desolate desert."

Theo's lips clamp together and he scowls for a moment. Then his expression smooths.

I recognize the signs of an incoming lecture and cut him off. "I know. You got here before the mob and the neon lights. It doesn't matter; they can't come here anyway."

"They can't normally come here." His expression becomes sardonic. "But if you die without an heir, they can. You should name an heir, now."

I sniff. "And name you, so you can kill me off and regain your place? No, thanks." I'm not as old as Theo, but I wasn't born yesterday, either.

He bows his head. "You know I can't do that."

"You've done it before." It's my turn for sarcasm. We've had this discussion several times, and I'm getting tired of it.

But I automatically jerk away when he gets in my face, moving faster than I can see. He snarls. "I've told you I can't do it again." He jumps back, bowing low enough that his head touches his knees, as though getting that close to me physically hurts. The prophecy probably smacked him. Tom stands in front of me, gun pointed at Theo's head.

"Why not?" Theo has said that before, without fully explaining. I've pushed him each time, and he's avoided it by bringing up a critical decision I have to make. I step to the side, around Tom. "Look at me. Tell me the whole truth, now." I push my will into him, just a little.

His body straightens with a jerk, his mulish expression returning. I capture his gaze and don't let him go.

Grimacing, he raises his chin but doesn't try to break our connection. "My sire was insane, driven to madness by breaking his place ties. Even so, severing my connection with him, followed by the power surge caused by the assumption of all his vampires, almost killed me. I thought I knew how bad it would be, but I was wrong. I screamed for hours, never passing out, and if I could have moved, I would have walked into the sun." His lips press together for a moment. "That is why the Queen is turned unbound. If you had been bound to me, killing me might have killed you. If you survived, you'd never attempt it again. If you are destined to lead all the vampires, you must be ready to bind and then kill at least once. Because some of our leaders are centuries older than I. They will fool you easier than I did." He shivers. "I will not be able to tell if their capitulation is real."

I don't understand his logic. Plus, I already took his vampires, and while it created a surge, it wasn't that bad. "But you would have bound me, not them. After I freed myself from you, they would have no bind on me."

Theo's mouth twists. "Ah, but they do. One of them turned my sire, and that vampire still holds a secondary bind on me. Or would, but you are free from that. The true Queen Unbound could survive breaking secondary binds, but it is unnecessary pain. She must save her strength for binding leaders, not breaking."

"The Queen is turned unbound to make it easier to take over? Is that what you're saying?" Captain Obvious strikes again. Dealing with Theo is exasperating. I have to drag every little thing out of him. But at least I don't fear for my life. Much.

"Exactly." He nods once.

My eye muscles are getting a workout, just keeping them from rolling. "Well, no kidding. The name pretty much implies that. Tell me something I don't know."

He scowls, an unusual show of strong emotion. "If enough of them feel threatened by you, or believe you are an imposter, they can join together and remove your power. Or, with the help of a powerful witch coven, kill you."

Removing my power will kill me, most likely. "How many of them have to agree, and what kind of effort does that take?" If that only requires agreement and cooperation, then I'm already gone. But I suspect that joining together means trusting each other. Few of my vamps trust each other; leaders will be a million times more suspicious.

"It's not a matter of numbers, but power." He shakes his head. "I don't know the specifics because none of them would tell me. They believed me too junior, too weak." He snarls. "I am neither, but I still remain ignorant. It is an intolerable slight."

I huff. "And they won't tell me because they need an advantage to take me out, right?"

"Correct." He winces. "My Queen."

The prophecy must have smacked him. Again. I don't care for the title, but the prophecy and the priestess are sticklers. Despite her initial reaction, the priestess isn't obsessed or fanatical, except when it comes to enforcing my reign. She refuses to give me the trials she originally demanded, saying that my assumption of Theoden's power is more than sufficient. While that might be so, I don't fully trust her. Or the rest of them, although Tom and George seem sincere. "Is there anything else, Theo?"

His lip curls again. He despises his new nickname, which has spread through the group like news of a billionaire on a bender at a high roller table. "No, my Queen." He bows and backs away to the door. Tom opens the door and follows him out, leaving me alone.

Despite getting more out of Theo, questions remain. Do I push and insist on initiation into the vampire leader secrets now or consolidate my position and press them at a later date? Individually, or in a group? The choices have advantages and disadvantages, and neither Theo nor the priestess will give me an accurate assessment. The rest of my vampires are underlings and employees and probably won't tell me unpleasant truths. I need allies and advisors.

The gargoyles have gone largely silent. Matias sends an occasional text, asking if I need help or training, but nothing more. I need the magic training they've offered, but I'm not sure the cost is worth it. Especially when they haven't told me what the gargoyles are costing our planet.

Karski has come to the tower with representatives of the major were species, meeting with me and my new advisory board. We have hammered out an agreement on handling disputes between our peoples. We've stuck strictly to that topic, and Karski treats me as a rival leader, not a friend. Which is a shame because even if we can't be friends, I could use a neutral sounding board with common interests and morals. Hopefully, if there's a mutual threat like a vampire leader invasion, Karski will be more cooperative.

Matias will tell me the truth, but from his alien perspective. That isn't necessarily bad—diverse opinions and ideas create a better basis for decisions. I don't know what his help or advice will cost, though, and I don't know if he really knows anything important about the other vampire leaders.

But if the vampire leaders refuse to accept Theoden, it will be decades—or even centuries—before they'll accept me. While I can afford the time, I suspect they'll act sooner than I like.

Unless I force their hands.

Maybe I should test the limits of my unbound status and take the fight to them. But Theo still challenges me, which doesn't bode well for an assault.

Black and white thinking isn't helping me. There's a lot of ground between hiding in Vegas and an attack. Sending a virtual meeting invitation is probably a first good step, no matter how much Theoden objects. I can get to know the other leaders on a surface level and use my hard-won bartender talents to lull their suspicions. They'll almost certainly believe I'm a low-class nobody, and therefore, they'll underestimate me. That will buy me time to investigate, find weak points in their defenses, and train my abilities.

I can also test my limits. I'm the Unbound Queen—it's time to find out what that really means without the chains of prophecy or tradition. And it's past time for a small indulgence, too. I've bound myself to this desk for too long—freedom beckons. I click the intercom button on my desk. "Tom, bring my new motorcycle around. I'm going riding." I've barely ridden my custom Kawasaki Ninja; it needs a proper test, too.

"Yes, my Queen. I'll have it and an escort in the garage shortly."

Riding alone would be better, but being Queen means security. "Excellent. Thank you." I leave my office, trot to my luxurious living suite, and pull out my new riding leathers. Gorgeous tooled black leather is supple under my hands and stiff over the crash protection pads. Red LEDs highlight portions of the design; I can activate the lights for safety or turn them off for stealth. Sliding the fitted leather on makes me smile with anticipation and joy, something that has been decidedly lacking in my life lately. I need to teach my vampires how to have conventional fun, to take the place of hunting humans, something I've forbidden.

After I buckle my boots—the heels light up, too—I text Tom that I'll be downstairs shortly. Looking at the names on my contact list, I grin and start a text group with Karski and Matias.

> Going riding—want to join me?

Maybe I can engineer a win-win for all of us. We can ride, then talk. But just speeding through the desert for an hour with friends is worth the risk of reaching out. And if they don't show up, I'll still have fun. I grab my helmet and ride the elevator down.

When the door slides open, Theoden stands there. "Going somewhere?"

The prophecy's anger simmers, but I control it. Still, I'm tired of Theoden trying to change me. "Yes. And it's none of your business."

His lip curls. "Aristocracy do not ride motorcycles. That is far beneath the dignity of the Queen Unbound."

I laugh. "I didn't fight my way to the top just to become someone else." Pushing past him, I wink. "This working-class queen has left the building."

I hope you enjoyed Char's story. I plan on writing more in the Vegas Underground series. Subscribe to my newsletter, Scott Space, to learn more and get some free short stories! https://dl.bookfunnel.com/dsdq7hxh1t

AUTHOR'S NOTE

I wrote the original *Working Class Vegas Vamp* to help process my feelings after my youngest brother experienced a major medical issue. He worked behind the scenes in the Las Vegas entertainment industry. Much of it is contract work, so there's little security and the jobs can disappear without notice. Me and my siblings took turns caring for him, crowded into his one bedroom apartment during his initial recovery and therapy period. We overlapped our stays, making a small space even smaller.

Night after night, between 2 and 4 in the morning, the upstairs apartment door would slam, one or several people would stomp across the floor, the sliding door would whoosh across the track and crash into the frame. Then the nauseating scent of marijuana and cigarettes would penetrate the terrible seals on our sliding glass door, followed by thumping noises.

One evening, my sister and I were trying to figure out what those people were doing. (FYI, my sister is an author too; she writes funny, lighthearted sci fi and fantasy as Julia Huni, and romcoms as Lia Huni.) First, we speculated that vampires occupied the entire apartment complex, because you rarely saw anyone during the day. Then Julia came up with the idea of drag performers kicking off their boots and relaxing after a long night of performances. That led, of course, to vampire drag performers, and it got wilder from there—speculating was a ton of fun, and gave us a laugh despite the grim circumstances.

Over the weeks, the idea simmered in the back of my mind and wouldn't let go. We got my brother into a residential therapy program—just like Char, I was thrilled to drop those apartment keys off forever—and we were able to relax a little. That's when I started writing. Because I'm known as a classic-style space opera author, and I didn't know exactly where the story was going, I published it on my blog in installments for free. After my brother's situation stabilized, the story grew to include my feelings about the current US administration. As a twenty-year USAF veteran, I will continue to support and defend the US Constitution against all enemies, foreign and domestic. Sometimes, that's through fiction.

Anyone who read the serial on my blog will note I've cut a lot out of the final version. Many of the early chapters were written as therapy, and weren't important to the story. I appreciate everyone who suffered through the serial version!

Although the story was born from trauma, I've really enjoyed writing it. I plan to write another book about Char, and probably more about the others, too. But I need to write *Time Guild 2* first!

A couple of additional notes:

Theoden's female werewolf limo driver is named after Virginia Hall, a WWII spy in Germany with a wooden leg. Virginia accomplished so much, because no one thought a handicapped woman was a threat.

Freddie the badger is named after a WWII Dutch resistance fighter, Freddie Oversteegen. She was amazing!

Alek the werewolf alpha is named after Jan Karski, a WWII Polish soldier, resistance fighter, and diplomat. He was key in getting the word to the Allies about the concentration camps.

All of these people were determined to fight facsism to the best of their ability, and accomplished truly great feats. I encourage you to look them up—there are books and movies about all of them.

I hope you enjoyed *Working Class Vegas Vamp*!

ACKNOWLEDGMENTS

My first thank you is to my sister, Julia Huni. She came up with the initial inspiration for this novel! While she's usually my first/alpha reader, she read this story on my blog with everyone else. So please don't blame her for any flubs.

Second, thank you to Dakota Nyght of Dakota Nyght Editing Services. We first met on Facebook fighting fascism in Montana, but have since connected several times in real life. She needed an example for an editing seminar during MISCON, so I offered my serial. She made several notes on the first three chapters that led to vast improvements, such as deleting several chapters and changing the tense from first past to first present. Since I usually write in third past, it was a big adjustment, and the story is better for it. I have a long way to go before I'm comfortable writing that style, I'm afraid.

Third, thanks to Paula Lester of Polaris Editing for proofreading. Sadly, I did the tense switch after she proofread, so again, all errors are mine!

Fourth, the therapists at Nevada Community Enrichment Program and the hard working people at Spencer and Hastings Houses in Las Vegas. Thank you for giving us peace of mind!

Fifth, my writing sprint partners who are always ready to commiserate or kick me into gear. Julia Huni, Hillary Avis, Paula Lester, Marcus Alexander Hart and Lou Cadle—thank you all!

Sixth, my husband, The Amazing Sleeping Man, who supports my writing 100%. Love you!

No thanks at all are due to Zoe or Shepherd Book, who demand walks no matter how inspired I might be, bark at every little thing, and constantly want attention. But regardless, life is better with dogs.

Finally, thank you to God for sending me on this writing adventure!

All errors are mine and mine alone.

AM SCOTT BIOGRAPHY

AFTER TWENTY YEARS AS a US Air Force space operations officer, AM now operates a laptop, trading in real satellites for fictional spaceships. Read her classic-style space opera science fiction for engaging characters with action, adventure, hope, and heart.

AM's writing cave is deep in the mountains of western Montana; check out Montana, The Amazing Sleeping Man, Zoe, their slightly crazy German Shepherd and Shepherd Book on Instagram. AM is also a volunteer leader with Team Rubicon Disaster Response.

Sign up for the Scott Space Newsletter and get free short stories, *Lightwave: Short Stories 1*. https://dl.bookfunnel.com/dsdq7hxh1t

The Folding Space Series is eight books long and growing! Start with *Lightwave: Nexus Station* or *Lightwave: Clocker*. There's plenty more adventure left in the Folding Space Universe—next up is the Time Guild Series. *Time Guild 1* is out now!

If you prefer YA stories, start with *Quinn of Cygnus: Lift Off* for an exciting coming-of-age story. Quinn's Quantum Fold Series is complete, but her story continues.

If not out adventuring, find AM in all the usual places:

Website: www.amscottwrites.com

Instagram: https://www.instagram.com/amscottwrites/

Facebook: https://www.facebook.com/AMScottWrites/

Bluesky: https://bsky.app/profile/amscottwrites.bsky.social

YouTube: youtube.com/@theamazingsleepingman

Email: am@amscottwrites.com

AM loves to hear from readers! If you find errors, please let her know at the email address above. She's on most social media, but somewhat irregularly, so if you ask a question or make a comment, please don't be offended if she doesn't immediately reply. She's particularly difficult to contact when deployed on Team Rubicon operations or out backpacking—cellphone towers don't exist in disaster zones or the wilderness!

www.ingramcontent.com/pod-product-compliance
Lightning Source LLC
Chambersburg PA
CBHW021158310726
48971CB00002B/693